ENTER PORTAL 2:

ATTACK OF THE RAEKEEM

Printed in Australia

Cover design by Jessica Chaplin

Typeset by Alana Lambert

First printed March 2024

This edition first printed 2024

Paperback ISBN 978-1-7637872-1-6

eBook ISBN 978-1-7637872-3-0

A catalogue record for this work is available from the National Library of Australia

ENTER PORTAL 2:
ATTACK OF THE RAEKEEM

A. J. ELKSNIS

Also by A.J. Elksnis

Enter Portal
Enter Portal 1: Portal to Liberty

For Ben, Tim and Ellie

Chapter 1

Jericho Williams was seated on the edge of his cot, scratching his chin stubble with his prosthetic fingers, watching a prison guard walk by his cell.

'We lacked the resources to produce the numbers I had in mind,' Jericho explained to the man interviewing him. This was the first attempt by a journalist agency to seek his side of the story since he was incarcerated. Since he and Sabre Company had tried to overrun the Universal Community. 'Greer sent us a Shifter, which we used to–'

'Escape the UC forces,' the journalist interrupted. 'You took advantage of the Kai-ol technology trade. We know all that, Mr Williams. People want to know who you really are and why you did what you did.'

Jericho gave the man seated by a card table opposite him a threatening glare. 'To reassemble and begin resource procurement in other realms,' he said, finishing his sentence. 'It's pronounced *Kee-yol*, and I am a Colonel, not a "mister".' He gestured to a pile of letters stacked on his narrow bookshelf. 'Though the attention is flattering, this ceaseless "fan mail" is littered with inaccuracies and exaggerations.'

Jericho eyeballed the twenty-something-year-old youth, disgusted by the latest "hipster" fashion. He was wearing skin-tight jeans cut above the ankle, no socks, plant-based loafers, a V-neck T-shirt, and facial hair shaped so close it looked like carpet. The final insult to Jericho's senses:

a tangled bun of hair tied at the very top of his head. 'Clearly, Mr Ponce,' Jericho continued with disdain, 'you don't know "all that".'

'It's Tronce,' the man said tersely as he stood to pick up the letters, printed from Williams' fan-sent transmissions. He took them back to the card table to inspect. 'There are people out there who want to read about Jericho Williams the villain, not Williams the two-dimensional, one-armed psychopath.' Tronce noticed the messages were sent from lawless outer rim settlements that had rejected UC society soon after the Great Migration.

'I see,' Jericho conceded with a reluctant sigh. He took his pillow, removed its slip and returned it to the head of his bed. 'You want to know me.' He folded the cloth, under the table, lengthways thrice.

'We need to give the reader a redeeming quality they can relate to,' Tronce encouraged, poised to take notes on his digital pad while it recorded audio.

'Come closer, boy,' Jericho grumbled, using the lock mechanism on his prosthesis to grip one end of the cloth. 'I won't be raising my voice or repeating myself.' Arms under the table, he began to twist the cloth with his good hand.

Tronce moved his chair closer. 'Pretend I'm your audience. Give me a reason to like you. Give me an angle that–'

Jericho flipped the table, tossing the letters, and looped the pillow slip over Tronce's head. Pulling him down, he locked both knees against his ears, yanking hard, cutting off his air.

'Throttled duck,' Jericho said with a chuckle, dominating Tronce's squirming attempts to free himself. 'That's the sound, the same sound everyone makes when they're being strangled.'

He pulled the cloth tighter and leaned down. 'You want to like me,' he whispered. Tighter still. 'How's this for a redeeming quality? Does this work for you?'

He took a deep breath, drew Tronce's head sideways to free one ear and shouted, 'How do you like me now?'

The cell door unlocked. Two guards rushed in and pinned Jericho to his cot.

Though his cell visits were now revoked, Jericho was allowed a face-to-face in the prison meeting room, while handcuffed and chained to the table.

A guard unlocked the meeting room door, and Jericho could see it was one of his Automated Machine units. Reprogrammed to serve its captors.

The journalist from two days ago was ushered in and he sat across from Jericho.

The door closed and locked.

'How's the neck, Ponce?'

Tronce opened his mouth to correct Jericho but only managed a pained whisper.

The chain pulled taut when Jericho leaned to cup one ear. 'What's that?' He gave an approving smile. 'My story must be quite lucrative for you to brave coming back here. Now.' He clapped, clinking his handcuffs, and searched the table before him. 'Where was I… ah, yes: Dennis Conroy, Luther Saint and I were soldiers of fortune. Our numbers – those we trusted – were dwindling. Sabre Company was literally perishing, despite the efforts of so many philanthropically financed poverty-eradicators and peace crusaders. The nail in our coffin was hammered in when those paying us to fight or create their wars were evicted from Earth.'

Jericho paused while Tronce cleared his throat. He twisted a cough lozenge out of its wrapping and gestured for Jericho to continue.

'When Branner released the first batch of his machines, we saw an opportunity, a way to turn the tide. We stole an AM and had it disassembled and analysed, only to find it couldn't be tampered with, not without the unit shutting down and becoming useless. We needed Branner's schematics. Saint and I stayed behind while Conroy joined the other once-powerful people in exile.

'We infiltrated a factory as technicians, with a little help from the late Commander Greer. Worth noting, actually,' Jericho said, pointing to the console Tronce was using to record the interview with a chuckle, 'he was defenestrated by one of Silica's heroes, Fiona Parker.'

'You're saying she threw him out of a window,' Tronce clarified. 'Her official report didn't mention that.'

'Kicked, actually. I saw the security footage. That wife-murdering sleaze finally got what was coming to him… but I digress. So there we were in the factory. I created a distraction' – he traced the burn scar over his scalp – 'that damn near got me killed, while Saint hacked the system.'

Jericho recalled duct-taping a metal-cutting lance to a crate. He had set the flame against a cable holding one corner of the catwalk on which he'd stood, thinking he would have time to move to cover before his distraction began. But a factory security AM came out of nowhere to apprehend him. The two of them grappled, the cable was cut and the hot end lashed Jericho's head.

'I wouldn't have made it out had Luthie not been there.' A nostalgic twinkle shimmered in Jericho's eye while he relived the thrill of the skirmish. His back pressed against Luther's, fending off AM after AM, until they fled aboard their ship and escaped with the data.

His gaze fell as he was hit with a wave of sadness, lips pressed ruefully. He glanced at his interviewer, seeing something in Tronce's face he hadn't seen in anyone's since his imprisonment. Lack of judgment. Even the other inmates hated him, hated Dennis Conroy more.

'Meanwhile, Conroy had gone to Silica,' Jericho continued, with a grunt. 'Made himself comfortable, backstabbed his way up the party ranks, poisoning every faction from the inside with scandals, paranoia and murder. When he was ready to bury his remaining opposition–'

'Wait,' Tronce said, raising his hand with a transfixed expression. 'Go back… You called him "Luthie", wh–'

'Let me finish,' Jericho said impatiently. 'Conroy gave Saint and I the order to enter Silica. Saint commandeered a resource carrier and we flew in with a crew of our own AMs. We programmed them to build a new factory and, in turn, an army.' He watched Tronce's furrowed brow relax into a realisation. 'What? Come on, out with it.'

'You loved him,' Tronce whispered.

Jericho's expression betrayed nothing while he leaned back. He'd opened his mouth to reply when black smoke bloomed around Tronce. Jericho's eyes grew wide at the horror before him.

Dark tendrils coiled outward, revealing a monster in the form of a serpent, rising two metres high, balancing on its tail, its mouth closing over Tronce's head, a ring of serrated teeth rotating, slicing through his skull. Tronce stared at Jericho, his jaw hanging limp. The cough lozenge rolled from his tongue to the floor. Spasms shook his body. Blood oozed down his pale face. The tendrils rolled inward, enveloping the serpent and its victim.

In a gush of smoke, two humanoids stood in its place, and the cloud dissipated.

The taller black-clad man's lips spread into a sharp smile. 'There is much I would like to discuss with you, Mr Williams.'

Jericho called out for the guard, but no one came.

'Dampening cloak field,' the other explained. 'Your captors and their surveillance can only see and hear the last five or so minutes of whatever you and this unfortunate chap were doing.' He gestured to his black rubber uniform. It shimmered and changed into tight jeans and a V-neck T-shirt. His hair rose into a topknot, and his face became Tronce's.

Jericho's eyes darted to the taller one. He clearly wasn't human. His eyes were white, but for pinpricks of black. Sharp bone protruded from each of his elbows. 'What are you?'

'We are Raekeem, and I am Lord Telsta,' the alien said. Another sharp grin. 'I think you might be interested in what I have to offer.'

San Francisco
VR House

Speeding through the forest, Lana revved her snowmobile when she saw an opportunity to take down her opponent. She veered toward a hillside, increased her speed and climbed a gradual slope that soon became vertical. Lana was travelling fast enough for her snowmobile to cling to the wall of ice. She looked down to her right to see her opponent matching her speed.

Ahead, the wall was curling like a wave. She swung her body and pulled on the handlebars before the lip of the ice curl and barrel-rolled her sled. Now inverted, flying over the lead racer's head, she reached with one hand, took hold of his jacket collar and let her momentum pull him off his vehicle. The man cried out when Lana released him in time to brace herself before her snowmobile landed flat. She sped on while he tumbled through the air and hit a tree. His sled veered sideways and careened over the hill crest.

Lana swayed away from the picket lines and slid through the finish tape, still leaning to keep the vehicle from tipping after her stunt. She turned sharply, riding the brakes to a sliding stop, throwing snow against the cheering crowd. Gloved hands were raised high, and the hoods and ears of their Ushanka hats bounced, while men and women called out her name. Lana stepped up onto her seat and thrust her hands high, soaking in her victory. She hopped down and lifted off her virtual reality headset. The game continued in her ears while she looked to the control room.

'That was incredible!' she said through excited breaths.

The team of programmers and engineers in the control room sat at their computers, staring in slack-jawed silence. They jumped when Rachel erupted from her seat.

'I want a go! Lemme go in!'

The two of them paused when the owners of the gaming company, VR House, entered the grey room. They looked to the padded wooden pillar and the AM unit wrapped around it on the floor.

'We've never seen anybody do that,' one of the women said. 'We'd like to use your gameplay in the promotion.'

Lana shrugged. 'Sure. I didn't break anything, did I?'

One of the engineers was checking the gaming rig Lana had been sitting on. It was attached to a mechanical arm that could swing, turn, roll and invert the gamer using it. The seat and handlebars could be swapped out for a body harness to give the gamer the feeling of being in space, or it could be used for flying and skydiving simulations.

'The Jock will need some repair, but the rig is fine,' the engineer said. 'You're good to go, Ms Navara.'

VR House had a partnership with the Branner Factory. The factory would send male and female base models called Jocks for testing, while the VR gamers got to interact with them in sport and combat games. Jocks had no personality programming and no facial features. They were robotic manikins with athletic physiques, which were graphically mapped inside the VR games to be any character, wearing anything, and given any scripted voice.

Rachel gave the sled racing game a go, and she and Lana left VR House an hour later. Lana wanted to go for a run, so she took the Golden Gate Bridge toward Sausalito, while Rachel took the car to pick up Sam from a lab at the Civic Centre.

It was March, and the end of the day was warm. The wind was strong. Lana's ponytail whipped behind her. The occasional pedestrian recognised her and waved as she ran by. People knew her, and they knew the work that she and her colleagues at the Portal Hub did. It was four years since Sabre Company had been defeated and everyone who fought them were world-renowned heroes.

The Hub was built into the mountain facing the Atlantic Ocean. Lana ran from the bridge to a path overlooking the water. The sun was setting, and the ocean waves were crashing against the rocks below.

A tone sounded on Lana's console, notifying her that a public service announcement was being live broadcasted.

'Statistical data, collected from one hundred Council-run focus groups across Earth and selected colonies, has yielded a disturbing shift in social prejudice targeting those of us categorised as "single". The Council is currently discussing countermeasures with Earth leaders as well as with all colony mayors.'

Lana arrived at the Hub, dumped her clothes in the washing machine and headed for the shower room. Meg Green, the most well-known journalist in the world, always delivered news with candid and considered professionalism. Today, her tone was severe.

'Investigations concerning causal links to national suicide rates were what prompted the need for a focus group campaign,' Green continued. 'People are no longer being driven to self-harm due to financial disparity. But singlism has once again reared its ugly head.' Her last words sounded angry. There was a pause, and Lana heard a frustrated sigh.

'It took the Wealth Sacrifice and Redistribution Initiative and a "campaign" for a spotlight to finally be shone on what's been happening to people like me for decades.'

Lana was washing herself with the volume turned up. She turned off the water when she heard what Green had just said.

'We've been bullied and alienated. Those of us who have to see a shrink and pop pills so we can get out there and be among you want singlism to stop.'

Lana dressed and carried her clothes to hang them outside. She was facing the bridge when she saw the traffic slowing to a halt. Pedestrians, cyclists, and runners all stopped.

'In many cultures, singlism has not only been acceptable etiquette for coupled people, it has been institutionalised and, until now, legalised. No more, a senior councilwoman promised me today. And I quote, "Discriminatory behaviour, such as making single people feel invisible, unimportant, incomplete, less than human, can and will be reported".

Severity of punishments will be discussed in the coming days. Until then, fellow U-Comms, respect your fellow human being.'

Lana heard soft clapping in the distance. Others joined. And soon, the Golden Gate Bridge became a mass show of solidarity.

Chapter 2

Portal Hub

Lana walked by the break room, where there was a pool table, arcade games, console games and a basic VR space. She stopped at Rachel and Sam's quarters. The door was open but the two of them had turned in early, after a long week of Realm travel, their consoles switched off. The latest world they and Lana had discovered was an advanced version of Earth. They dubbed it Theotech because the society there was heavily religious and technologically progressive. These were not cohesive attributes, however. For that reason, Theotech was in a state of social loggerheads.

Lana arrived at her quarters, picked up her plush red panda teddy and lay down on her bed. Holding it comforted her, but she soon felt her earlier mood returning. Rachel had suggested they go to VR House to unwind and debrief. It'd been fun, but the feeling was back, the feeling of inaction where action was due. Due in Theotech.

The global population in the Theotech version of Earth was divided into four groups, one occupying half of the planet's continents, while the other three, all religious groups, were divided between the remaining lands. Thousands of sub-religions were aligned under what resembled, but were not identical to, Home Realm's Buddhism, Hinduism, Christianity, Catholicism and Islam. Buddhism and Hinduism had joined, and somehow, Christianity and Catholicism had aligned as well. Islam remained separate. Though the fourth group, the non-religious, occupied half of the planet, they comprised three quarters of its population.

Each religious affiliation was colour-coded, and their people had to wear an armband indicating the group they belonged to. They lived only in their designated lands, and there was very little interaction between groups. If a citizen wanted to change their religion, he or she was welcomed into whichever interested them.

Lana turned onto her side and thought about the man she had seen yesterday, who seemed to have packed all of his material possessions and left his religion. She'd wanted to observe his transition to wherever he was going, so she and Rachel had followed him.

Like biologists studying an animal in the wild, they had watched from a distance while the man walked out to the city limits. He had eventually stopped walking and sat down on one of his bags. Soon, he was approached by what looked like police from the religious group he was leaving. They warned him not to loiter, and when they saw he had no armband, they asked him which religion he belonged to. He said, 'None. Not anymore.' The officers escorted him down an alley and, when they caught Lana and Rachel watching, told them to move along.

Lana asked what they were going to do with the man. And they stared at her as though she were stupid. 'Move along,' they repeated. They left, and Lana wanted to follow, but Rachel reminded her that their mission in Realms was to observe and learn. They were not to intervene. Lana reluctantly agreed, and the two of them returned to Home Realm.

Unable to sleep, Lana got up, took her wrist console and left her quarters. She crept by Professor O'Conner's room, down the hall and up to the Shifter Command level. She programmed the destination and a mercury sphere expanded in the portal room below.

Lana returned through the portal two hours later and sneaked back to her quarters. She undressed, climbed into bed and closed her eyes. She managed to get five hours sleep before the sun rose.

The smell of fresh coffee was drifting from Rachel's mug. She stopped at Lana's door in her tank and trunks and knocked. Taking a sip of her long black, she wiped her blue-tipped fringe away from her eyes. She had let her natural dark hair grow out. Only a couple of centimetres of blue remained.

'You must've had a long run,' she said to Lana. 'You're usually the first up.'

Lana moved to the edge of her bed and gazed at the floor. 'I went back.'

'Theotech?' Rachel joined Lana on the bed. 'You can't keep doing this.'

'I know.'

'You need Pete's authorisation.'

'I know,' Lana groaned like a scolded teen. 'It's logged. Nothing went wrong. Rache, you won't believe what I found.'

'Lana, if something had gone wrong and the Council got wind of it…' Rachel went through the motions, trying to get Lana to understand the importance of protocol. 'Even without the Kiyol mandate, we couldn't possibly help people in every Realm, in every situa–'

'I know!' Lana's exclamation caused Rachel to jump and spill her coffee.

Rachel was breathing quickly while her hot coffee soaked through her top.

'Sorry, sorry.' Lana pulled some tissues from the box on her bedside table and wiped Rachel down. 'Theotech has viable solutions to conflict.'

'They've segregated themselves into a social standstill,' Rachel retorted. 'The non-religious are overpopulated. Conflict is inevitable.'

'That's what I thought at first. But we didn't dig deep enough. I found out more about their history, and I think it's worth another look.'

Rachel listened to her friend, and while considering a return mission, she looked across the room at Lana's wall-mounted collection. Each item was from a different Realm. She stood from the bed to take the hand axe Lana had found in Forest Realm. She felt the weight of it while she drank the rest of her coffee. 'Okay,' she said, nodding. 'I'll go back there with you.'

'Thanks, Rache.'

'But last night…' Rachel returned the axe and strode to the door. 'That was your last unauthorised trip.'

'Won't happen again.'

Rachel paused at the door and turned. 'Lana, I know you went back because you thought you could help that man. But we signed up to explore new worlds, not to change them.'

'I didn't sign up for this,' Lana said, masking her frustration with a matter-of-fact tone. 'I was literally made for this.'

'I know,' Rachel said apologetically. She took a moment to regard the young woman she personally trained to be a skilled combatant. Professor Peter O'Conner's Augmented Human project was indeed a success. Lana was able to withstand hostile environments because Pete infused her skin with organic silicon carbide, which allowed her cells to harden, armouring her entire body. As long as she could react in time, Lana was practically invulnerable. She now had years of field experience in Realm travel, and she also maintained an excellent level of fitness. She had all of the tools necessary to help those who were in danger. *But she's on a leash*, Rachel thought. *We all are. No intervening, observation only.*

'Get something to eat,' said Rachel. 'Then we'll go to Theotech together.'

She returned to her quarters. Once dressed, she was about to go and find Lana when she remembered she had to take her pills. She found the jar of tablets that Professor O'Conner had had made specifically to treat her condition, called Mitochondrial Memory. The medication was supposed to reduce the number of episodes and, if taken over the course of a year, Rachel could potentially be free of them. Every episode drew her into a memory that belonged to her mother, her grandmother, her great-grandmother, and so on. Some memories were happy, some were mundane, but some were horrible and traumatic. It was now eleven months since Rachel had started taking her medication. Her last Mitochondrial Memory had occurred over three months ago.

One of the women in her ancestral line had been a medic in the First World War. The memory took Rachel into the hospital among the wounded and the dying. Shellfire could be heard in the distance, and although Rachel was experiencing the memory from outside her ancestor's body, she could feel what that nurse felt.

Through her ancestor, Rachel was holding a soldier's bloodied hand while he shook through his last breaths.

'Please, tell my wife I love her,' he said. 'Tell my boy to be strong.' His eyes glazed over. Tears were streaming down Rachel's cheeks.

The memory had faded, and Rachel had woken to her partner Sam holding her while she wept.

Rachel gazed down at the yellow, oval-shaped pill in the palm of her hand. She didn't know if her next episode would be worse. But the thought of stopping them from coming to her ever again convinced her to swallow the pill.

At that moment, she heard Professor O'Conner's voice from the comms speakers in the corridor. He requested all Shifter operatives suit up and report to the portal room.

On her way there, she came alongside Lana. 'Sorry. We'll have to reschedule Theotech.'

'It can wait,' said Lana. 'This sounds serious.'

They made their way up the corridor and joined two AMs who were suiting up in the portal room. Lana and Rachel opened their designated gear lockers at the wall and equipped themselves with side-arms and assault rifles. Although intervention was prohibited in alternate Realms, self-defence was not.

'The Kiyol have reported a possible threat to our Realm,' said Sam over the comms speaker. She was up on the Command level, programming the portal that Lana, Rachel and the two AMs were going to travel through. 'We sent a drone. Visibility is about thirty per cent. Very dense pollution. I'm dubbing this one Haze Realm.'

Sam and Peter O'Conner always forwarded reports to the Kiyol, and vice versa, as part of the agreement that was formed over eight years ago. The Kiyol developed the first Shifter device, and they had been exploring alternate universes parallel to theirs for two decades. If they expressed concern about anything Realm related, it was imperative that Rachel, Lana and the others follow their lead.

'They need us to check out the state of our planet in a Realm they've just returned from,' said Sam. Her tone was grave. 'That version of the Kiyol home world has been destroyed.'

Haze Realm

The portal opened and the mercury sphere expanded, reflecting the evening light. Lana and Rachel stepped out, followed by the two AMs. Their hands rested on holstered weapons. The air was poison. Rachel and Lana wore face masks to protect their eyes and lungs from the yellow haze that obscured the streets like a fog.

Rachel watched the topographical readout from the drone Pete had sent on her console. It was fragmented, showing empty spaces between an otherwise familiar map of San Francisco. Though Lana and Rachel still visited Melbourne Realms, different versions of SF had become their focus these past months.

Rachel nodded to the AMs. 'You two head that way. Lana and I will scout to the east.'

The soldiers confirmed and they parted ways.

'What did this?' Lana murmured, stepping over human skeletal remains.

A Kiyola warrior and Realm Traveller, Jihna, had sent Lana and Rachel video footage to review before they entered Haze Realm. What Jihna had recorded was a horror to behold. A close version of Amestae, the Kiyol home world, was destroyed. The majestic and beautiful Leetheria City had been levelled, the surrounding lands burnt.

Lana heard the split-second hiss and whistle of a fast-travelling object descending toward her. She sidestepped, caught the feathered end of an arrow shaft, and pulled Rachel behind a streetcar. Another arrow struck where they had been standing.

'Support, we're under attack,' Rachel called to the AMs through her comms. 'Find high ground. We're pinned down.' She tapped at her console to bring up a partitioned feed linked to the AMs' chest cams. After climbing a stairwell to access the roof of a single-storey building, the AMs immediately drew a line of sight on the archer. The camera then panned to a woman ascending a fire escape to the roof. She pulled two short black poles from her backpack while creeping toward the archer.

'Hold your fire,' Rachel commanded, and tapped the video feed to zoom in. She watched the archer turn and fire a badly aimed arrow. It flew over the young woman's head when she rolled toward him. She rose and struck his bow with both poles, swung her arms wide and brought her weapons together hard against either side of his head. He swayed, discombobulated, before dropping to his knees.

Rachel felt Lana tap her arm.

'We're being flanked,' she said, nodding to either side of their cover.

'We're not here to fight!' Rachel called out to the figures approaching through the yellow mist. 'Who's in charge?'

'I am.' The voice came from their left. Lana aimed her pistol at the head of a short, muscular man. Rachel lowered her gun and pressed her hand down on Lana's.

The gang leader stood before them, brandishing a long, crudely fashioned blade. 'Take their weapons.' Two of his crew approached, holding makeshift spears. An arrow whistled through the haze and glanced across his jaw, ripping the breathing mask from his face. He swore, pulling his shirt over his mouth. 'We've got them, you idiot! Stop shooting!'

'Your archer's down, Benson.' A woman's voice came through the mist, high across the road. 'Leave now or the next one's going in your brain.'

'Is that you, Jess?' the gang boss called out. He signalled for his men to back away. 'Why don't you come down, and we'll–'

'Now!' Jess yelled.

'We need to talk,' Rachel called out to Jess.

There was a moment of silence. 'Top floor. No tricks.'

Lana looked up through the haze to the silhouette on the roof. 'I like this girl.'

The AMs arrived to see Jess seated across from the gang leader, Benson, with Rachel and Lana at either end. They seemed to be waiting for somebody to speak first. Rachel nodded to the late arrivals to stand guard, and the AMs took position at the stairs, mindful of the gang members waiting below.

Jess looked from Rachel to Lana, noting their clean urban camouflage uniforms and new-looking face masks. 'I saw the shiny ball you came from.'

'That was a portal,' said Lana.

'We saw it too,' said Benson, crossing his arms over his broad chest. 'So you're, what… time travellers?'

'No,' Rachel answered flatly. 'Same time. We're from a different version of your world.'

'An alternate reality?' Jess asked.

Lana nodded. 'Ours exists parallel to yours and countless others.'

Benson raised his eyebrows at Jess.

'It doesn't matter whether you believe us,' said Rachel. She looked to Jess, the more accepting of the two, and gestured to the yellow haze outside. 'How did this happen?'

'The air was poisoned by pollution,' she said. 'Almost every evergreen species of tree died. Only deciduous species survived. Then the Raekeem came.'

'Benson,' one of the gang members interrupted. 'The Mutated heard us. They're filling the street.'

Benson nodded. 'Block the door downstairs.'

'Mutated?' Rachel asked.

'They're people who can breathe the haze, but they're like zombies,' Jess explained.

'Who are the Raekeem?' Lana asked.

'An alien race,' Benson answered. He clenched his fists and stared at the table. 'Governments were taking measures to protect the rich during the environmental collapse. Domes were built, but then these huge alien ships came down, one for each major city. Turns out their soldiers were already here, hiding among us. They can change what they look like.'

Lana watched him relive the invasion in his mind. 'Clearly they didn't come here to take over the planet. What did they want?'

Jess leaned on her elbows. 'They rounded up all of the intellectuals, the spiritual people, the artists, took them up to the ships… did something to them, then dropped them back here empty.'

'Empty how?' Lana asked.

'Drained their minds. Took all that makes us… us. Once they had what they needed, they pumped a toxin into the atmosphere. Then they left.'

'Why did they target certain kinds of people?' Rachel asked.

Jess shrugged. 'I don't know. But they took more kids than any other age group. Two eight- and ten-year-old Tibetan kids who somehow escaped described what the Raekeem were doing. I remember seeing it on TV. The translator speaking for them said the Raekeem were harvesting…' She hesitated. 'They said they were harvesting the "third eye".'

Chapter 3

Home Realm
Silica

The Black Bird was dispatched to intercept an unidentified ship flying low, thirty-five kilometres outside of Liberty. It had been flagged for entering Silica's airspace without authorisation.

Chesh, the pilot of the Black Bird, dialled through radio frequencies while repeating, 'You have broken airspace protocol. Land immediately. Respond or we will open fire.'

Captain Renee Riley was sitting in the co-pilot chair. She waited while watching the comms dashboard. No reply. 'Fire a warning.'

Forward cannons emerged from armoured compartments on either side of the Black Bird and fired. The blasts erupted above the unidentified carrier, and it deviated, dipping to the roof of an abandoned factory.

Chesh and Renee watched the alien ship slow before its stern doors opened. A long object the size of a shipping container dropped and crashed through the roof of the building. The craft's nose tilted for a steep ascent, activating a portal unlike any they had ever seen.

Renee stared into the dark cloud expanding with sinuous lengths, reaching, twisting around the carrier before consuming it.

Chesh activated the ship scanners, unable to get a reading after it disappeared.

'Bring us over the building.'

The Black Bird hovered low, beaming lights into the gaping hole below. 'The object is emitting a jamming signal. I can't get a read.' Chesh studied the alien pod through the night-vision camera trained on it. 'It's open, whatever it is.'

'Take us down. Safe distance.' Renee tapped at the ship comms. 'Security Division, this is Captain Riley of the Black Bird, requesting an emergency response team. Sending coordinates now.'

'Copy that, Captain. Coordinates received. Response team ETA: twenty minutes.'

Rowan Navara and his wife, Fiona, pulled into the driveway outside their two-bedroom home. The doors of the silver sports car swung upward and Fiona stepped out, her high heels clicking on the concrete. Rowan loosened his tie and was about to follow when he heard his wife's comms beep simultaneously with his.

Fiona sat back down into the plush seat and looked at the car clock: 21:45. 'Better be important.'

'I'll get someone to cover,' Rowan offered and opened the link to the car dashboard console. A holographic display of Renee beamed against the windscreen.

'Hey, guys, we've got a situation,' she reported. 'Thought you might wanna take a look.' She hit play on the recording Chesh had made of their pursuit and the mysterious black portal.

'What is that?' Fiona tapped "zoom" to get a better look.

'Some kinda freaky teleport,' said Renee. 'Lana and Rachel are away on Realm Recon. We're headed into space to search for any other ships.'

'We'll join the response team,' Fiona volunteered and ended the transmission.

'Heck of a way to cap our anniversary.' Rowan turned the car back on and backed onto the road. He'd been putting aside credits for this, his dream car, for years. Any excuse to drive it and drive it fast gave him great boyish pleasure. He thumbed a button on the steering wheel, and selected "Access Test" to use the fast lane on the highway he and Fiona now entered. This random test required him to tap the same thumb button twice when a small green signal appeared on the windscreen. He then had to wait three seconds and tap four times. He completed the test and was granted entry into the fast lane exiting the city.

Rowan disconnected the drive control link from the Driverless Road Safety Leader, pushing the accelerator to reach one hundred and thirty kilometres per hour. Had he failed the test, his car wouldn't have allowed him to disengage from the DRSL. And any road law infringement outside the DRSL would automatically cause his car to decelerate and pull into the emergency lane.

'Did you hear Charlie and Lex are expecting?' Fiona hit the Security lights to blink at the front and rear of the car, giving them right-of-way. They passed the DRSL car leading the auto-drive-linked traffic, and the line of cars soon retreated into the distance.

'Good for them.' Rowan couldn't detect any hints in his wife's tone, but he couldn't help a feeling of apprehension.

'I'll send them a card,' Fiona said distractedly while tapping on a data pad. 'There are a few seats left for a flight tomorrow. I say we do this thing tonight and gee'et.'

Rowan chuckled at Fiona's Texan pronunciation of "get". 'Let's do it.' He breathed a silent sigh of relief, thinking the mention of Charlie and Lex had been headed for "let's have kids" territory.

Rowan and Fiona had planned to take a morning flight to Soumia, a tropical colony, in two days. Tonight's interruption had convinced her that they should start their vacation early.

They sped along the hill crest, and the factory rose from the horizon between the black and the stars. It was an ominous scene. The rusted walls and broken windows were illuminated by the headlights of three vehicles.

Rowan parked and Brad Hawkins walked over to brief them.

'Anybody gone in yet?' Fiona asked, removing her earrings. She dropped them in her purse and threw it into the back seat of the car with her shoes.

Brad nodded to the building. 'The response team is inside now.' He took a moment to admire the high-powered vehicle, while Rowan and Fiona opened a case of tactical equipment in the boot. 'You must'a saved some serious credits for a ride like this.' He looked up and nodded to Rowan's bow tie. 'What's with the outfit?'

'Anniversary.' Rowan armed himself with a pistol and shotgun.

He and Fiona changed out of their formal wear, and into Kevlar-woven clothes. Rowan put on an armoured vest and handed one to Fiona. 'So, what's inside?' he asked.

Brad handed them each a comms earpiece. 'All signals are jammed by whatever it is they dropped through the roof. The team will shut it down if they can.'

Rowan turned on the torch attached to his shotgun, lighting the bird-poo-speckled concrete at his feet. An eerie feeling crept over him. He stole a glance at the windows of the factory's second floor. A figure retreated. He followed Fiona to the factory doors and took aim while she opened. He checked the interior and signalled that it was clear to enter. Her boots echoed against the high ceiling of the ground floor. He moved to a stairwell while she checked each corner of the open space.

'Response team, backup has arrived,' Rowan called out. No reply. He crept around the assembly machines and the empty shells of family-sized vehicles. He paused when his torchlight beamed over two bodies in the stairwell. Battery fluid was splashed against the wall and trickling down the steps. Fiona arrived beside him, and they exchanged a concerned look. They proceeded up the stairs and stopped when they found two of the surviving AMs standing guard. Light from the vehicles outside shone through the floor-to-ceiling windows. Rowan could see the two AMs were uninjured. One was holding a sword, looking with a furrowed brow at the battery fluid dripping from it.

'What happened here?' Rowan asked. 'Report, soldier.'

Someone lunged at Rowan from the shadows and knocked the shotgun out of his hands.

Fiona advanced from the stairs, and was struck down. She squeezed off one stray shot before her weapon clattered across the floor.

Rowan was kicked in the back of his knees. He fell. He now saw four AMs, and they began to shimmer in the light. Their uniform gradually faded, turning dark, transforming into black rubber straps wound around their slim physiques, covering most of their bodies. Dark veins coursed beneath their pale skin. Their hair was black, their eyes white with small pupils.

The sword-wielding one stepped forward and spoke in English. 'I am Sentinel Kordin. We are the Raekeem.' His lacklustre tone suggested he was beginning a speech he had given dozens of times before. He looked to be in his early thirties. His deep-set, intelligent eyes wandered with disinterest over the two humans before him. When he spoke, he revealed a forked tongue.

'You have a choice,' he said, wiping the blade clean against his leg before returning it to a sheath on his back. 'The same choice I offered those machines.'

A female Raekeem leaned forward, bringing her face close to Fiona's. She licked Fiona's cheek, took a step back and spat on the floor.

'Xera, please,' Kordin chided impatiently.

Xera grimaced at the taste on her tongue, baring sharp teeth.

Fiona edged closer to Rowan. They exchanged a glance when they heard a commotion outside. Fiona's gunshot had alerted Brad and the others.

A tone sounded from a console strapped to the inside of Kordin's wrist, and he tapped a button to read a text transmission. He signalled for two of his fellow Sentinels to go downstairs.

Fiona could hear a subtle hum coming from the floor above. *These aliens are here to protect whatever they dropped through the roof,* she thought.

Kordin returned his attention to his captives. 'Your choice is simple: you can leave with or without your heads.'

Fiona feigned injury from being knocked down earlier. She leaned into Rowan while she reached to his back and pulled the pin on a flash grenade strapped to his belt.

Rowan felt her movement and held her arm, tapping his finger once, twice, and on the third, she tossed the grenade a metre high. They covered their eyes. The flash grenade blew, blinding the Raekeem.

Xera swung her sharp elbows in Fiona's direction. Fiona sidestepped, and the wooden crate behind her took a slash instead. The two grappled and swung each other's weight, turning in circles, each trying to dominate the other, until they fell to the ground. Fiona threw her legs around her opponent's head. Xera's sharp teeth bit through Fiona's leather boot. Fiona released her, and Xera kicked her off. They rose. Fiona blocked Xera's low and high flick kicks, ducked under a roundhouse and rose under her crotch. Taking Xera's weight across her shoulders, Fiona threw her, spinning, into a barrel roll. Fiona twirled mid-air and landed the heel of her boot in Xera's abdomen, sending her over a dusty table and into a stack of chairs.

Rowan had, meanwhile, dealt lightning-fast Wing Chun roll punches into Kordin's chest and face while he was blinded by the flash. Kordin staggered away and drew a short knife from his belt. Sidestepping, Rowan squared his shoulders and readied his hands for a swift disarm.

Kordin advanced, feigned a straight stab and jerked the blade out, slashing Rowan across the chest. Rowan clenched his teeth through the stinging pain and swung a roundhouse kick across Kordin's head.

Kordin spat black blood and turned, hearing boot steps approach from behind. He couldn't react fast enough to avoid Fiona.

Leaping from a straight sprint, she brought her knees to her chest, rotated her body into a corkscrew spin and kicked her feet hard into Kordin, sending him through a wall. Plaster exploded across a desk as he broke through the factory office, crashed through a whiteboard, bounced off a desk, rolled over a chair and slammed into the opposite wall.

Rowan patted the dust from Fiona's leggings when she picked herself up from the floor. 'Nice launch.'

They heard the rushing boot steps of an AM team, and Brad came up the stairs. Rowan looked to Fiona. 'Where's the other one?'

Fiona cast around for the Raekeem woman she had fought. 'Uh-oh.'

They both saw a black cloud forming in the office. Xera was helping Kordin onto his feet while their teleport consumed them, and they vanished.

Kordin and Xera arrived aboard the Raekeem mother ship. Xera had set coordinates for the sick bay, and a medic approached carrying a syringe of black liquid. The two each took an injection as they groaned through the pain. The stem cell accelerant regenerated their damaged muscles and skin tissue.

Kordin undressed and threw his uniform across the room. The medic attempted to assess him and Kordin pushed him away.

Xera clenched her teeth while the serum took effect. The bruises around her abdomen began to fade. Her nose twitched from traces of Fiona's scent.

'That could have gone better,' she growled. Lengths of rubber coiled on the floor as she unwound the strips of her uniform and followed Kordin to a washroom.

A fine spray of water jetted from the ceiling. Kordin breathed through a wave of frustration before he pounded his fist into the metal wall.

'We completed our mission, Kordin,' Xera assured him. 'We delayed them long enough for the payload to–'

'That is not what angers me,' Kordin snapped. He saw her flinch and raised a hand in apology. 'Come. Wash.'

The two of them had developed an intimate relationship after many years of friendship. But Xera belonged to a lower clan, so an official bond was forbidden. It was believed among the Raekeem that blood lines had to remain pure. High clans only mated with high clans. Of course, this rule did not apply to the Lords of the Raekeem.

Telsta was Kordin's Lord, and he chose whomever he wanted as his concubine. Unfortunately, those chosen often did not return from their Lord's chambers unscathed. Many died from their injuries.

'It is not the humans who anger me either,' Kordin said. 'Although I will kill that man if our paths cross again. It is this mission. It is a foolish—'

'Kordin,' Xera whispered and glanced back at the sick bay. 'Be careful what you say.'

'Let them hear. I don't care anymore.' He leaned against the floor-to-ceiling window and gazed out at Silica. From space it looked like an eyeball, with its city populating just one spot on the white planet. The mother ship was cloaked, positioned far from space traffic.

'What do we gain?' Kordin argued. 'What do these people have that we cannot find elsewhere?' He looked back at Xera when she did not respond, and waited for her opinion.

Xera focused on washing herself with gel from a dispenser. 'I agree,' she whispered, hesitantly. 'Our being here makes no sense. But it is not ours to question why.'

Kordin felt Xera's hands massage his neck muscles. 'You called out to her last night,' he said.

Xera's gaze did not leave the white planet. 'Mother haunts me still.'

Kordin knew little of the incident. He had enquired about Xera's mother, who'd been head of a lower clan and a skilled technician working on Telsta's command deck. He'd been told only that there was an accident, and that she died before medical aid could be given.

'She would be proud of the woman you have become,' he said, and left the washroom to get dressed.

Kordin turned to see that Xera hadn't moved. He told her he would find her later, and she nodded, still staring out into space.

Kordin decided to deviate from the corridor that led to his quarters and took an elevator to the senior officers' deck. He walked along a row of three doors, each bearing the symbol of his clan, an inverted triangle inside an egg shape. The first two were locked, and the third was in use.

The first quarters belonged to Kordin's late father. The second was his uncle's, who was said to have vanished during a secret mission. The third was Feen's, his only living blood, the youngest of the three brothers.

Kordin entered his family code on the pad of the second door. His lost uncle had rewired the standard lighting and connected it to old lamps found in human worlds. They all turned on automatically, illuminating the room with a warm yellow hue. The red-carpeted floor and leather couches offered a musk that could not be found anywhere else on the ship.

Kordin picked up a small wooden carving of a bird. It was one of many ornaments and trinkets standing on shelves that held hundreds of paper-bound books. A wave of nostalgia washed over him, while he recalled the many nights his uncle would read to him. Kordin would hold the bird, mapping its form with his small fingers and staring across the room, imagining the scenes his uncle described.

'Get out.' A voice came from the door.

Kordin turned to see his uncle, Feen. He calmly returned the wooden bird to its spot, facing it outward, exactly as it was.

'You have no business being here,' said Feen.

'I will find out what happened to him,' Kordin promised and stalked out.

Chapter 4

Rachel shot the hinges while Lana took a running leap, planted her feet into the door and rode it like a surfboard across the concrete, aiming her P90 into the factory interior. Rachel followed her in with the shotgun Rowan had left on the floor below. The clap and grind of Lana's entry echoed back to them from the rear wall. They both wore masks, in case the alien capsule they were here to investigate was a chemical weapon like the one the Raekeem had used to pollute Haze Realm.

Rachel signalled to the AMs behind them to check the far end of the matte black, minibus-size capsule. She couldn't discern what material it was made of, but its thick reinforcement ribbing had obviously protected it from the fall. Glass and support beams from the broken roof lay crumpled beneath it. Lana's gaze followed a pigeon flying up through the gaping ceiling. Rounding the broad side of the container, she found two curved doors. They were already open. She turned on the torch attached to her P90 and shone it into the dark interior, illuminating two rows of three cylindrical tubes standing against the walls. She and Rachel entered, stepping sideways, back-to-back, checking each of the tubes.

'They're people,' said Lana. 'Rache, these three are Council members serving the current term.'

'Hank.'

Lana spun around when she heard Rachel's scared tone. She helped Rachel pull on a pod's door handle. The frosted rubber seal gave, and the door swung open. Rachel shouldered her gun and peered closely at her old friend and former Captain, Henry "Hank" Drake. She pressed her fingers to his neck to check for a pulse. Nothing.

Hank's eyes snapped open. He latched his ice-cold hand onto Rachel's throat and lifted her off the ground. Lana tried to pry away Hank's fingers, but he back-fisted her in the face.

Rachel took her knife from the sheath at her back and slashed Hank's arm, opening the skin to reveal electrical wires and tension cables. She could hear the rapid boots of the AMs approaching. Her eyes bulged as his grip tightened.

Lana's axe blade came down on Hank's arm. She chopped two more times, and Rachel fell with the severed hand still holding her throat.

Lana dragged Rachel out of the container, while the Hank-bot stepped out of the capsule. She tossed in a fragmentation grenade and ordered the AMs to close the doors. There was a dull bang a second after they did. A cacophony of startled pigeons took flight from the rafters of the factory, and feathers drifted.

Lana pried the robot hand off Rachel's neck. Rachel coughed and tried her comms to see if Lana's grenade had knocked out whatever was jamming their signal. 'Brad, come in.'

'Rache, we're on our way up. What's the commotion?'

'Some kinda robot replica of–'

A jarring blow hit the doors from inside the container.

Rachel equipped her shotgun when the doors swung open. The Hank-bot emerged from the smoke. Wires sparked from its damaged legs. Lana and the AMs opened fire. Rachel aimed and delivered a slug to its head. It dropped to its knees, its body smoking as it fell. Rachel stood over it, ready to fire again.

Lana rolled the bot onto its back and used her axe to cleave the artificial flesh enough to reveal writing and symbols printed across its chest plate. With the camera on her wrist console, she recorded an engraving that read "IDBot 5", followed by two lines of alien script. A screen displayed red digits counting down from eleven seconds.

'Oh shit!' Lana exclaimed with a backward step. 'Bomb!'

'Everybody out!' Rachel called through her comms.

Lana fired at the nearest window, shattering the glass, before leaping through it and onto the veranda roof. Rachel and the AMs followed, and they ran along the slope. They dropped and slid off the gutter to the ground. The sheet metal rocked beneath Lana's feet when the IDBot detonated.

The explosion ripped apart the alien pod, setting off a chain reaction in the remaining robots. Glass and metal supports were projected in all directions as the factory roof and walls bulged and were blown apart by the radial blast.

Earth
San Francisco

A four-unit security detail arrived at the portal room. They took positions behind the transparent blast panels that rose from the floor, surrounding the platform in the centre. A bright flash lit the room and a portal expanded on the platform. Rachel and Lana rolled out, and dust, chunks of concrete, and metal debris followed with them.

The portal closed. The blast shields were lowered. Lana crawled out from under a sheet of corrugated iron, and Rachel helped her to her feet.

Rachel coughed and waved the medical team away when they arrived by her side. 'I'm fine.'

Sam initiated clean-up from the control deck once everybody was clear of the podium. The circular piece slowly rose, separated into curved panels and dipped inward, pouring the rubble into a deep well.

She followed the dirty footprints along the corridor to the washroom. 'What happened?' She looked both women up and down. They were caked in dust. 'Did you find what the Raekeem dropped?'

Lana shook pebbles from her hair. 'We found robot doubles.'

'Exact replicas of Council members…' Rachel paused, kneading the tender muscles in her neck. 'And Hank.'

Sam's head jerked back in surprise.

'They all must've had bombs in their chests,' Lana added. 'There was no time to disarm them.'

'I'll prep a briefing with everyone,' said Sam as she left.

Lana and Rachel took a shower. Soon the room was steamy, and the floor was coloured grey from the dust that had clung to their skin.

'I have a feeling this is the beginning of something very bad,' said Lana.

Rachel gave her a long, pensive look. 'I have a feeling the bad began months ago. They had to study our leadership, the current Council members.'

Once clean, they dressed, and Rachel said she would go and call Hank to make sure he was actually Hank.

Lana needed to talk to Sam up on the Command level. She rubbed a towel into her hair while Sam finished typing and sent a briefing schedule to her dad, Lana and Rachel.

'The briefing's in an hour,' said Sam. 'You should go get some rest.'

'Too wired after that. Hey, did you hear about the countermeasures against singlism?'

'I did,' Sam replied slowly. 'But I don't really understand it because I was never aware of it. I've been in one relationship after the other my whole life.'

'Well, I've only been out in the real world for a few years.' Lana shrugged. 'So I've only been in one relationship, with that cyclist guy, remember?'

'Yeah, he broke it off,' Sam recalled, but elbowed her encouragingly. 'You gonna get back on the horse?'

'No. And to be honest, I only dated him because it was what everyone else seemed to be doing. I went into it knowing that people get hurt doing this thing we're expected to do, knowing that people become depressed about the outcome, and that they keep doing it even though it takes away a piece of their self-worth every time they fail at playing "the dating game", at "getting back on the horse". Gotta get back in the race to get that "partner" status! Gotta get married, get a car, get a house, get those accessories, whaddya call 'em? Oh, yeah: children. Gotta build up that social status! Gotta get another car, a bigger house–'

'I know.' Sam laughed at Lana's advert voice. 'We think we're a progressive society, but we're still acting out a centuries old, outdated, socially constructed script.' She leaned into Lana inquisitively. 'But are our expectations, our social pressures, really that oppressive?'

'Well, yeah,' Lana said with a furrowed brow. 'Nobody wants to admit it, but the truth is: single women are seen as lepers and single men are seen as sexual predators. The way we judge people according to how they live is 1690s Salem archaic.'

Sam didn't have an answer to the problem. 'The Council can't ban couples, though I guess there's no actual need to couple. Adoption, insemination–'

'No, no, no…' Lana breathed patiently. 'Genuine love, what people like you and Rachel have, is *real*. It should be nurtured. I don't think being in love and starting a family is what makes people think they're better. Love is real and children are the future, but status? It's nothing. Marital status is a fake fucking badge of honour.'

'Language, please.' Professor Peter O'Conner entered the room while looking over his glasses at Lana. And before she could protest, Pete said, 'I agree. And in terms of love dynamics, it's not just single people who are discriminated against. Harems, quads and people who are in open relationships, they're ostracised too. People hate ambiguity. Anything other than having a soulmate means you're a swinger, a pervert or a loner.'

Sam and Lana exchanged a surprised look, and Sam felt her cup of coffee leave her hand. 'Hey, get your own–'

'Just a sip,' Pete said, eagerly pressing it to his lips and drinking deeply. He took off his glasses and rubbed a knuckle into each closed eye. 'I was up all night helping to write up a Proposal Vote with all the colony mayors, the Council, and Hutch Branner as well, concerning marital status…' He looked down his nose again at Lana. 'And its incremental banning from any further official use in UC society.'

'Pff! What?' Sam chuckled. 'Dad, nobody is going to vote yes to "ban" marital status. *Titles* have been around for thousands of years.'

'They will if they don't want our allies to abandon us,' Pete stated matter-of-factly. 'Oh, yeah: the Kiyol and Laicians were there weighing in as well.'

Lana's jaw dropped and she glanced from Sam's frozen expression to Pete. 'They're going to pull out if we don't deal with singlism?'

Pete drank the last of the coffee before handing the cup back to Sam. 'They see it as a violation of freedom, and are frankly disgusted that we let it run unchecked for so long. Their societies are older than ours. They went through all the isms, eradicated them one by one, brutally in some cases. Singlism was one of the first to go in Kiyol culture.' He glanced at Sam, somewhat disappointed. '"Titles",' he huffed. 'Honestly, Sam, we barely survived the fight against Sabre Company without help from our allies, and now we're facing an alien threat. "Oh, but we have marital status!" Yeah, that'll send 'em packing.'

'Ease up, Dad. Until this morning, I didn't know singlism was a word. And I sure as shit didn't know our allies cared about how we treat each other.'

Sam wasn't just testy about him drinking her coffee, she was engaged in a mental battle between the socially, culturally and traditionally conditioned side of her and her innately compassionate side: *Have I said and done things to single people that made them feel like they're worthless?* In the next moment: *I have the right to be called somebody's wife if I want to be seen that way. Seen that way? What am I, distantly related to a royal family, demanding legitimacy?*

She gazed, bewildered, into her empty cup and spoke her next thought. 'Marital status has been rooted in and maintained in a lot of cultures for a long time.'

'So was slavery.'

Sam's head jerked up at her father's retort.

'Wars were fought for people's "right" to keep slaves, to maintain their social status and their slave-trade wealth.' He crossed his arms. 'I'm sorry, but did you really think stopping singlism was just about protecting people's feelings?'

'Yes,' Sam confessed. 'But try pitching all that to the whole of the Universal Community. We're not as evolved as we like to think we are.'

'True, yes.' Pete placed a hand on his daughter's shoulder. 'I apologise for being irate. It's been… a day.' He let out a tired sigh. 'I know what we have to do to shake people out of their entitled fantasies will be challenging. It hit home for me personally. I loved your mother, my *wife.* I was proud to be her *husband.* But I'm not willing to hold on to such titles so desperately, at the expense of everyone else's freedom. And that's ultimately the point the Council will try to communicate to everyone: freedom is worth the sacrifice. Ethnographic data never lies. Ubiquitous treatment of people on a societal level determines how we live our lives, how we are *allowed* to live our lives.'

He paused to let Sam and Lana consider the gravity of what must be changed. 'Marital status is a social caste system. The only argument in favour of keeping it hasn't got anything to do with how long we've been perpetuating it. It's about how popular the tradition is, how the "majority" has been enjoying it as' – and he nodded at Lana – 'a badge of honour. A decade before the Great Migration, there was a social shift.' He gave Sam a knowing look. 'Remember? Your mother and I, everyone who was coupled, were the *minority*. We all knew there were too many people making too many people on this too-small planet for far too long. A lot of people stopped having babies, and more stopped getting married. So many that billions of people like Lana, people like Meg Green, and now me – we who have no "other half", who are seen as half of a person, if a person at all – were the *majority*.'

'Now that the population problem has been solved, the colonies are growing,' Sam deduced. 'People are starting families again. The social dynamic has reverted back.'

'This Proposal Vote, properly implemented, should help bring respect for our fellow U-Comms back into the forefront of everyone's mind,' Pete stated resolutely.

'Heck of an ultimatum,' Lana breathed. 'Stop being a bunch of pretentious pricks–'

'Language.'

'–or stand alone in the galaxy, a single race, among potentially predatory ones like the Raekeem.'

'"Single", very good.' Pete chuckled, and said over his shoulder on his way out, 'I'll see you two at the briefing.'

Lana was gazing out of the window to the portal room below. She turned back, and Sam gave her a "What's up?" look.

'Did you…' Lana stopped. 'This isn't the time. I'll bring it up later.'

'Uh-uh.' Sam pulled a chair over. 'I know you almost got crushed by a building today, and we're in for a fight against who-knows-what, but you know the rules: we deal with shit better when we deal with it now. Right now. Sit.'

Lana hung her head and dropped into the chair. 'Did you always want to be a scientist?'

'Not at first.' Sam thought for a moment. 'My mother took me to ballet lessons when I started school. I was good, so I thought I'd grow up to become a professional dancer. But then the girls arrived,' she said, gesturing to her breasts. 'And I fell victim to top-heavy discrimination.'

Lana forced a smile.

'What's bothering you?' Sam asked.

Painful considerations made it hard for Lana to look anywhere but the floor. Even thinking of what she had to say hurt, and she was afraid of what Sam might think. She felt her friend's hand rest on her knee.

'Lana, it's me,' Sam encouraged. 'Say whatever–'

'I can't do this anymore.'

Sam leaned back in surprise, but then rolled her chair close to Lana. 'You want to resign?'

'I don't want to. I have to.' Lana lowered her voice in case Rachel was close by. 'I'm supposed to help people, Sam. I can't just observe.'

'Lana–'

'I can't watch people get hurt. These places we go to, these people we see… We're not talking about animals in the wild. They're people and some of them need help.'

'What happened in Theotech?' Sam asked.

Lana slowly recounted her visit back to the world where the religious and the secular lived in separate populations, while Sam listened closely…

Chapter 5

The sphere retracted, and Lana made her way along an outer city street. It was 05:00. Nobody was around and there were no police on patrol. Crime was very low in the cities, due to the division and colour-coding of religions.

The sun began to rise, and Lana found the alley where she and Rachel had last seen the man escorted by law enforcement. She followed stairs down to a body of water, where an amphibious plane was docked. When she approached, an officer stepped out and called to her, pulling his side-arm.

'Stop right there.'

Lana raised her hands. 'I was called to duty at short notice,' she said. 'I've been assigned to join you.'

The man peered at her suspiciously. 'You got ID?'

Lana patted her jean pockets and shrugged. 'Like I said, short notice.'

One of the other guards handed him a wand that Lana guessed was used for detecting explosives. He tossed it to her. 'You know the drill.'

Lana caught it, pressed a button on the handle and waved it over her back, sides and boots.

'We're late,' the guard called, satisfied. 'Climb aboard.'

Engine noise sounded. Lana moved along the passengers and was relieved to find the man she'd been looking for was unharmed. She sat down next to him. He seemed very nervous, watching the two officers at the head of the plane. He gave Lana a quick glance and didn't seem threatened, perhaps because she wasn't armed with a baton like the other two.

'I'm Lana,' she said, and held out her hand.

The man looked at it. 'Paul.'

'You don't shake hands as a greeting where you're from?'

'Oh.' He smiled. 'No, we don't display any… well, anything toward each other in public.'

'I see.' Lana spoke her next words quietly. 'I'm not an officer. I lied to get aboard.'

'Figured that.' Paul gripped the arm supports of his chair when the plane skimmed the water's surface. It shuddered when its wings took to the air. Lana looked down at her pinned hand, and Paul's crushing grip.

'Um…'

'Sorry.' Paul released her and wiped the sweat from his brow. 'So, why did you come aboard?'

'I saw you being taken away. Are these other people secular?'

Paul looked about at the other passengers. 'They wouldn't be on this plane if they weren't.'

Lana kept an eye on the officers. 'Paul, where are they taking us?'

'Across the bay. We're not far from the Majority border.'

'Have they hurt you?' she asked, looking over Paul's body. He had a wide build, like he'd spent most of his life working heavy-lifting jobs.

He seemed surprised that she would ask. 'No. They're standard escort security for religion departure.'

'Then why are you so tense?'

'I've never been on a plane before.'

After fifteen minutes of silence, Paul looked out of his window at the land appearing beneath the clouds. 'Hey, look at that.' He breathed a sigh of relief. 'We're here.'

Lana saw that artificial basins had been built to extend the city further into the sea. A long-nosed train sped along its magnetic rail, between high-rise apartments and neon-lit businesses.

'Why are you leaving your religion?' she asked.

'It doesn't allow homosexuality,' said Paul. 'None of the religions do.'

'Did you leave family back there?'

'My parents, my sister.' Paul braced himself and clenched his teeth when the plane skimmed over the sea, then let the water take its weight. He exhaled again once it stopped bobbing. 'I'm allowed to visit them. But the officials will probably question me more about the men I was with. I'll never give them names.'

Lana was disgusted by the archaic system where sexuality could in any way determine what community you were allowed to belong to.

After disembarking, Lana explained to the guards that due to air travel sickness, Paul needed help carrying his luggage, and she offered to guide him to public transport. Once clear of the dock, she asked him about the division of religions, and their separation from the majority of the world population. Paul answered her questions, but warned her that his information might not be accurate, due to his religion having tailored their records and education to fit their ideology. He suspected other religions did as well.

'Thank you, Paul.' Lana shook his hand when they arrived at the taxi bay. 'And good luck.'

Paul wrote down his contact details on a piece of paper and handed it to her. 'Look me up. We'll have coffee.'

'I get it,' said Sam. 'Theotech has its problems. And if we intervene, maybe give them advice on more inclusive education and voting for public change to eliminate discrimination, they might benefit, sure. I question what we do here sometimes. The situations you guys have to walk away from… it can't be easy. But it's Kiyol technology we're using here. They set the ground rules.'

Lana remembered the meeting Ambassador Jainon had called after the conflict against Sabre Company. Everybody on the Shifter team had forgotten all about the agreement. Even Henry Drake, who had struck the deal on Professor O'Conner's behalf, was unprepared when Jainon arrived in San Francisco.

Jainon hadn't forgotten, and it was her duty to remind the professor that the words spoken in his absence were binding. All Shifter technology was to be returned to the Kiyol following the defeat of Sabre Company.

The meeting had gone on for hours. Lana and every member of the team gave first-hand evidence of the good they had done, and the knowledge they had gained. All the while, Jainon had listened patiently. She requested a recess to speak with her colleagues via comms and returned some time later to deliver their verdict. It was agreed that the Shifter team would be allowed to keep the technology on one condition. And that condition was what changed the work Lana had come to love during her time as a member of the team.

No more interfering in Realm culture in any way. Observation was now the Shifter team's prime directive.

'Have you talked to Rachel about this?'

Lana shook her head solemnly. 'I will. It's just, with all that's been happening…' She saw that Sam wasn't buying her excuse. 'I don't want to let her down.'

Henry Drake's voice sounded in the corridor as Rachel walked by with her comms on speaker. She was stress-eating an apple fritter on her way to the briefing room when her former Captain answered.

'Hank, are you alright?' Rachel couldn't help her rapid speech and concerned tone. She'd known Hank for many years. 'You tried to kill me, so we had to blow you up, and the other IDBots blew up as well, and the whole factory came down.'

'Who is this?'

'It's Rache. So, you're alright?'

'Of course I'm alright,' Hank replied wearily. He sounded like he'd just woken up, and probably had, because he was in Alaska trying to enjoy his retirement. 'A whole factory, huh?'

'It was… I won't get into it,' said Rachel, breathing a sigh of relief. 'We'll fill you in later.'

'Alrighty. Thanks for calling.'

Lana watched Rachel walk on. 'I mean, will she be alright without me?'

'Just tell her what you told me,' said Sam. 'She'll understand.'

When Sam and Lana arrived, the rest of the team were already assembled in the briefing room. Hutch Branner had also been called in to assess the photos Lana took of the IDBot.

'So there could be more of them?' Sam asked when she found a seat.

'We saw two empty cylinders,' Lana said, with a glance to Rachel. 'That's two robot doubles looking identical to, most likely, two people in positions of power. And they're wandering around ready to blow.'

There was a list of possible candidates in Pete's head, but he decided to raise a more pertinent issue. 'What if the Raekeem have been here for years? Sabre Company may have been working with them.'

Rachel shook her head. 'There wasn't anything about the Raekeem in Jericho Williams' memory.' She had delved into the mind of the Sabre

Company Colonel to find the location of the General, Dennis Conroy. She knew everything he knew. And she guessed the Raekeem would have seen the SC militant force as a threat, and attacked them as well, had they still been around.

'Can't be a coincidence,' said Sam.

'What?' Lana asked.

'The Matter Portal is temporally disabled.'

Rachel leaned forward abruptly. 'What? How?'

'The Kiyol reported it an hour ago,' Pete explained. 'Some kind of disruption wave passed through the site and fried everything at their power relay station.'

Sam nodded at Lana's frustrated expression. 'Your Shifters won't be able to produce anything you've replicated until it's repaired, which could take months. Which makes me think–'

'It's them,' Rachel agreed.

Lana tapped at her console, connected to the large screen projector, and brought up a freeze-frame shot of the IDBot's open chest. 'Safe to assume the markings on the IDBot are Raekeem.'

'I sent your intel to the Kiyol,' said Sam. 'They agree; the script doesn't belong to any known dialect, alien or human.'

'Can you zoom in on the symbols below IDBot 5?' Hutch Branner asked Lana, squinting at something that caught his eye. The visual zoomed in on a group of three symbols. 'Those are signoff imprints. We use them for completed units at the factory. Standard testing approval. But I've never seen this type of machine before. The only other guy who ever made...'

'Crone,' said Pete.

Sam looked from him to Hutch. 'Who?'

'Howard Crone.' Hutch scratched at his grey beard. 'He was a student of mine, back before I left teaching at the Science Academy to start my factory. Howard was making basic bots for commercial use. He comes to mind because he was building robotic statues of historical figures for museums... Never did anything sinister like this, though that would explain why the bomb timer you saw displayed English numerals.'

Lana stood at the same time as Rachel. 'Where can we find him?'

'That's just it.' Pete looked to Hutch and back to Lana. 'You can't. Howard disappeared a few years ago. His wife and daughter, too. They vanished.'

Chapter 6

Cranes lifted rubble from the demolished factory outside Liberty. CAM units were tasked with searching for any Raekeem technology. Brad was using a lance to cut through a pinned girder, which was too long for the crane to lift in one piece. Once he was through, he stepped back and waited for the giant claw to carry away one section. Beneath it was a crumpled steel box that was padlocked. He used the lance to cut the lock, lifted the lid and fished around the damaged contents, finding four rectangular cases and four consoles.

After inspecting each item, Brad reported his findings. 'Rache, I found what look like medical supply kits and one working console.'

'Do a search for the name Howard Crone, with a "C", on the console for me. He could be the guy who built the IDBots.'

Brad wiped the dust-covered screen to better view the search. 'Says "Asset Objective Complete", and then there's numbers.'

'Could be Realm coordinates,' Rachel suggested. 'Send those through to me.'

San Francisco

'You were right.' Sam spoke over her shoulder to Rachel. 'They're coordinates… to an alternate version of Los Angeles.' She opened a portal to the coordinates Brad had found.

'I'll go suit up with the oth–' Rachel saw a reconnaissance craft drop from a compartment in the portal room ceiling and into the mercury sphere. 'Woah, what happened to the drone? Its bottom is melted.'

'Radiant heat,' said Sam. 'We sent it to Storm Realm to check on Kingston.' She watched the camera feed while the craft flew high over the alternate LA. 'Wildfires, or "bushfires", as the Aussies call them, had covered the city in smoke. I sent the drone to the nearest affected area. The link to their internet news showed that the whole country is on fire.'

The data hack commenced and information about the Realm was sourced from satellites and towers. Sam carried her data pad, following Rachel to the armoury where Lana and two AMs were preparing. 'The drone has done its sweep,' she reported. 'The Realm is fairly similar to what we found in Storm Realm four years ago: dense pollution, overpopulation.'

She typed the coordinates into the Realm database and titled it "Smog Realm".

Kiyol Home World
Leetheria City

Ambassador Jainon was escorted to her transport by the Kiyola warrior Jihna. A cool breeze blew against their purple skin. Jainon stopped before the ship ramp to take in the fresh scent of the vast plantation fields. The crops which supplied food to the people of Leetheria City were arrayed in a ring surrounding the inner district. The great waterfall ranges sparkled in the distance, beyond the animal reserves and townships.

'It worries me that the Matter Portal has been disabled,' Jainon confided. 'Have the engineering crews begun their repairs?' She looked at Jihna, tilting her head curiously. 'You have not spoken a word since we left the Council hall.'

'My apologies, Ambassador,' said Jihna in a monotone. 'I must be tired.'

A Kiyola warrior approaching the platform guards caught her eye. The warrior was Jihna. The real Jihna she thought she had thwarted.

A Kiyolo security guard stepped aside when Jihna hastened from the steps leading to the landing bay.

'Jihna?' He looked her up and down. 'Why have you changed out of your uniform?'

'Somebody drugged me last night. I woke very late.' Jihna nodded down at her two-piece sleep wear. 'I hurried here to…'

The Kiyolo spun around, and Jihna looked to where he was staring.

'Jihna,' he said, 'If you are here, who is that with the Ambassador?'

'Activate the anchor beams!' Jihna shouted, and ran to Ambassador Jainon.

The IDBot Jihna pulled a retractable staff from her belt, switched to the rifle function and fired a plasma round at her approaching target.

Jihna threw her body sideways into a mid-air spiral, landed, and rolled under the next shot. She rose and covered the gap to her double by completing a forward summersault, locking her legs around the IDBot's head. She swung her upper body across the ramp and threw the machine, burying the crown of its head into the tail of the ship.

A shocked Jainon stared down at her would-be assassin as she was hurried down the ramp by the pilot and guided toward the approaching guards.

The IDBot stood back up, placed its hands either side of its crooked head and snapped itself back into alignment. It glared at Jihna and advanced, landing a lightning-fast punch to her chest. Jihna fell backward and rolled across the port. She fought to breathe air into her winded lungs while her double dropped on top of her, pinning her with a knee on her chest. It raised its weapon high, poised to strike, while the staff activated a spear tip.

Jihna bared her fangs and bit deep into the machine's leg. Sparks flew from between her cheeks and she spat out electrical wires. The spearhead came down just as she was able to shift her shoulders. The blade snagged her top and stabbed into the metal platform. Flat on her back, Jihna drove her knee into the IDBot's spine.

The machine tumbled forward and turned awkwardly, having lost motor function in its damaged leg. It looked down at the cream-coloured top caught in the spear and retrieved the weapon. Jihna had climbed the wing of the ship and dropped behind it for a surprise attack. She brought her arms under its armpits, locking its head.

'Now!'

She held the struggling IDBot for a second more and a plasma blast struck its chest. She released and the guard fired a blast into the side of its head. Spasms shook the machine's body while it lay on the ground.

The guard stood over the IDBot, aiming his staff. Jihna rolled the body to reveal scorched wires hanging over its belly and an armoured chest plate lined with alien writing.

'Give me your blade and the power cell from your staff. Quickly! I must disarm the bomb!'

He gave her the knife, unloaded the palm-sized energy capsule from his staff and handed it over. Jihna activated the knife's blade-heating mechanism and it turned white hot. She cut away her double's chest armour to uncover the bomb timer. It was counting down from twelve seconds.

The metal plate came away after a firm tug, and Jihna found the chemical-based explosives ready to react and detonate. She cursed when she saw that one of the two small cylinders of liquid she lifted out was attached to a booby-trap lead. After cracking the guard's power cell open, Jihna poured the acid within over the IDBot's chest. The liquid sizzled on contact and the chest sank concave, consumed by the glowing ooze until there was nothing left but molten steel and wires.

The guard breathed a sigh of relief. 'Well done.'

'I did not know that would work.' She held the cylinder, severed from its lead, up to the light to inspect the dark substance. She handed it to him. 'Have this chemical identified.'

'The Ambassador is safe,' he reported. 'I am sorry, Jihna. We all thought it was you.'

'An exact replica,' she replied, studying the remains of the IDBot. 'The human Council were to be targeted as well, but that threat is gone. There is one more assassin unaccounted for that we know of.' She rose to her feet and paced quickly toward the nearest communications station. 'Of the allies in this galaxy, only one target remains.'

Aqua Sierra
Kulete City

'You called for me, Ma?' Prince Ohkwai Chillo entered the Records Hall, where his mother, Queen Sienta, waited by a column of spinning rings. She spoke to the columns and they glowed, turning the rings in response. Four of the sixty columns slowed, and the rings aligned to reveal sets of Laician symbols.

Chillo read the information his mother requested from the records. He let out an impatient sigh and returned her judgmental gaze.

'What is the meaning of this?' she asked sharply, her long finger stabbing at the column. Her eyelids blinked upwards with a narrow brow of stern expression. All industries within the royal domain were required to report production data, communications and other important pieces of information, and it was forwarded to the Records Hall every day. Promotions in any field were one of those other important pieces of information. And Chillo's son had been promoted to Pilot yesterday.

The Prince rolled his eyes. 'Calm down, Mother. He has enrolled into Exploration Studies.'

'No grandchild of mine will fly into space,' Sienta warned. 'How can you let him do this?'

'It is perfectly safe.' Chillo tried to calm himself, frustration brewing against yet another of his mother's attempts to control his family. 'You know Kida's mother is from the legged line. Kida is legged, which means he can fly our spacecrafts. It is a great honour to the schools of science and technology for a royal to choose to become an Explorer.'

Sienta swished her tail and the fin along her spine flexed its vibrant colours, betraying her panic. 'Exploration Studies?' She jabbed her finger back at the columns. 'It says Pilot. That means combat.'

'There must be some mistake,' Chillo lied, thinking, *I will speak to the administrator who disregarded my express instruction not to report Kida's promotion!*

Sienta's brow furrowed deeper and she tilted her head. 'Kida is just a boy. He is not ready for the dangers outside our waters. What if his hydration suit fails? That has happened, Chillo. It could happen to your son.'

'The ships have failsafe mechanisms. There are backup suits on board. All Pilots can abandon their crafts and teleport back to our seas if they need to. There is nothing to worry about.'

'Yes, what is it?' The Queen spoke in a shrill voice, looking over her son's shoulder toward a messenger at the door.

'Urgent communication, madam.' The young Laician woman swam swiftly to a communications console by the record columns. 'Shall I open the link for you now?'

'Who is it?' Chillo asked.

'Kiyola Warrior Jihna, my lord.'

Queen Sienta nodded, and the messenger opened the link.

The comms tone vibrated through the Records Hall and Jihna's voice came through. 'Greetings, Queen Sienta. I wish to warn you of a possible threat to your family.'

Chillo's mother shot him a "You see?" look. He ignored her. 'Chillo here, Jihna. Is this related to the aliens called the Raekeem and their attack on the humans?'

'There has been an attempt on our Ambassador's life as well,' said Jihna. 'The assailants are called IDBots, and if these machine replicas have been sent to my people and to the humans as prominent figures… people from each of our allied societies—'

'You believe one may have been sent to pose as one of my family,' Queen Sienta deduced. 'This is most troubling. Thank you for informing us.' She looked to her son. 'Alert the Royal Guard.'

Chapter 7

Smog Realm

The portal opened, and four AMs stepped out of the rippling mercury. They formed a line and saluted when Rachel approached. She and Lana had found an abandoned building in downtown LA to use as their base.

'At ease.' She gestured to two AM tech specialists, who had already used their consoles to hack into Smog Realm's version of the internet. 'They are our eyes and ears in this Realm. You're on guard detail. Keep this building secure while we locate Howard Crone.'

Lana received a message from Sam, and she read it out while sitting on a workbench. 'One of the IDBots made it to the Kiyol home world. The target was Ambassador Jainon.'

Rachel was stunned. 'How did it get from Silica all the way to Ameetac? Are they alright? Did they stop the bomb in time?'

'Nobody was hurt. It was a copy of Jihna,' Lana read from her console. 'The real Jihna fought it and managed to melt the bomb before the chemical reaction detonated.'

'The Laicians will be the next target.'

'Got a hit,' a tech unit reported. She'd assumed Howard would have a phone, and knew that many Realms had phone service providers, which held customer information. She was able to bypass all internet security and firewalls to find Howard's account.

She brought up a satellite map and zoomed in to street level. It was tracking, in real time, a car travelling along a highway overpass.

The tech unit calculated how long it would take to close the distance in the four-wheel drive Lana had procured upon arrival. 'We're fifteen minutes from this location.'

Rachel nodded to Lana. 'Let's go.'

Howard stepped out of his car and walked to his apartment. Once inside, he paced quickly to the door leading to a basement. He descended stairs to a narrow corridor crowded with stacked boxes and empty shelves. Entering a service elevator, he pressed the down button, counting the contents of a yellow envelope while he descended. The cash he had taken from his bank account amounted to twenty thousand dollars. He arrived at his basement lab, and motion-activated lights blinked on, illuminating tables and shelves cluttered with electrical equipment and explosives. Three rows of IDBots slept mounted in cylindrical capsules.

Howard uttered a routine greeting, and male and female voices responded in unison from within their capsules. 'Good morning, Howard.'

He powered on the computers and picked up a framed photo from beside a monitor. He wiped the glass, eyes growing hot at the sight of his smiling daughter. 'Daddy's gonna bring you home, honey. We're almost there.'

A flash of light blinded him, and he dropped the picture. He blinked at a young woman standing before him as she lowered her torch but not her side-arm.

'How did you…' Howard spied the elevator roof hatch hanging down before the doors closed. *She must've shimmied down the shaft cables.*

Lana retrieved the photo frame. 'Mr Crone,' she started. 'I'm from–'

'Give that back!' Howard cried, overcome by emotion when he saw the broken glass obscuring his child's face. His chin wrinkled, and his bottom lip trembled. 'What more could you possibly take from me?'

Lana handed over the picture and holstered her gun. 'Calm down. I'm not going to hurt you.' She pressed two fingers against Howard's temple, and a wave of his thoughts, feelings and memories surged through her mind.

Images and voices took her back to Home Realm. She experienced everything from Howard's perspective.

Howard was startled by a black cloud expanding in his yard beside the pool. Ink-like tendrils reflected off the water's surface.

'What is it, Howard?' his wife asked, standing beside him.

'I don't know.'

A scream came from their teenage daughter's bedroom, followed by thudding steps approaching from the hallway. A man and woman dressed in business attire carried her into the lounge while she fought to break free. They threw her to the floor. Howard lunged at them, and the woman struck him hard. He fell beside his daughter, and the pale-faced intruders took hold of his wife while the room was engulfed in a black cloud.

Howard and his family were forced down into chairs and their wrists were bound. Silhouettes approached through the light that shone from the floor. One of them spoke calmly, without threat. 'You're going to help us, Mr Crone.'

'Who are you?'

'We are the Raekeem.'

Howard glanced from his wife to his daughter, relieved that they were uninjured.

'We need your talents,' said the man. Now his tone darkened. 'If you refuse to build what we need–'

Lana felt an inertial pull when Howard's memory surged forward to the present location.

Howard watched his wife's glazed eyes as he pressed against the wound in her chest, trying to stop the bleeding. He cradled her and blinked through tears.

'Do your work, Mr Crone... or your daughter's death will not be as swift.'

Lana gasped for air, brought back to the present by the sound of the elevator door. Rachel entered, aiming her side-arm at Howard.

Lana raised her hand. 'I'm okay.' She regained her composure, and turned to see if Howard was alright. 'I'm sorry for your loss, Mr Crone.'

'How...' he breathed. 'How did you do that?'

Rachel looked around Howard's workshop and up at the unsettling display of sleeping IDBots. They were just base models of adult males and females, but they were alive.

Lana stepped to Rachel's side and related briefly what Howard had suffered. Rachel listened, while paying wary attention to the middle-aged man. She didn't holster her weapon. One of his creations tried to kill her. She didn't care what he'd been through. What was happening now, as a result of his actions, was her priority.

Rachel approached him, speaking evenly. 'You need to tell us everything you know about the Raekeem.'

Howard returned the frame to his desk. 'And who exactly are you people, huh? You barge in here with your mind-reading and your demands…'

'We're friends of Hutch Branner and Peter O'Conner,' Lana explained. 'Your machines have attacked us and the Kiyol.'

'I had to. You saw what they did to my wife,' he said, voice trembling. 'Abbey is all I have left. Save her and I'll tell you whatever you want to know.'

'Fine,' Rachel conceded, trying to hide her anger. 'In the meantime, my team is going to clean out your shop. Everything goes before the Raekeem can use it.'

'Of course.'

'Did they take Abbey aboard their ship?' Lana asked him.

'No.' Howard clenched his fists. 'They gave her to one of the gangs here in the city. Their salesman owns a club. He deals drugs… and traffics minors. I took out all the cash I have.' He pulled the envelope from his jacket and dropped it on the workbench. 'The Raekeem created an account to cover all the materials I needed for the Identity Robots. I did what they wanted. They're done with me.'

Rachel nodded to the envelope of cash. 'The salesman would've killed you and taken your money. I've seen it before.' Memories of months spent serving with the Liberty Underground before the liberation of Silica came to her mind. Slavers often accepted ransom. And they often reneged on the deal.

Lana studied the photo of Howard's daughter. The girl looked to be one size down from her own.

'I've got a plan,' she said to Rachel. And she turned to Howard. 'I'm going to bring Abbey back to you.'

She saw in Howard's eyes that he took her words as a promise she intended to keep.

Raekeem Sentinel Ship

Lord Telsta sat in a high-backed chair watching his Lead Sentinel, Feen, pace back and forth before him.

Feen glared down at his nephew and Xera. They were the only surviving members of the squad sent to deploy the IDBots in the world the Raekeem called the Three Kingdoms. They stood at attention, four steps down from Telsta's platform, accompanied by a new squad of six Sentinels. The hall was dark, illuminated only by lights along the perimeter and in a diamond formation in the centre, beaming from beneath steel grates lining the floor.

Xera couldn't stop her muscles from trembling, the subtle quiver of her long mane of hair betraying her anxiety. Kordin caught her perspiring scent. He guessed that she feared execution. Raekeem who failed their Lord were often cut open and left to bleed to death.

Feen stepped down, letting his boots clang loudly against the steel steps. His pointed ears caught the sharp intake of Xera's breath. Kordin was completely calm. This irritated Feen. Everything about his nephew flew in the face of Sentinel discipline. He set a bad example for younger Raekeem. He always wore his hair loose about his shoulders, with his fringe partially obscuring his eyes. All of the women on the ship loved his bad-boy attitude. Some of the younger male Sentinels were beginning to style their hair the same as his.

'Explain yourself, Sentinel!' Feen barked at Kordin.

'Our carrier was pursued by a human vessel,' Kordin replied with confidence.

'And you did not shoot them down?'

'We left the ship to secure the payload.' Kordin looked up to Lord Telsta and back to Feen. 'We delivered it as you ordered.'

Even now, in the most precarious of situations, Kordin saw a way to discredit the man who, instead of encouraging him through his years of training, instead of being an inspiration in his father's absence, had been his tormentor.

'Four of us teleported to the payload. The rest of my crew escaped.'

Feen brought his face close to Kordin's. 'Your ship could have been tracked back to this carrier! You should have ordered them to fight!' He moved on to Xera. 'And what of the IDBots?'

Xera's lips moved, but no words came.

'The contents were dispatched while we engaged the enemy,' Kordin stated flatly. 'Any that did not deploy must have been faulty in design. We should never have had a human build them.'

Lord Telsta spoke before Feen could react to this insubordinate retort. 'Perhaps you are right.' His next words came deep and slithering, his eyes wandering over Xera's body. 'You did well. Both of you.'

'My Lord.' A voice came over the ship comms. 'Our last Sentinel dispatch has returned from the next world. Scouting is complete.'

'I will view their findings now,' Telsta replied with haste. His eyes lingered on Xera until he turned to face a large viewing screen on the wall behind him.

Kordin and Xera received a brief "saved by the bell" glare from Feen.

A version of Earth was displayed, showing humans walking busy streets. Most wore business attire, and they were on their way to and from office buildings, eyes cast down, giving way to fellow pedestrians and traffic, seemingly without having to look. The view shifted to homeless people pushing their belongings in shopping trolleys.

'Useless, dead souls,' Telsta grumbled. 'Why do you waste my time? Is it not obvious we or one of the other Lords have already harvested these weaklings?'

Feen accessed the report issued by the returning team. 'My Lord, this world has received no prior visitation, according to our records.'

'Another society of self-imposed slavery.' Telsta watched the display blur with a haze of grey cloud and dense smog as the camera probe zoomed out of the city, crossed the globe to another country and flicked to a video feed following a man walking a busy street. 'So predictable.'

Telsta sighed in disappointment, but continued watching the man, who looked to be no older than thirty, talk to himself, staring down at a small photo in one hand, carrying a briefcase in the other. His tie was askew, his expensive suit gleaming in the sunlight. He wept, returning the photo to his pocket and looking to the road of speeding cars. A truck horn blared. He stepped out, and Lord Telsta's croaky laugh echoed through the hall. The impact startled nearby pedestrians. They stopped and stared. None of them approached the body. Then they turned away, hung their heads and kept walking.

Lord Telsta chuckled through a bout of coughing. His lungs wheezed until he pressed a breathing mask to his mouth. 'Oh... oh my. How amusing.'

Feen could not ignore the pressing urgency that the failed IDBots presented. 'My Lord, it is plain to see that there will be little essence, even if we harvest the children. Shall I prepare for the next phase?'

Telsta did not reply. He was intrigued by a man on the display, seated on a park bench, typing at a laptop. The man looked up every now and then, suspiciously eyeing off people passing by. 'That one, right there.' The image focused and stayed with him. Telsta's long black tongue licked his thin dark lips. 'Bring it to me.' He glanced at his Lead Sentinel. 'Conquering the Three Kingdoms will take some time. I require sustenance. Something fresh to bolster my strength.'

'Very good, my Lord,' the voice from the comms replied. 'Sentinels will deliver the essence to you directly.'

'No!' Telsta growled. 'I will harvest it myself.'

Feen was irritated by the delay, but he nodded and ordered everybody back to their stations.

'Feen,' said Telsta. 'You will not punish Kordin or Xera. They are to be commended for their efforts. And as for the next phase... assemble the fleet.'

The man typing at his laptop was startled to find two people dressed in grey suits standing behind him. Their strong arms hooked under his shoulders, dragging him over the bench and across the grass, behind a tree. Onlookers did not stop to help him. Instead, they walked fearfully on.

A black cloud appeared in front of Telsta. Long tendrils reached in all directions before receding and vanishing. The man was on his knees, shivering with fear. He blinked around at the dark room and gasped when he saw Lord Telsta grinning down at him.

'What were you doing there, human?' Telsta asked gently.

'What is this?' He looked around the dark room and the columns of light beaming from the floor. 'Where am I?'

'I can smell hope... mmm, some fight hidden within.' Telsta's snake tongue flicked, and his smile grew wider at the horror it brought to the man's face. 'I saw you typing your thoughts, human. Do you hope to one day share this hope, to encourage others in your caged society to…' – Telsta's thin eyebrows rose – 'refuse this "slavery"? Do you truly believe your kind would dare bite the hand that feeds you?'

The man swallowed hard. 'The hand that feeds… feeds only lies and false hope.'

'*Arbeit macht frei*,' Telsta replied in a parental tone.

The man was surprised that this alien creature knew human history.

'You seek freedom, do you not?' Telsta asked kindly. He smiled when he saw the man's eyes soften, as though he believed mercy was about to be bestowed.

Telsta could not wait any longer. He stepped away from his chair, stood over the man and, salivating between his words, said, 'Death is your freedom.'

Black tendrils circled him.

The man shrank from the clearing smoke. A taller figure loomed over him, and he let out a guttural scream. A seven-foot serpent stood in Telsta's place, balancing on its tail. Long barbs lined its thick carapace, and its head opened to a circular mouth full of serrated teeth, dripping viscous ooze. It dropped onto the man's chest and reared up as its tail arrived behind it, pinning him to the floor.

Screaming echoed through the dark hall. The creature's mouth latched over his head, twisting, slicing with its teeth.

Blood dribbled into the man's earlobes. His eyes stared into nothing.

Chapter 8

Smog Realm

Lana rolled her eyes in drug-induced delirium, acting her part as the college student picked up in a club owned by Nelson Abbot. He was the mafia salesman Howard had described, and Lana was posing as the product.

She was in a limousine being driven along an arterial road. When it rose to a crest, Lana saw thousands of makeshift buildings at the bottom of the hill and along the river. According to information the techs found on Smog Realm's internet, the poor in this city lived in homes made of any structural junk they could find. They had to rebuild their homes every year because flooding brought torrents of destructive waves through the river. Safely built atop the hill were the mansions, villas and suburban villages, the homes of the privileged. Golf courses, club halls, pools and spa houses were only accessible to them via private roads.

Nelson Abbot was smoking a cigar, the pungent, sweet smoke clouding the sunrays beaming through the car windows and skylight. He was watching the last of a stock market report on a TV screen imbedded in the limo's bar. A news broadcast came next. The anchorman greeted his audience jovially, and the live feed showed a row of nine men and women, kneeling, hands bound behind their backs, black hoods covering their heads.

'Today's public execution features some of the lowest scum of society: scammers and hackers. Let's see their faces.'

The men and women were unmasked, and the camera zoomed into each of their faces, displaying a detailed side graphic of their history and their known connections.

The view returned to the first in the long row of criminals. One by one, they were shot in the back of the head. The camera followed each one closely until the ninth was dead.

Lana groaned as though she were about to vomit.

'No, no, no. Not in the car.' Nelson found an ice bucket and pushed it into Lana's hands. 'How much did you give her?' he asked his henchmen.

'Her drink must'a already been spiked,' one said. 'She was like this when we found her.'

Their boss pushed aside a lock of Lana's hair and took her chin, turning her head left and right to inspect her features. 'What's your name, sweetheart?'

'Where… where am I?'

Nelson took in Lana's tight peach dress, cupped her right breast, squeezed, and then felt her side and buttocks. 'She's perfect, boys. You check her purse?'

'No ID. No cell phone.'

Nelson took a lollipop out of his jacket pocket. 'Here you go, sweet cheeks. Suck on that for now.'

The limo arrived at the Abbot Mansion, and the four of them went inside, followed closely by the armed driver. Lana gazed up at the chandelier hanging from the ceiling two stories above. She staggered, and one of the guards took her weight, under her shoulder. She pressed the candy end of the lollipop into the palm of her right hand and made a fist, with two fingers either side of the stick.

Nelson trudged up the stairs, loosening his tie. 'Get her washed up. I want her ready for bidding in an hour.' He heard one of his henchmen grunt and turned to see him drop to his knees, holding the back of his neck.

The other reached into his jacket for a gun. Lana took his arm, spun under it and pulled him face-first into a marble pillar. She snatched his gun and aimed it at Nelson. He ran up the stairs and screamed when Lana shot him in the leg. She waited and listened. The house was silent.

Nelson watched Lana climb the red-carpeted stairs, aiming the gun at his chest.

'Give me your phone,' she said, coolly.

Nelson handed it over. 'Please… don't kill me.'

Lana threw it down, hard enough to smash it to pieces. 'Where are they?'

'Who?'

'Let's try the other leg.'

'Basement! They're in the basement!'

A door closed below them. There was a jingle and a clink of keys dropping into a china bowl. A second later, a woman's voice called out in alarm, 'Nelson?' She made her way to the stairs and gasped. 'Oh, my! Please don't kill my husband!'

'Cut the crap, Lenore,' Nelson said through gritted teeth. He pushed his matted fringe away from his eyes. 'She knows.'

Lana could sense the woman's panic, watching her reach into her handbag. 'Uh-uh. I wouldn't do that.'

Lana held out a hand. Lenore handed over her bag.

'The basement,' Lana said to Nelson. 'Key or code?'

He retrieved a card from his pocket. It trembled when he held it out to her.

Lana took it and motioned for his wife to move. 'Both of you, upstairs.'

When they arrived at a bedroom with a balcony view, Lana opened the doors and checked the street. The coast was clear.

'Do you have any idea who we are?' Lenore yelled.

'That's enough,' Nelson said with a warning tone, while holding his stinging wound.

An adjoining room had a sheet hung on the wall, a mounted camera pointing at it, and a laptop next to a printer. Lana stepped over bundles of rope to investigate. She picked up a page titled "Priority Customers". Light glinted from vials next to the printer, which were labelled "Scopolamine". The drug was used to treat motion sickness. There were over a dozen boxes.

Lana held one vial between finger and thumb. Her eyes narrowed, and she turned to Nelson.

'Oh, shit,' he breathed.

Lana had read somewhere that scopolamine could also make anyone highly susceptible to suggestion. She picked the rope up from the floor and approached the couple.

'Take off your clothes.'

'Let's talk about this,' Nelson pleaded. 'Name your price.'

Lenore crossed her arms and glared at her husband. 'You weak, pathetic—'

She squealed when Lana pressed the nose of the gun into her temple.

'Take. Off.' Lana clicked the gun hammer into firing position. 'Your. Clothes.'

A man wearing a white cashmere sweater walked his Brussels Griffon beside the Abbots' perimeter fence, speaking irately into his cell phone. 'Three million today, and another three next month. No. No more. We go higher and I'll have a target painted on my back. Call me when it's done. Bye.' Pocketing the phone, he swore when the dog slipped through the fence bars, leash trailing behind. 'Damn it, Cinnamon, get back—'

Eyes locked on Cinnamon's interest, he froze, for across the yard were a naked man and woman hanging from the Abbots' balcony.

Nelson snapped awake at the sound of barking. Blood from his gunshot wound had dribbled down his chest. The rope tied around his ankles bit into his flesh.

Lenore moaned through the tape across her mouth. Her eyes widened when she noticed the camera from the upstairs studio. It was set on a tripod on the front lawn. Their feed was always connected live to wealthy buyers across the world.

The recording light was on.

Lana helped Howard's daughter, Abbey, into the four-wheel drive. Abbey hadn't let go of her since she released the girls from the Abbots' basement. She climbed in beside Abbey and drew a blanket around the girl's shoulders.

A nine-passenger van arrived to collect the other captives. Once everyone was quickly secured, Rachel gave the order to both AM drivers to move out.

Lana held Abbey, ignoring the pain in her arms and shoulders from the exertion of hoisting Mr and Mrs Abbot into inverted suspension while they were unconscious. She met Rachel's gaze. She knew Rachel saw what she had done. Her friend didn't judge her or warn against any wrongdoing. She looked to Abbey for a moment and turned back to watch the road.

Later, when they returned to their base, Howard took Abbey into his arms and wept. Chief Medical Officer Jolie was called in to Smog Realm. She directed her team of AM medics to treat the girls for dehydration, starting them on a regimen of food and drink that would help purge the drugs they'd been given. Having served with Rachel and Lana for many years, Jolie barely needed to communicate with them. They all went to work, setting up temporary bedding, making each girl comfortable.

'Give them all an hour, then we can take them to Home Realm and admit them for further treatment,' Jolie recommended.

'Thank you,' said Howard. Having worked with Hutch Branner, he'd had many opportunities to study AMs. How close they were to human never ceased to impress him. Jolie's amber hair was tied back into a ponytail with a plaited ridge. Its oils glistened in the light, as real as human hair. And her body movements were as fluid as any adult female's.

Rachel motioned for Howard to step away with her. Once out of Abbey's earshot, she spoke seriously. 'We've arranged for you to meet with the Council Security Division. Jolie and the AMs will stay with your daughter.'

'I need to stay—'

'That was the deal.'

Howard opened his mouth to protest and stopped.

Lana approached him and Rachel. 'How's Abbey?'

'Fine, thanks to you.' Howard shook his head in disbelief. 'I don't know how you did it. Those kids owe you their lives.'

'I'm glad I got there before they were sold.' Lana glanced back at the AM tech specialists. 'We ran a hack trace on the list of aliases the buyers use, found their identities and sent it all to the authorities. They'll be able to subpoena transaction records and arrest all of the politicians, mafia bosses, oligarchs, and… what's a "Cardinal"?'

'Oh, wow.' Rachel shook her head, too shocked to explain. She raised her shoulders at Howard. 'What happened to this world?'

'There was a global financial crisis a couple of decades ago,' he replied distractedly, looking back to see his daughter's face one more time. 'Somebody invented something called "cryptocurrency". It allowed criminal organisations to abandon conventional money laundering and maximise their profits completely unhindered. They're buying entire governments, corporations, institutions. I doubt any subpoenas will be made.'

Lana's posture straightened defiantly. 'Then we should find them ourselves and–'

'Lana.' Rachel raised a stopping hand. 'We talked about this.'

The silent tension was cut when a tech called out a report from the next room.

'Ma'am, we have received a message from Ohkwai Chillo on Aqua Sierra. His personal guard are tracking what could be the missing IDBot.'

'I need to take Howard to the Council,' Rachel told Lana. 'Look, I know it sucks, but we can't–'

'Go.' Lana nodded. 'I'll head to Aqua Sierra.'

Chapter 9

Home Realm
Aqua Sierra

Kintai and Julis, Chillo's personal guards, travelled along the rise of the ocean floor, pulled by a torpedo-armed diving craft. The underwater formation, once a mountainous island, took them close to the surface of the sea.

They were following an aquatic craft headed for Kulete City.

Julis adjusted the trajectory of their craft to intercept it. Once they were within firing range, Julis launched two torpedoes.

The enemy craft attempted an evasive manoeuvre, dipping left and increasing its speed. A hatch opened and the occupant was ejected with a flurry of bubbles. The twin torpedoes followed the empty pod another three meters before hitting it. Two impact spheres expanded from the explosion, sending the IDBot into a hurtling barrel roll.

Julis slowed their craft to ten knots, and they descended to investigate. Kintai gasped when she saw the body of Ohkwai Chillo bounce along the ocean floor. He rolled through a cloud of sand, disturbing a sea serpent. The serpent slithered out from the sand bed and across the rocks.

'It is not our master, Kintai,' Julis assured her. 'That is a machine assassin. We must try to disarm the bomb inside its chest.'

He turned on the craft's polar directional fans to keep it stationary and swam down. Kintai followed, aiming a pulse rod at the body drifting between the boulders imbedded in the sand. She nodded to Julis, while he pulled a knife from his belt.

There was a bright flash above them. Kintai was about to look up when the IDBot stirred. Its eyes snapped open, and it kicked its broad fins to propel itself into Julis. It latched its hands around his neck.

Julis stabbed the machine in its shoulder and escaped. Kintai fired a sustained pulse beam into its chest. It was pushed into the rocks, pinned by the beam.

Kintai tapped the comms unit in her ear when she saw Lana swimming down, wearing a black and silver wetsuit and breathing mask. 'We have the assassin.'

Lana could barely see the IDBot struggling under the beam. Afternoon sunlight came from behind the underwater mountain, casting a wide shadow. She noticed the rod Kintai was using to pin the IDBot. Its function seemed to ignore Newton's laws, and Kintai was able to keep it steady with very little effort.

'We need to use this to defuse the bomb,' said Kintai, taking a small vial from a pouch on her chest strap. 'It will only work in the open air.'

'There is a shallow plateau at the top of the mountain,' said Julis.

Lana swam down and took position, ready to grapple the IDBot Chillo. Julis drew out wrist binders, and he nodded to Kintai.

She turned off the beam and swam back to the dive craft.

Julis bound the IDBot's wrists behind its back and pulled it up from the rocks with Lana's help. The two of them swam hard, holding the robot tight while following the mountainous rise leading to the plateau. The IDBot squirmed and fought their hold. They were almost at the top when it snapped the cuffs and head-butted Julis so hard he drifted, unconscious.

Lana felt the IDBot's webbed hand latch onto her face and rip off her breathing mask. She tried to kick away, but it held onto her with one hand and pulled Julis' knife from its shoulder with the other. Lana engaged the organic silicon carbide in her cells to harden her skin. The IDBot sliced Lana's wetsuit from her neck to her sternum. She drove her knees into its chest and pushed away.

A second later, Kintai slammed the nose of her dive craft into the IDBot's hip at high speed. She released and let it plough the Chillo replica into the mountain. She and Lana swam at the assassin, took one arm each and hauled it to the plateau.

Lana broke the surface, coughing and spluttering. She leaned all of her weight onto the IDBot while it squirmed and flicked its tail. Kintai twisted her repelling rod and its lights turned from green to red. She was balancing on her tail in the shallow water, steadying her aim. She fired a sustained laser and sliced an oval shape on the IDBot's chest, a centimetre from Lana's knee. The robot tried to roll free, so Kintai dropped on top of its tail and handed Lana the vial of liquid.

Lana held it between her teeth, pinned the machine's shoulder, and yanked the oval of synthetic flesh and the plate of armour from the IDBot's chest with her free hand. She popped the vial's cap with her thumb and was about to douse the bomb when Kintai grabbed her wrist. The bomb timer was counting down from thirteen seconds. Kintai leaned over the chest cavity to carefully remove one of the explosive capsules connected by a trip-wire. She pointed to the other still in the IDBot's chest and nodded for Lana to proceed.

Lana began to pour the corrosive liquid. But the IDBot struggled. The first drop dabbed on its chin, hissing as it ate through artificial flesh. The IDBot rolled backward and flung its tailfin into Lana and Kintai. The impact sent them both into the water.

Lana rose from the foaming sea. One side of her face was red from the cold slap. Her eyes widened when she realised the IDBot Chillo was gone. Only the wind and the lapping waves could be heard. Lana spun around at a sudden splash, saw a rising gush of water and the IDBot flying in an arc through the air. Its body rotated horizontally, swinging its broad fin across the water's surface. Lana jumped, kicked her legs forward and lay herself out like a plank in mid-air. The machine's tail breezed beneath her chest. She turned her hips, alighting on one foot before quickly springing off, kicking her other leg to complete a cartwheel flip. She pounced on the IDBot's back and drove both elbows into its head. It collapsed and, for a few seconds, its limbs became rigid while it shook like it was having a seizure.

The red digits in its chest were counting down from five seconds. Lana turned to flee and saw Kintai rise from the water at the edge of the plateau.

'It's gonna blow!' Lana screamed.

She spear-tackled Kintai into the waves and side-stroked down, pulling until Kintai could reorient and kick her tail. She took hold of Lana and sped them deeper, further from the mountain.

A dull thud reached their ears. Lana glanced back and saw the water turn white as boulders flew through the air and plummeted into the sea. A surge of bubbles rushed past Lana and Kintai, and the two of them rolled and bobbed in the underwater shockwave.

Kintai found Julis while Lana swam to the surface. She saw the wind blowing a high cloud of steam. And she looked up when she heard an engine. A Laician spacecraft descended from the sky and flew over her.

Lana's chest rose and fell while she tried to catch her breath from the exertion of her fight against the last known IDBot.

This is just the beginning, she realised. The battle against the Raekeem was yet to come.

San Francisco
Unity Building

After the success of the Wealth Sacrifice and Redistribution Initiative, the tallest skyscraper in San Francisco, previously known as the Transamerica Pyramid, was repurposed and renamed to become a city hub for the Universal Community. The top floor of the Unity Building was the Situation Room.

AM Unit Commander Lincoln had arrived in San Francisco, having flown from Riga, where the Council were now serving their term. He entered the meeting room and completed a head count of all who were present.

The holographic projections of Ambassador Jainon and Prince Chillo were accounted for, along with projections of all the Council members in Riga. Physically present were Rachel, Jolie and Howard Crone. They all listened to Howard relating his experience of being abducted and then being forced to work for the Raekeem. Having been taken aboard their ship many times, Howard knew their security protocols, their chain of command and their motives.

'Raekeem soldiers are called Sentinels,' Howard continued, glancing to Rachel every now and then for some moral support. Though he had at first found her intimidating, he was grateful that she and her team had found him and his daughter.

Howard wasn't used to speaking before so many people, and he wasn't entirely certain of his future. He didn't know if they were going to lock him away for building the IDBots. *If so,* he thought, *who would take care of Abbey?*

'They infiltrate worlds to steal resources, and not just materials, people as well. They keep them as slaves. Their Lord, Telsta, considers the human amygdala a delicacy. So part of their mission is to harvest the brains of creative individuals. I also heard one of them say that consuming the amygdala slows his aging.' Howard paused to swallow his disgust. 'Telsta commands the mother ship, which is cloaked. There are four other Lords commanding other ships. But they are on their own quests of carnage.'

Noting Howard's obvious anxiety, perhaps due to the presence of Commander Lincoln, Council member Varteja spoke gently. 'Mr Crone, we understand that you were under duress, and we are very saddened to hear of the death of your wife. You will not be subject to persecution.'

'Thank you.' Howard breathed.

'But you will be watched,' said Lincoln. He glanced at the holographic display showing footage from Howard's underground workshop. 'How did they infiltrate the world you were in?'

Howard had plenty of time to get his head around the concept of travel between Parallel Universes, having spent years trapped in Smog Realm with his family. 'The Sentinels use holographic technology: slim consoles attached to their uniform that enable them to create an artificial appearance, a kind of cloak that covers their entire body.'

'They can look like anyone?' Rachel asked, with an alert glance to Lincoln.

Lincoln turned abruptly and walked out of the room.

'That's correct,' Howard answered, noticing the murmurs of alarm rippling through the room.

When Lincoln returned, two of his security detail followed. 'Jolie, Rachel, please remain seated,' he said. He sent a quick message through his comms to his personnel in Riga. 'Members of the Council, please stay in your seats while security performs a brief pat down.'

'Is this really necessary?' a Council member asked, frightened. The threat had suddenly become less *there* and more *here.*

'I'm afraid so,' Lincoln answered dispassionately.

Jainon and Chillo both ordered their guards to do the same. Once Rachel and Jolie were patted down, Lincoln ordered a sweep of the entire building.

Chillo waited until everyone was settled. 'My son has just informed me that the last IDBot self-destructed.' He raised his voice over more alarmed murmurs. 'No one was harmed. My people are safe.'

Rachel noticed a relieved but uncertain look on Jainon's face. 'All we can do now is prepare,' Rachel offered. 'We have no other leads to the Raekeem who are hiding here, or to their mother ship.'

'You have nothing more to tell us, Mr Crone?' Jainon queried, watching Howard with her passive jade eyes.

He shook his head. 'I've told you everything I know.'

'Very well,' Varteja said. 'Thank you for speaking to us. Go and be with your daughter. This meeting is adjourned. Everybody, please keep your link communications open for hourly updates on the situation.'

Jolie and Lincoln parted from the others and made their way to the elevators.

'This is bad,' Jolie whispered.

Lincoln glanced back at Howard with a grave expression. 'It's worse than anyone is willing to admit.'

They entered a compartment and descended. Jolie was thinking of soft targets, but there were so many, on so many different planets. 'Where do you think they'll strike?'

'They'll target our defences.'

'The Branner Factory,' said Jolie.

Lincoln turned to her, nodding solemnly. 'Can you clear your schedule? We should secure the factory and its airspace.'

'Of course. I'll let them know we're—'

'No, we can't tell anyone,' Lincoln cautioned. 'We have to assume the Raekeem are monitoring our communications. Issuing a task force to fortify the factory will only tip our hand. We have to get there ourselves and secure Hutch Branner's hard drives, his schematics, everything.'

'Without raising… suspicion.' Jolie realised now that Lincoln was the only one who hadn't been frisked. 'How do I know you're not one of them?' She moved into a defensive stance. 'This is exactly the kind of infiltration talk a Raekeem operative—'

'Sentinel,' Lincoln corrected. He loosened his tie and unbuttoned his shirt. 'Howard said they're called Sentinels.'

He pressed Jolie's hand to his chest. She could feel the metronomic beat of his pump. Like all AMs, Lincoln's battery fluid was circulated to prevent congealment and clotting. His body heat was insulated by his synthetic muscles and skin tissue.

Jolie moved her hand to his ear. She had reattached it after he'd lost it to a Sabre Company Captain.

'Definitely you.' She breathed. 'So our reason for going to the factory could be a routine diagnostic of our neural systems.'

'Good thinking.' Lincoln buttoned his shirt. 'I'll notify security individually once we get there.'

Jolie nodded. 'I'll speak to the staff and prepare them for evacuation.'

Lincoln had detected an increase in Jolie's body temperature and realised what was happening. It had been some time since either of them had been alone together and for good reason. It was not yet socially acceptable for AMs to be seen expressing anything other than camaraderie toward one another. Lincoln had been avoiding Jolie for so long, he had forgotten the danger.

'Lincoln, I want you to know…'

'Jolie–'

'I know.' She met his eyes. 'We can't…' She gestured to the space between them, her mouth waiting for her next words to come. She sighed instead.

Lincoln turned away. 'Everything we do is programmed.' He couldn't hide the frustration in his voice. 'Why did Hutch Branner allow–'

He thumped the wall with an incensed huff. Due to his programming, he was tripping over sentence structures. 'We shouldn't even be able to think about it.'

'We're designed to be like people,' Jolie reasoned. 'We're actors. We have a role. We play it. How can it be wrong for us to let this play out?' She shrugged, perplexed. 'Maybe he made a mistake with us.'

'Mistake?' Lincoln turned back to her in surprise. 'Hutch Branner doesn't make–'

Jolie pulled Lincoln against her and kissed him. He fumbled for the panel and hit the "stop elevator" button, a second before she pinned him against the doors. She unbuttoned his shirt and kicked off her shoes.

Lincoln's eyes dropped to the bulge in his pants. 'I didn't know it could do that.'

Chapter 10

Aqua Sierra

A portal opened two metres above the sea, and the setting sun lit the mercury gold. Lana dropped out of it and plunged into the waves. She oriented her body down and was stunned by the vibrant colours of the Laician city below. Bright blue, pink and purple bio-luminesced from the domed buildings and cylindrical towers.

A figure ascended toward her. It was Kintai, coming to greet her.

'Welcome to Leetheria City.'

She guided Lana down to the largest dome, the Royal Palace. Guards stationed in the towers blew into long valved instruments. They were the dungchen-like horns Lana had heard Chillo's warriors blow before they helped to defend Otami Palace.

Lana and Kintai swam through the open palace doors. Their archway was studded with pearls and they were made of woven reeds, a mesh to keep wildlife out of the interior.

'Are you as sore as I am?' Lana asked Kintai as they entered the foyer, massaging her own neck.

'More so, I imagine,' Kintai admitted, tilting her head. 'I was told you have a natural ability to armour yourself.'

'Only my skin,' Lana explained. 'A blow like the one that IDBot gave us still does muscle damage.'

'That it did,' said Kintai, shrugging her shoulder with a wince.

'Did I almost blow us up?'

'You could not have known it was booty-trapped.'

'You mean booby—'

Lana gasped when Kintai opened the next door, taken aback by the opulent beauty of the dining hall. Rippling light from the glass ceiling illuminated the stone floor. The walls were studded with shiny minerals, arranged in swirling, organic patterns.

Kida, Chillo's son, sat opposite Julis at a polished stone table. They both rose and waved, calling their greetings through linked comms as Lana and Kintai approached.

Lana expressed her thanks for the dinner invitation. And she observed the practice of seating when the two male Laicians sat back down. She swam over to her backless chair and lowered herself onto the sculpted-coral cushion. Taking the curved, coral-padded belt of woven reeds, she used the hook and notch to secure herself to the chair as Kida had. She could feel a continuous underwater current. It was more subtle in this enclosed hall than outside, and she guessed that there was some kind of perpetual mechanism creating the artificial movement. Without a current, Lana supposed, these gilled creatures would suffocate.

'Was that you in the spacecraft today?' she asked Kida.

'Yes. I recently graduated Flight School.' Kida smiled shyly and adjusted the comms attached to his ear. He gestured to the platters of various fish, seaweed, coral and fungal cuisine, all expertly displayed in giant, half-open clam shells. 'Please, help yourself.'

Lana smiled. *Now the tricky part.* Since visitors from dry planets had become more and more frequent over the years, various apparatus had been customised to accommodate their needs. Lana had changed out of her damaged wetsuit into the most fancy-looking bathing suit she could find at such short notice. She also wore a membrane that lined her entire body in a transparent film. It allowed her to push food into her mouth without taking in a lungful of water.

Lana waited for Kintai to go first and observed their dining etiquette. They didn't place foods onto their own plates, but simply reached over and forked one item at a time to eat. Lana followed suit and decided to try the coral first, with the intention of leaving the fungi till last.

The coral was similar in texture to crunchy lettuce, and the fish was delicious. Lana had noticed earlier, when Kida had stood to greet her, that he had a pair of scaled legs instead of a tail.

'I thought all Laicians had tails,' she said. 'Are there many variations of your species?'

'There are many within different clans across the planet,' Kida explained. 'It took a while for us to understand that evolution will always take its own course.'

'By "a while",' Julis said gravely, 'he means there was some conflict in the beginning, between the legged and the tailed.'

'But now we embrace variation.' Kida gave Lana a small smile. 'We encourage interspecies mating.'

Lana's eyebrows shot up and she swallowed a piece of squid without chewing. She coughed while a communications tone sounded.

Kida touched a stone on the table. It glowed white, and they all looked up when a holographic display expanded above the table.

'Sorry for the interruption, everyone.' Rachel appeared with clouds drifting behind her. A ship flew by and Lana guessed she was in San Francisco, on one of the Unity Building landing platforms. 'Howard Crone has recommended we return to Haze Realm. It's our best bet at finding more information about the Raekeem. We leave in the morning.'

'Copy that,' said Lana. 'I'll be back soon.' She set her fork down and gave Kida a short bow. 'Thank you very much for the meal.'

'My pleasure.' He released his chair belt and rose. 'Our experts are analysing the wreckage of the craft that the IDBot arrived in. We'll let you know if we find anything of use.'

Black Bird, en route to San Francisco

Aboard the Black Bird, Renee walked through the diner to the gym. Brad was doing sets of kettle bell lifts. He finished and asked her to spot him while he lay down to bench press.

It had taken Renee some time to get used to her old Captain, Henry Drake, no longer being leader of their group. But the others respected her and trusted her to captain the Black Bird as proudly as he had.

'You think the Raekeem will target the shifter facility?' Brad asked, and hefted eighty kilograms.

'They'll see our realm travel technology as an asset worth destroying.' Renee held her hands out, ready to guide the bar back into its cradle. 'They've been targeting each of our allies. Their next move can only be–'

'Invasion.' Brad breathed out with a grunt. He lowered the bar steadily, close to his chest, and heaved it up again.

'Those brain-harvesting bastards are picking one heck of a fight,' Renee said. 'Three against one.' She reminded herself that her people, the Kiyol and the Laicians had already faced extreme adversity together. This was not the first test of their alliance.

'Cap.' Chesh, the pilot of the ship, walked into the gym. 'Impulse engines are powering down to full stop. You'll be good to go in ten.'

'Thanks, Chesh.' Renee was going to teleport ahead to the Portal Hub to personally run a security assessment. She helped Brad set the bar into the cradle.

'Why do we have to stop the ship to portal out?' Brad asked, standing to shake his arms loose.

'Rachel said portals always open stationary in time and space,' Chesh explained. 'Open it while the ship is moving and all that travels through the sphere will be taken to wherever the portal destination is, leaving a great big gaping hole in our hull.'

Haze Realm

Jess watched the new stranger, Sam, a scientist in her late twenties, assemble what she called a mobile purifier. The base of the machine was bolted into the asphalt. Its lid separated, and a white balloon escaped from its top, followed by a connected tube two hand lengths wide. It floated to a height of thirty metres. The electric motor hummed to life, and the haze around them began to clear.

The area was guarded by a squad of five AMs. Two more were stationed inside the abandoned building where Lana and Rachel had discussed the Raekeem with the Haze Realm survivors. Jess had returned to the street periodically, eager to learn more from the strangers. Particularly the one called Lana. The archer Jess had knocked out was said to rarely miss his target. Word was spreading that Lana had snatched his arrow from flight.

Lana removed her mask, and Sam waited for her to take a few breaths.

'Air's clean,' she said. Her nose twitched. 'Smells pretty bad, but it's breathable.'

'Eck!' Sam put her mask back on. She looked to Jess when the young woman took off her mask. It was the first time any of them had seen more than just her eyes. Her nostrils flared and her full lips parted when she breathed in purified air. Sam could have already guessed from Jess' almond-shaped eyes, but her now visible features showed that she was Middle Eastern.

'The air is… cleaner than I've ever breathed outside.' Jess knelt down to inspect the machine. 'Can you bring us more of these?'

'It's a temporary solution,' said Sam, and she gave Lana a look that wasn't very hopeful.

'It will take at least fifty years for the soil to recover and for the trees to re-grow,' Lana explained to Jess. It occurred to her that Forest Realm, the home of Tinba, Mehra, their parents and Anook, could be a viable refuge for Jess and the others. 'Sam, what about Forest Realm? It's safe there now.'

'The Raekeem could strike at any moment,' Sam cautioned. 'The resources it would take to relocate these people, the number of AMs…' She met Jess' pleading eyes and stopped.

'Please,' said Jess. 'We won't survive here much longer.' A timer beeped on her wristwatch. 'I have to get back to my group.'

'I'll go with you,' Lana offered. 'We should at least be able to help a few of you.'

'A few?'

The AMs standing guard whipped their rifles in the direction of the voice. The gang leader, Benson, emerged from the haze, accompanied by three of his crew. The AMs barred their way.

'Let them through,' Lana ordered.

'I've got forty women and children living below ground,' Benson argued. 'You have to take them.'

'Benson, this is Dr Samantha O'Conner,' said Lana. She saw Jess' eyebrows rise when she spoke Sam's last name.

'What's the plan here, Doctor?' Benson asked Sam insistently.

'I'm escorting Jess to her home,' Lana said to the AMs. 'If these guys give Dr O'Conner any trouble, shoot them.' She nodded to Sam and made to leave.

'This is my territory!' Benson shouted and took Lana roughly by the arm. 'You think you can–'

Before anyone could react, Jess swung a left hook across his jaw. She yelled in his ear, 'Do not fuck this up for us!'

Benson staggered back against his men while Lana pulled Jess away.

Sam stepped in. 'Everybody calm down. Let's talk inside.'

Jess stormed off into the haze and Lana followed, pulling her mask back on. 'What was that about?'

'Benson is my uncle. We're not close.' Jess' voice became muffled when she replaced her mask. 'Your friend is right; the Raekeem are preparing to attack your world. Maybe you should concentrate on defending yourselves.'

'I'll do what I can to convince the people who can help,' Lana promised.

Jess' eyes were tearing up at the slim prospect of survival. She hid her emotions from Lana and guided her up a ladder at the rear of a truck. She scanned ahead with her binoculars.

Lana gazed along the street. What she saw looked like a moment frozen in time. The cars were still in their lanes, hardly damaged, windows intact, ducos faded from years under the sun. Heads of skeletons rested against windows, on dashboards and steering wheels. Bones baked white.

'Cool axe,' said Jess, pointing at the hand axe holstered on Lana's hip.

'I found it in Forest Realm,' said Lana. 'It's a war-torn world, but the people there are rebuilding. They could use your help.'

The two of them walked on, and Jess asked questions about Lana's world. All the while, her eyes instinctively scanned ahead, watching for booby traps set by other survivors. 'What year did the Wealth Sacrifice and… What's it called?'

'Redistribution Initiative, WSRI,' Lana prompted. 'It was thirty years before the Great Migration, so around the early 1970s.'

'So your people achieved space travel outside the solar system in the 2000s. How?'

'Freedom. Up until the 70s, corporations controlled every government, and every government controlled each continent of people.' Lana thought for a moment, trying to come up with the most accessible way of explaining how innovative people and industries were able to excel so quickly. 'What's the easiest way to control a person?'

Jess shrugged, her mind still reeling at how early and fast Lana's world had developed.

'Time,' said Lana. 'Take away a person's time and make it yours. Have them work for you and pay them little to work a job they have no passion for. A job that offers no personal growth or opportunity to learn anything of use. And make them work that job for their entire life. That's how you control entire countries. Do that, and every generation will be conditioned never to innovate. They're born into an establishment instead of an emergent, evolving society. We broke the establishment. Rebuilding began and innovation took us out of our solar system.'

Jess' route took them to the financial district, through an office building, up broken escalators, to a set of dirty glass doors. 'There's something you should see,' she said.

Lana followed her along cubicle workstations. She could hear typing further on. They came upon a woman, seated, wearing a headset. Dried bloody finger marks dotted the keys. The woman stared at a blank, dust-covered screen. Lana was shocked by her skeletal form. She was practically flesh and bone. And yet she could somehow sit up straight. Her bludgeoned fingers deftly hit keys, and dust drifted from her wiry hair.

A man typed at a dead computer in the cubicle opposite. Lana waved a hand before his eyes. No reaction. She gazed across the other pod stations and saw at least a dozen others occupied, the tops of their heads visible. Many had lost their hair. All of them were emaciated.

'I found them last year,' said Jess, staring sadly at the workers. 'I came back with food, tried to snap them out of it. But they wouldn't stop working. I pushed them off their chairs. But they all got up, sat down, and went back to work.' Jess turned to gaze out of a window overlooking the financial district. 'I've seen other workers standing on the street corners, waiting at traffic lights, waiting for the signal to walk.'

'How are they still alive?' Lana asked, taking one last look at the computer operators before they left.

'One of the men in my group is a scientist,' said Jess. 'He thinks there's some kind of nutrient in the haze that the Raekeem ejected into our atmosphere. It could be enough to sustain them.'

When they reached the street, they crossed an intersection and entered a park. Lana heard a metallic creak and saw a playground swing pushed by the wind.

'So I'm guessing the average life expectancy is high in your world?' Jess asked.

'One hundred and thirty is the average,' said Lana, and she turned around to find that Jess had stopped in her tracks, gawking.

'You're shitting me,' she hissed, so as not to attract any dangers lurking in the haze. 'Ours was seventy-five before the Raekeem came.'

'The people in my world were on a similar path,' Lana admitted. 'Pollution was contaminating our soil, reducing nutrients. It wasn't just carbon pollution. They were emitting every bad chemical you can think of in high volume, and it was literally killing everything that needs clean air. They brought it under control after the WSRI. It took a few seasonal cycles but the soil was eventually restored and food became nutrient-rich. Also, people had time to exercise and time to spend with their families. All of that equals less stress, which means longer life...'

She was distracted by movement in the haze before them. They had left the park and were crossing a road.

'So, besides people and the toxic air,' she murmured, checking their rear, 'what other threats do you usually come across?' She saw something dart through the haze and pulled her side-arm with her right hand. She unsheathed her axe with her left.

'Mutated people and mutated animals,' Jess answered. She took her kali sticks from her pack and pressed her back against Lana's. 'The worst is a kind of Rottweiler-hyena hybrid the Raekeem brought here. We call them war-dogs.'

Lana heard the distinct scratch of nails and the scrape of paws.

'We're surrounded,' Jess whispered. 'Three, maybe four.'

'I'll teleport us back a ways to get the jump on them,' said Lana, tapping with one finger on her console.

'What?'

The war-dogs converged, running in for the kill. Lana fired off a round, pulled Jess to her side, and they disappeared in a flash. They reappeared on the road, fifteen metres back. The dogs barked at one another, confused, until they caught the scent of their prey wafting through the haze.

Jess stumbled to her knees as though the ground had been pulled from under her. Lana saw the mist shift, and a dark figure approached at speed. She took aim with her pistol and fired. One dog went down. She fired on another. Her tactic was foiled when the remaining three separated, climbing over mounds of rubble.

Jess and Lana walked slowly, each broadening their peripheral vision to its maximum extent, watching the seven feet of clear sight available to them. Quickening paws circled, and the panting of hungry predators could be heard, dangerously close. Their deep growls were followed by ferocious barking.

Lana decided to conserve her ammunition, holstered her pistol and held her axe with both hands, ready to swing. A tail whipped past, and one of the two dogs ran close to her flank. Yellow mist swirled at chest height. A large male flew through the haze, jaws open, teeth bared. Lana spun, pulled Jess down and swung her axe over her head. The war-dog sailed over, yelping when the blade landed in its chest. Lana pulled her axe free before the weight of its body hit the road. Both she and Jess were breathing hard. Jess pressed her back against Lana's and tried to ignore the terror pounding in her chest.

Intense growling came from somewhere off to their left and was ended abruptly with a blow that sounded like a mallet hitting meat.

Lana heard boot steps approaching. 'Don't come any closer,' she called, not taking any chances.

'Jess, are you alright?' A man's voice came from the figure obscured by the haze.

'We're okay, Hal,' Jess called and returned her weapons to her pack.

The man called Hal emerged from the yellow mist carrying a steel pole. 'The Professor sent me to find you,' he said. 'Where've you been?'

Hal's tone was rough, but Lana couldn't tell if he was truly upset. Breathing even a little of the haze had made her own voice sound strained.

'I was with the people I told you about,' said Jess. 'This is Lana. She's one of them. They want to help us.'

'Thanks for the assist,' said Lana. 'We were very nearly war-dog chow.'

Hal gave her a humble nod. 'You seemed to have everything under control,' he said, gesturing to Lana's bloodied axe.

Bare feet padded along the road behind them. Jess froze and gave Hal a sideways glance. 'Mutated.' She tugged at Lana's arm. 'They'll want all this meat. Let's move.'

Lana glanced over her shoulder while hustling alongside Jess, and she could see men and women running to the war-dogs. Their skin was pale yellow, tight against bone and muscle. What remained of their clothes hung off them, dirty and tattered.

'The Mutated have good hearing and an even better sense of smell,' Jess explained to Lana while they ran. 'Always out in numbers. Nobody who takes them on lives to talk about it.' She slowed to a jog when the Mutated could be heard devouring the war-dogs.

'Those people…' Lana breathed, listening to the carnage. 'They can digest raw meat?'

'Professor O'Conner says the haze has caused an "adaptive mutation",' Hal said, ushering her to keep moving. 'Come on. He'll be excited to see you.'

Lana stopped in her tracks.

'Did you say… O'Conner?'

Chapter 11

Rachel, Sam and their guard of four AM soldiers accompanied Benson and his men into the underground tunnel network. They were given a tour of the living areas and introduced to the dozens of families hiding within. Many children were born with defects, and most of the adults were slowly starving to death. Rachel had seen these kinds of conditions in other Realms before, worlds torn apart by war. But Sam had never witnessed anything like this.

After they'd excused themselves to speak privately, Sam wiped tears from her eyes. 'Okay, so…' She exhaled a long breath, trying to pull herself together. 'The Press will need to be notified when we're ready to present our aid proposal to the public. It'll be a hard sell. Maybe the Council could send us supplies reserved for disaster aid.' She was so affected by Haze Realm's struggle that she was speaking as though she had completely forgotten their prime directive.

Rachel felt it incumbent on her to pose some logical questions. 'How do you think people will react to this kind of aid? Do you think the Kiyol will allow us to become some kind of inter-Realm relief organisation?'

Sam shook her head, too overwhelmed to offer a reasonable answer. She saw another child and tried to avert her eyes, to protect her heart from breaking, but she couldn't. The little boy was playing with a teddy bear darkened by many years of filth. Orange light from fire burning in dustbins reflected from his glazed eyes.

'They'll all die if we don't help them,' Sam said finally. She watched the boy rock the teddy bear in his arms. 'I don't know how we can convince the Kiyol, but people back home… they remember Silica. They trust in what we do.'

Rachel followed her partner's gaze and a lump in her throat came with an unexpected wave of guilt. She had actually convinced herself that this was not Home Realm's problem, that she should pull her team and walk away from it. *This world might have recovered, had it not been for the Raekeem*, she reasoned.

'You guys stay here,' Rachel ordered the AMs. 'Sam and I will go and speak with the Council.' She nodded to Benson when he approached. 'We're going to try and get your people out of here.'

Benson crossed his arms, hugging himself while casting his eyes to the ground. When he looked up at Rachel, his eyes were watering, and his jaw twitched. He managed a nod and left to organise his people.

Rachel glanced at the Realm stay-duration timer on her console. 'Lana hasn't checked in.'

'Your friend who left with Jess?' one of Benson's guards asked. 'She's in good hands. Jess is a tough kid. Her parents died young. She and her brother lived down here with us, until…' She took a moment, a hint of regret clouding her eyes.

Rachel took a step closer. 'Ma'am, if somebody here harmed Jess and the boy in some way, it's important that you tell us.'

'What? No, nothing like that. He slipped out one morning, went wandering around on the surface. We searched for him. Just before nightfall we found blood, a shoe… His.'

Sam gasped and covered her mouth.

'Jess wanted to keep looking, widen the search. The next day, we were hit by the Mutated. Lost two men. Benson had to call it off.'

Rachel shrugged. 'Believe me, you would have lost more people had he not. I've been in his shoes.'

'I thought so too, but Jess packed up and left. Never came back. She's had it in for him, for us, ever since.'

Lana followed Jess and Hal into a dilapidated building, entering a lift. 'There's power to this building?'

'Only to the basement and this elevator.' Hal hit the "B" button, and there was a disconcerting groan before the lift descended. 'We installed a filtration system in the air ducts. You can take off your mask now.'

'That group of war-dogs didn't have a meathead,' Jess commented. 'All smarts.'

Lana gave her a curious look.

'The smart war-dogs stay lean and turn on the muscular ones,' Jess explained. 'There's always one that fights for the right to take more meat from a kill. That's the meathead. It's a vicious cycle.'

'Dog-eat-dog world,' Lana agreed. Sam's voice came through her comms. 'Hey, Sam. I know, we're late. We ran into trouble.'

'Are you okay?' Sam asked.

'We're fine.'

'Benson has advised that you stay indoors if you don't think you can make it back before nightfall. Rache and I are returning to Home Realm to speak with the Council.'

'Copy that.' The elevator arrived at the basement and the doors opened to a long corridor.

Jess gave Lana a brief tour of their living quarters and facilities. 'These used to be storage rooms for old stuff, like art and statues.' She swung her backpack onto the shoulders of what Lana assumed was a copy of the Venus de Milo.

They proceeded to the last room, which looked like a chemistry lab, and Hal introduced her to a man leaning over a microscope. Lana couldn't believe her eyes. It was Professor O'Conner, but he looked to be at least ten years younger. And she thought she could see some kind of transparent film covering his lab coat. It shimmered, now and then, across his hair and skin. She attributed it to the fluorescent lights and the haze affecting her eyes.

'Finally, you're back,' said Pete. He was about to give Jess a stern lecture on the dangers of the city when a teenage boy entered the lab. He didn't speak, just rushed over to Jess and hugged her.

'I'm alright.' She squeezed him and gestured to Lana. 'This lady is one of the strangers I was telling you guys about. She says her people can save us.'

'Save us how?' Pete asked Lana.

'Relocation.'

'To where? The whole planet is contaminated.'

'We can talk about it in the morning,' Jess chided and motioned to Lana. 'Come on, let's find something for you to eat.'

Lana followed her, and she nodded to a corridor leading away from the sleeping quarters. 'Bathroom is down there.'

Lana massaged her neck and glanced over her shoulder. She caught Hal watching her from the lab. He turned and spoke to the Professor.

'So…' Lana tried to sound casual. 'Are you and Hal…?'

Jess looked up while setting down her gear. 'Oh. No, Hal and I are just friends. He saved Ryan and found me when I left the tunnels. He's like our big brother.'

Lana recognised a familiar-looking cylindrical pod on the far side of the lab. It was a similar design to the capsule in which she'd spent her first years of incubation. 'What did you tell him about me?'

'Hal?'

'Your Prof–' Lana stopped herself. 'What did you tell Pete?'

Jess shrugged. 'Everything you and your friends told us about your world. Except for how you guys populated other planets. I can't wait to–'

'Don't tell him anything else,' Lana snapped. She saw Jess flinch. 'Sorry, I would just prefer to answer any questions Pete might have about my world myself, okay?'

'Sure… I guess.'

Home Realm
Planet Darwin
Branner Factory

Lincoln and Jolie had arrived at the factory a day apart. After Lincoln received his neural systems check-up, he announced to the staff that he would stay to conduct routine security analysis. When Jolie arrived, she covertly informed all personnel in the building of her and Lincoln's suspicions regarding Raekeem infiltration.

'That explains it,' a technician commented. 'I assumed the Commander was here to follow up on our report on the SAM sites.'

'What report?' Jolie asked, dreading the possibility that the Surface to Air Missile sites – installed after the Sabre Company attack – were inactive.

'The AMs tasked with testing and maintaining each site disappeared,' he said. 'We reported it last week and received a reply from the Commander's secretary saying he would see to it personally.'

'I think that's everybody,' Lincoln said, returning to Jolie.

'You knew about this?' Jolie exclaimed, as quietly as she could, given the magnitude of the bad news.

Lincoln ushered Jolie upstairs to the break room so they could speak privately.

'I checked the sites yesterday,' he said gravely. 'Sabotage. They'd take weeks to repair. I considered shutting the whole factory down, making it look like production has stopped. But we have units in storage. The Raekeem will see them as military assets and attack anyway.'

'Best we can do is wait and react when the time comes,' said Jolie.

Lincoln walked to a window that overlooked the assembly lines. All of the units ready to be programmed were being given basic start-up directives so they were ready for evacuation. Lincoln had defended this place, where he and Jolie were born, when Sabre Company attacked. They fought and they won. *This time*, he thought sadly, *we'll have to let it burn.*

'Hey.' Jolie tilted her head to one side, watching Lincoln. She saw defeat. 'Branner will rebuild,' she assured him. 'There are enough of us to hold our own in this conflict. Together with the Kiyol and the Laicians, the Raekeem don't stand a chance.'

Lincoln gazed back at her, and forced a wry smile, which faded when the walls shuddered from a distant explosion.

The room went black. A rising tone designed to alert without causing panic began. A higher, pulsing pitch sounded before the alarm peaked. And again, louder. Rumbling like cannon fire vibrated through the ceiling, followed by shuddering impact after impact. The evacuation alarm died. A moment of silence.

BOOM.

Silica
City of Liberty

Emma Palmer looked up from her coffee and waved when she saw her roommate approaching from the street.

He was tall, so it wasn't hard to spot him while she was seated at an open-air café. The two of them had agreed to meet during Emma's lunch break. She was working in Resource Procurement in Fiona Parker's department.

The Liberty magazine poking out of Emma's purse caught her friend's eye when he sat down. The front page displayed a familiar face.

'Can you bring your big-time-celeb brother to the work party?' he asked.

'I'm sure he can tear himself away from training to join us,' said Emma, and added proudly, 'He's competing in the Desert Race.' Dogs among the café patrons started barking in unison. She had to raise her voice. 'Pretty stiff competition this year.' She pulled out the magazine, and she knew by the expression on her brother's face that he didn't approve of the status he was given. 'Luke is happy to be called a hero, but not a celeb—'

Emma was interrupted by a vibration. She could feel it under her feet and saw ripples in the black of her coffee.

Her friend felt it as well, and when he looked around, he caught his reflection in the stainless-steel coffee machine a few metres away. It was shaking, and the table they shared wobbled. 'What is that?'

Emma stood and walked onto the street. A shadow creeping along the road drew her eyes to the sky. Her jaw dropped at the sight of an enormous saucer-shaped carrier ship. Its approaching mass sent shudders through windows and foundations below it. A deep bass tone thundered through the streets and thumped Emma's chest.

Then the ship stopped moving, and so did everything else.

The dogs continued their warning growls and barks at the giant intruder. Pedestrians stepped out of stores and homes to see what was going on. Cars pulled over, and heads poked out of open windows. Everybody stared. At first, the mood was wonder. It soon became trepidation. Then there was a collective gasp when four aqua lines beamed down like lasers from the saucer's keel.

'Everybody find cover!' Emma cried out and ran to the nearest gawkers who weren't moving. 'Indoors! Now! *Go!*'

San Francisco
Portal Hub

Professor O'Conner spoke to his daughter through the inter-Realm comms link. 'Good to hear, Sam. See you soon.'

'How did they go?'

Hutch Branner arrived at the door to the control deck, pulling on a faded blue baseball cap. Pete recognised the hat from photos of Hutch in magazines and press events. He'd been wearing it since his twenties.

'The Council have agreed to request public opinion. If the majority are in agreement, a relocation team will be assembled.'

Hutch picked up a cup of tea he'd left sitting on a bench to cool. 'I'll issue a statement of support.'

'Speaking of, I hear Meg Green organised you and the others to speak about the marital status vote,' Pete said with a contemplative look. 'I'd like to join you.'

Hutch sprayed Earl Grey and coughed. 'Y-you? In front of cameras?'

'Nobody will notice an old geezer standing next to the wealthiest single man in the world...'

'Believe me, people pay attention when they see you,' Hutch said with an encouraging slap on Pete's arm. 'It'll be an historic moment. One I'm proud to be a part of.'

'It's a good opportunity to honour the people who built their lives up by themselves,' Pete noted, 'without government assistance, without tax exemptions, during those generations when people were being paid to have children.'

'Which created overpopulation.' Hutch chuckled. '"Oh, let's get a bank loan for a house we can't afford, and let's have kids we can't afford to feed or put through school because the government will pay for all that." I'll add it to my speech, and remind everyone that by creating overpopulation, old-world governments forced us to spend valuable resources to find other habitable planets and ship people off Earth.'

'Professor.' Chesh's voice came loud over the deck comms. The Black Bird was parked on the platform outside the facility. They had arrived fifteen minutes ago. 'The Raekeem are invading. I've sent a live feed to your console.'

Pete hit the link on his console and a holographic camera view enlarged to show a Raekeem carrier ship hovering low over Liberty.

'Look at the... size of that thing,' Hutch murmured, peering over Pete's shoulder.

'How did they get to Silica undetect–' Pete saw lasers shoot down from beneath the saucer. 'My stars and garters.'

Renee burst into the room, followed by Brad and two AMs. 'Mr Branner…' She glanced at the news feed and back to Hutch. 'We've lost contact with Planet Darwin. They're under attack.'

Hutch's eyes were wide. He sank into a desk chair and pulled off his cap. 'I should've known. They've been watching, casing out our defences.'

Pete put his hand on his friend's shoulder and looked back to Renee. 'Has Commander Lincoln–'

'He's at the factory.' Renee spoke quickly. 'Professor, I have to lock down this facility.'

'Do it, but I want a sweep of every room. Make sure everybody here is human or AM.'

Amestae
Leetheria City

Jihna ducked under her sparring partner's swinging staff, jumped into a backward summersault and blocked the next volley of jabs directed at her abdomen. The parrying clangs echoed off the curved walls of the training hall. Sunlight beamed through the glass ceiling.

They halted their sparring, breathing heavily, listening. Both warriors felt vibrations in the stone floor. They left the hall and descended stairs to a courtyard, where they saw children gazing up and pointing at something that shrouded them and their concerned parents in darkness. The shadow drew Jihna's eyes to the clouds. There hovered a Raekeem carrier.

'Sound the alert.' She pushed at her sparring partner, who stood staring like the others. 'Go!' she shouted.

Parents rushed away with their children, and the siren brought others out of their homes into an ordered line. They followed the path to the tunnels beneath the city.

Jihna raced up to the command platform, where warriors were already assembling, forming ranks, and were soon ready to receive orders. She met other high-ranking warriors at a console linked to signals emitted from other star systems. They were monitoring the images displayed on the hologram. The human systems were preparing defences, and a Raekeem carrier hovered low above the surface of the Laician Ocean of Kulete City. Waves heaved and fell beneath its hull, and as they saw holographic light beam down through the water and into the city, the same blue hue fell upon their position at the command platform. It expanded like a translucent, intangible sheet of holographic information. Jihna and the others moved outside and looked up to watch a giant figure shimmer into view.

'People of the Three Kingdoms. I am Lord Telsta of the Raekeem. Surrender now and there will be no unnecessary deaths.'

The other warriors looked to Jihna, unsettled by her stillness. Immediate action was normally her instinctive reaction. She stood with fists clenched, staring up into the alien's face. At his arrogant guile. The lie was so obvious it sickened her.

Jihna turned to her fellow warriors.

'Prepare for battle!'

Haze Realm

Lana shared a meal of bread and beans with Jess and Ryan before bed. She watched Jess cradle her brother's head in her lap while he slept, combing her fingers gently through his hair.

'How old?' Lana whispered.

'Thirteen.' Jess smiled down at him. 'Pain in the ass sometimes. Not his fault, though. A lot of kids started showing signs of brain dysfunction when the pollution got bad, even before the Raekeem hit us.'

Lana took Jess and Ryan's bowls to stack up on hers.

'You'll find some towels in the corner of the washroom,' said Jess. 'I left a pair of my pants and a shirt. Should fit you.'

'Thanks.' Lana's nose twitched at the bitter haze toxin that had stained her clothes. She took the bowls to the washroom sink and undressed.

After a thorough scrubbing in the shower, she was towelling when Hal backed in through the washroom door with a trolley of instruments from the lab. Since the Top Freedom law was passed in Home Realm a decade ago, nudity was taboo only within Asian and Arab cultures, so Lana didn't cover up. She found it odd; in most Realms, displays of violence were more acceptable than the beauty of the human body.

Hal was startled and apologised for forgetting to knock first.

'Don't stress,' said Lana. 'Hey, that pod in the lab…'

'It's an incubation chamber,' he said.

'We have the same technology in my world.' Lana found the change of clothes Jess had left out for her. 'It's used to create Augmented Humans. Were you…?'

'Yes,' Hal said. He turned to Lana in surprise and quickly averted his eyes. 'The Professor found me here about twelve years ago, when I was still in incubation. Luckily, the machines were pre-programmed to follow through with my birth process. Pete only had to run the education simulations and basically be my parent.'

'The same project was done in my world.' Lana couldn't understand how or why the Professor O'Conner in this Realm could appear to be ten years younger than hers.

Hal saw Lana's console when she collected it. 'So that's like a walkie?'

'It can also teleport people and open portals.'

'Wow. So you're from the future.'

'No.'

Lana gave Hal the explanation she must've given a dozen times before. There was a roughness about him, Lana noticed. His tone was polite but non-committal. He seemed to be trying to mask his lack of ease. His body language was guarded, even now, when there was no danger. He would become still from time to time, as though he was listening out for anything irregular. And everything about him told Lana he was ready to fight at any time.

Her console beeped an incoming communication. She checked the caller ID and hit the comms receiver. 'Hey, Rache, what's up?' Panicked, raised voices drowned out Rachel's first words. 'Say again. I can't hear you.'

'You have to get back,' she called. 'They're here. The Raekeem are invading Home Realm.'

Chapter 12

Home Realm
Planet Darwin
Branner AM Factory

A Raekeem drop ship fired on the building from the air. Shafts of evening light beamed through the ceiling to the assembly room. Flashes of Raekeem blaster fire threw the shadows of fleeing technicians against the walls.

Lincoln took cover behind the bulk of machinery that had been used to build him, so many years ago. Sparks flew from severed electrical cables beside him. He and Jolie had shot two Sentinels, but more were teleporting in.

Lincoln rolled out of cover, shot down a Sentinel and continued firing, providing Jolie an opportunity to follow the last AMs to the stairs. She and the AMs descended to the basement floor and stopped to receive instructions. These AMs were new and hadn't yet received their programming. Even if they had been armed, they wouldn't have been able to help defend the factory without training programs. Each wore the blue medical scrubs they were given after assembly.

Jolie typed a directive into her console and sent it to all of their neural transceivers. The AMs assumed a paired formation line and jogged down the evacuation tunnel that stretched on four hundred metres from the factory. The tunnel had been built after Sabre Company attacked, and it doubled as a storage space.

'There's one more!' Lincoln called from the top of the stairs.

Jolie hustled up to him and crouched to follow him back to a computer terminal. It was powered by a separate system that was hardwired to batteries beneath the concrete slab they were standing on. Lincoln popped up from the terminal and fired on the approaching Sentinels while Jolie accessed the security cameras.

'Where? I can't see anyone,' said Jolie.

Lincoln glanced at the six small video displays and pointed to the bottom right corner.

Jolie selected it and zoomed in. She saw a gas canister explode. A sheet of metal that had fallen from the ruptured ceiling slid off a female AM. She was lying on a conveyer belt, ready to receive scrubs. The legs of the conveyor track buckled under a fallen support beam, and her unconscious body rolled to the floor.

'I can't get to her,' Lincoln called while firing on another Sentinel.

Jolie could see that the AM was complete. *She's connected*, Jolie realised. *I can program her combat—*

A deafening explosion threw her sideways to the floor. The blast from the drop ship had shot through the gaping roof and ruptured the wall four metres above her head. She and Lincoln scrambled back to the stairs. She glanced over her shoulder to see a huge chunk of concrete plummet from the wall. It crushed the terminal they were hiding behind, and they tumbled down the stairs, followed by bouncing debris and a plume of concrete dust.

They got to their feet, and Jolie found the nearest terminal. Lincoln continued running for the tunnel before skidding to a halt.

'What are you doing?' he called.

'Hold them off for one minute!'

Jolie accessed the AM unit programming through the terminal options and tapped through tabs to reach the combat training protocols. The unconscious AM upstairs was the only soldier physically connected to the system, so her file was easy to find. Jolie backspaced the unit's designated number and typed in a name she thought would best suit the level of combat expertise she was about to give the new soldier. She knew that the most highly trained fighters humanity had to offer trained in Virtual Reality. All of their skills were recorded for use in AM combat programming. Units were given general combat abilities and specialised skills, such as aircraft piloting, base jumping, or heavy weapons training.

Lincoln shot down a Sentinel that was descending to the basement and drew the next one's fire away from Jolie by darting across the corridor to take cover behind a girder. He crouched and fired blind. The Sentinel cried out. Lincoln strafed out of cover and finished off the wounded Raekeem. Arriving at Jolie's side, he opened his mouth to tell her to hurry up when he saw the list of combat programs she'd transferred to a file called "Talon". She'd uploaded… *everything*.

'Done. Let's go,' said Jolie, and the two of them ran for the tunnel.

The drop ship ceased fire while the Raekeem soldiers searched the factory for survivors. They hurtled over fallen machinery and support beams. One stood over a female AM unit lying on her side. A cylinder of battery fluid had broken and spilled against her, dyeing her shoulder-length hair pink. It hung across her Southeast Asian features. The soldier assumed she was inactive and turned to leave.

Talon rose silently behind him, gripped his head and snapped his neck. She lowered him to the floor, took his weapon and moved on to her next target.

The Sentinel in charge spoke into his comms. 'Danin to carrier ship. Scan the surrounding area. Eliminate any escapees. Plant explosives on the remaining loadbearing pillars.'

Blaster fire sounded. Two of his squad fell. He caught a glimpse of a naked woman darting behind machinery and reappearing to kill two more of his team. All Sentinels blasted at her last known position and took cover when she returned fire.

Electrical sparks illuminated the dark, lending blinks of light to the lone AM who had reduced the Raekeem squad to eight. Talon rolled over an intact conveyor belt and pressed her back against a cylinder of battery fluid. Two Sentinels had flanked her and were closing in on her position. She dropped to the floor to avoid fire from one of them and shot the other in the chest. The cylinder burst and fluid splashed over her. Talon pushed away from cover, her slick body sliding through a narrow gap between fallen debris. She intercepted and sweep-kicked a running Sentinel. He fell on top of her, and she avoided the jabs of his spiked elbows. She jammed her weapon into his chest and fired. Now armed with two blasters, Talon rose from the floor and shot down two more Sentinels.

Danin climbed a support beam and jumped from it, through a broken window, and rolled through the glass. The agonised cry of his last Sentinel convinced him to remain crouched. He aimed his weapon at the windows. *She will come, but there is time to disable her weapons.* He used his console to remotely shut down all blasters in the vicinity but his. Quickly moving to the door, he pushed through toppled chairs then spun around at the slightest sound of footfalls.

Night fell, and the wind drew storm clouds over the factory. The drop ship beamed a searchlight through the exposed roof.

Talon stood motionless in the shadows at the opposite end of the corridor, watching the leader of the Raekeem squad. Her bare feet padded quietly along the carpeted floor once he turned his back. She watched him twist his forearm to check his console. It showed a timer counting down from three seconds. Talon ran beside the corridor wall, hopped and planted one quick foot after the other, climbing two metres high before launching herself at Danin. The force of her tackle sent the two of them crashing through the wall. They hit the floor a second before the explosives detonated.

The building shuddered, and the floor tilted beneath them when the supports gave way. Danin shoved Talon, wiped plaster dust from his eyes and pushed off from the wall to strike her hard in the head. She used the momentum of the blow to turn her body and whip her leg, landing her heel against Danin's kneecap. He cried out and fell against an overturned chair. He lurched at her and swung his elbow spike, slicing her calf when she tried to deflect it. Talon grappled Danin's arm with one hand, took hold of his hair and swung his head into a doorframe. He fell limp. She dragged him along the floor and up to a window ledge, where the night air was cool and heavy rain was falling.

A fork of lightning lit the ground below, and Talon saw a length of factory roof that was bent down, offering a steep slope to the ground. She pulled Danin and jumped from the ledge. The factory caved in on itself, and a dust cloud rose, enveloping them. Talon hugged Danin close and rotated her body, using him to cushion the impact of hitting the roof slope. She landed blind and felt the sliding inertia of their escape. They shot ahead of the dust cloud, jettisoning off the roof three metres over the ground before landing on gravel.

Talon blinked through flashes of jagged lightning reaching across the sky. Thunder drummed seconds later to a sharp clap. She rolled off Danin and checked his pulse. He was broken but still breathing. The rain washed over her, and she looked back to the place of her birth, where only a mountain of rubble remained. She removed Danin's console and accessed his comms, only to find that all options were in an alien language. Talon's machine brain compared its database of known written languages and quickly locked in patterns and similarities, until eighty per cent translation accuracy was achieved. She typed a message to the drop ship, telling them the target site was destroyed. She requested a craft be sent down and ordered the drop ship to leave.

Talon used Danin's comms to search for a friendly signal. A voice crackled, and she tried to dial through the static.

'I repeat: this is Commander Lincoln. Requesting assistance. Respond.'

Talon opened her mouth, but no sound came out of the speaker in her throat. *Damaged during the fight.* She decided to tap on the console screen, communicating in Morse code. Her head rose at the sound of engines. The unmanned Raekeem craft she had ordered came in for landing. Squinting through a blast of electricity between two clouds, she watched the bird-of-prey silhouette circle above. It descended upon her. Its jutting beak tracked her before it landed deftly, casting her in shadow. Its armoured fuselage and sizeable rear propulsion cowlings suggested it was capable of interstellar travel.

This mechanical predator was a most welcome sight. Because it was hers to commandeer. If she could.

When Danin woke, he was being dragged up the cargo bay ramp. Talon stopped at the armoury and took a Raekeem uniform before hauling her captive all the way to the cockpit. She lifted the immobile Sentinel, while he groaned in pain from numerous broken bones, into the co-pilot seat.

Talon dressed herself in the black, mummy-wrap-style rubber top, pants and shoes, which seemed too big at first. Then she flinched when they automatically tightened to hug her form. The excess rubber lengths hung at her sides like tassels. Talon guessed there was a hidden battery-powered sensor that retracted wires imbedded in the rubber.

She returned, dropping into the pilot chair, and studied the readings on the screen. The markings on the panels before her, as well as on the overhead switches, were Raekeem symbols indicating each function. Talon drew on her programming to identify practical engineering. She spotted what had to be the engine primer and a row of switches that were on/offs for separate ship functions. All of them were lit because the ship was already active.

Danin breathed through clenched teeth, watching the machine that had beaten him. He couldn't hide his smirk when she reached for the landing gear lever. Then he realised she had caught his reaction. He cursed at himself. Talon's fingers left the landing gear lever and found a switch. She flicked it and the loading bay door closed behind them. This lit up the previously inactive steering controls, which Talon gently pulled back to begin their ascent. She returned to the landing gear lever and gave Danin an appreciative look before pulling it. A groan sounded beneath them while the ship's legs retracted into the hull.

The symbol for communications proved elusive. *Another Morse code message to Lincoln to request his coordinates*, she thought, *and we'll see what this beautiful beast can do.*

Danin used his tongue to search behind his molars. His eyes darted to Talon when she held out a capsule in the palm of her hand. It was a chemical pill, likely a Raekeem version of cyanide. He glared at her when she let it roll out of her hand onto the floor.

The wings extended with overlapping armoured panels. Talon pushed the controls forward to fly the ship over the decimated factory and on to Lincoln's coordinates.

Haze Realm

Benson was standing at a flaming bin with his men. It was cold in the train tunnels, but spirits had been high since they'd been told they would be relocated. Everybody was huddled close, faces lit orange by rubbish burning in the steel barrels positioned by their huts.

Benson saw Lana portal in with two civilians either side of her.

'Well?' he said. 'Did your Council agree to–'

'I don't know,' Lana interrupted, speaking quickly. 'I'll relocate all of you myself if I have to. Right now, we have a bigger problem: the Raekeem have invaded my world.'

Benson hung his head and stared into the flames. 'It was only a matter of time. Is there anything we can do to help?'

'We need more intel. Is there anything else you can tell us?'

'I'm sorry.' Benson shook his head. 'I've already told you everything we…'

He saw Jess emerge from the shadows behind Lana and couldn't believe who was holding her hand.

'Hi, Uncle,' Jess' brother murmured shyly.

'Can we stay with you until we leave for the other world?' Jess asked.

'Of course,' Benson stammered, and he nodded to the shacks toward the rear of the tunnel. 'Someone will see that you two get a bed.'

Jess stopped and turned back to him. 'Sorry about…'

'Forget it. Welcome back.' Benson pushed his fingers through his nephew's hair and messed it up like he used to. 'Good to see you again, buddy.' He glimpsed an appreciative look from Jess before she left, and he hoped the two of them might restore the bond they used to have.

Another flash of portal light beamed against the walls and vanished. Hal and Professor O'Conner approached.

Benson watched the two men enter the light. The first looked to be around thirty, and the other was middle aged.

'Follow Jess,' said Lana. 'There's bedding–'

'There is something I must tell you,' O'Conner announced. 'I am Raekeem.'

'It's alright,' said Hal, and stepped in front of him when Lana released the clip holding her axe in its holster. 'He's not dangerous. I've known him all my life. He's been like a father to me.'

Benson and his guards were immediately on edge, moving to protect the nearest of their unarmed people.

Lana didn't draw her axe, but her hand was ready. 'I knew something wasn't right.'

'My name is Oskar,' the disguised Raekeem man said, stepping forward. Everyone fell silent. Only the licking of flames and the crunching of rocks underfoot could be heard while tunnel dwellers busied themselves with packing food, filtered water and belongings.

Lana gasped when Oskar's visible skin faded to pale grey. Black veins coursed beneath wrinkles of advanced age. His hair was long and white. The lab coat he wore shimmered into a double-breasted black rubber uniform bearing a crest: an inverted triangle inside an egg shape. 'I was a Science Officer. I have pertinent information.'

Lana glanced from Oskar to Hal. 'Both of you are coming with me. You're going to tell us everything.'

Chapter 13

Luke Palmer spoke through his comms linked with Renee in San Francisco. 'We've assembled all AM soldiers we have here in Liberty.' He looked to his sister, Emma, who was dressed in body armour and strapping on a thigh holster.

'No sign of the Raekeem here yet,' Renee confirmed.

'Any word from Lincoln or Jolie?'

'No,' she said. 'And we can't spare units to search for them.'

'The Raekeem will most likely test our defences before committing to a full offensive,' Emma said. Her words came out in a flat monotone, and she shivered at the sound of her own voice: robotic, obedient, bringing back memories of mind-controlled service to Sabre Company. 'Have we had any communication with Telsta?'

'Not yet,' said Luke. 'Rachel has advised the Council to capitulate. They'll stall the Raekeem while we figure out a plan of attack.' A message came through his console, and he relayed it. 'Rachel's bringing inhibitor nodes now.'

Portal light shone from the hallway outside the armoury, and they went out to greet Rachel. Emma shot a finger to the trolley of cylinders she pushed. 'What do they do?'

'The Kiyol advised that although Raekeem teleportation looks different to ours, the same physics apply,' Rachel explained. 'So these nodes will stop them sending in any ground forces.'

'Any *more*,' Luke corrected. 'They may already be here.'

Aboard the Raekeem carrier, stationary above Liberty, Lead Sentinel Feen oversaw the assembly of his forces. One hundred jets were fuelled and ready in the hangar. The pilots were being briefed on attack formations.

'Sentinel Xera,' Feen barked. 'Where is your Squad Leader?'

Xera looked for him among her fellow squad members. 'Unaccounted for, sir. Shall I–'

'No.' Feen walked off abruptly. 'This ends now.'

Xera watched Feen before leaving to follow him at a discreet distance.

Kordin stood at the main console on the carrier brig, panning through screens linked to the Raekeem database. The dozen console operators stationed there barely noticed his presence. They were captured humans who were drugged and conditioned to work eighteen-hour shifts.

Kordin read the file on his uncle Oskar. Oskar belonged to an ancient clan renowned for their exclusive knowledge of the Dark Sciences. He was deployed to a world where a human by the name of Peter O'Conner was to be abducted and persuaded to contribute his Augmented Human Project to the Raekeem. His work was to be re-engineered. However, Oskar had failed the mission. He never returned. To Kordin's disappointment, that concluded the file. He quickly scanned through the mission logs that the deck operators were able to locate upon his request.

'Kordin.'

He tensed at his uncle's tone and slowly turned to face him.

'Your squad are assembling without their leader,' Feen growled. 'Your callous disregard for your duties–' He looked over Kordin's shoulder to the console screen. 'You're accessing restricted records.'

'Tell me what you know about Oskar's mission,' Kordin demanded.

'I give the orders, you pretentious little–'

'Uncle,' Kordin interrupted. 'Tell me what happened to him.' He tried to suppress his emotion, as Raekeem men were supposed to.

Feen pressed his lips together, trying to contain his anger. 'You are so much like Oskar and nothing like your father. If he could see you now…' He shook his head in disappointment.

'What happened to Oskar?' Kordin demanded through clenched teeth, his heart thumping in his chest. 'Why did he not return from–'

'We harvested the humans and left Oskar in that world to rot,' Feen admitted, glaring at his nephew.

This challenged Kordin's preconceptions, lending him pause, slowing his pulse. *Feen is… not to blame for what happened to Oskar?* 'Telsta ordered you to abandon him?'

'No. I gave the order.' Seeing his nephew's jaw slacken, a blow dealt, brought Feen pleasure. He pressed for more, latching his hands down on Kordin's shoulders. 'Hear this, boy: Oskar's obsession was infecting the minds of our scientists. He was driving them to find a way to revert us back to the way we were.'

Kordin felt the weight of Feen's muscle. A lifetime of battles had given him superior strength. It was partly why Kordin never challenged his uncle outright.

'Oskar was weak,' Feen spat. 'The Raekeem, *my* Sentinels' – he thumped a clenched fist against his chest – 'are the very weapon all worlds fear! You…' He tilted his head and bunched his features in disgust. 'You are not worthy.'

Kordin slapped his uncle's hand away, shouldered past him and kept his back turned. 'You betrayed your own brother, Uncle. Our family.'

'You are officially stripped of rank,' Feen stated, with a satisfied exhale.

'I have Telsta's favour,' Kordin replied impatiently, back still turned.

Feen raised his voice with proud authority. 'From this day, you will tend to the war dogs.'

'He will not allow–'

'You will shovel their muck. You will sleep in their pens.' Feen leaned to Kordin's ear and whispered, 'And you will never see your precious Xera again.'

She was there, standing in shadow. Kordin had seen the light on her hip when he turned away from his uncle.

'You hear me now, don't you, boy? Oh yes, *she* has our Lord's favour. Slated to be his next concubine, but not before I… have my way with her.'

Kordin threw his head back into Feen's on the last word, breaking his nose. Blade out, Kordin slashed. Blood sprayed the nearest operator.

Making no attempt to close his open jugular, Feen punched Kordin in the face and grappled him.

The deck operators did not react when Feen cried out. Black ooze dripped between Kordin's fingers, pressed over his uncle's mouth. He clenched his teeth through the pain of Feen biting his palm. Sinking his blade up under Feen's ribs, he twisted it.

Feen clawed at Kordin's neck and shoulder then fell limp, staring at him with blank eyes.

Kordin let his uncle fall. Tears of rage streamed down his face. His eyes rose to meet Xera's open stare.

She looked from Feen's body to Kordin. The operators continued to work. She was very still while she thought through what must be done.

'You're Lead Sentinel now,' she said, and tapped at the menu screen on a console to initiate a teleport. She turned to Kordin. 'This did not happen.'

Kordin watched his uncle become enveloped in a black cloud. It retracted into thin air. Feen's body dropped out of the receiving teleport outside and plummeted to the human city below.

Xera took Kordin's bitten hand and kissed his wound, bloodying her full lips black.

Chapter 14

Rachel and Luke patrolled Liberty's streets, which had not been so deserted since Sabre Company occupation. They were with a team of AMs, deploying inhibitor nodes to establish the matrix web as they progressed through the east side of the city. Emma was doing the same in the west with another squad of AMs.

Rachel looked up at the stars, only to see the Raekeem ship looming above. Her eyes narrowed and focused on a person falling from the carrier. A distant thud sounded when they hit a roof.

Luke swept the torchlight beaming from his assault rifle over an alley, scanning it, and moved on. When his light caught something in a shop window, he stopped abruptly. 'Hold up. I saw movement in that clothing store.'

Rachel signalled the AMs to cover the street intersection and moved to position herself at the door. Luke entered and she followed. Their torchlights threw the shadows of mannequins on the walls while they checked the interior.

'Security Division,' Rachel called out. 'Anybody here?' Her aim jerked toward an opening door. Two boys came out, squinting. 'What are you doing here? Where are your parents?'

'They're underground,' the older one said. 'It got dark before we could make it to them. Thought it'd be safer to leave in the morning. Please don't report us. We didn't break in. Our parents own the store.'

'Go outside,' Luke told them. 'The soldiers will take you to shelter.' He gave the AMs the order through his comms.

The younger kid stopped. 'Wow! Luke Palmer and Rachel Navara!' He went back, found a pen from behind the shop counter and held it out to Luke. 'Can you sign my hat?'

'I hope you beat the aliens, so we can see you race,' the other boy said.

Rachel signed the hat after Luke had finished. 'Now go,' she said. 'And stay with your parents.'

'Thanks!' the younger one called over his shoulder and pulled the cap over his head.

'I'll never get used to that,' said Luke, shaking his head and smiling.

Emma's voice came through their comms. 'Rache, Luke, we're done here. All nodes deployed. We're heading back.'

'Copy that.'

Luke followed Rachel through the store and stopped to look back at something.

'What?' she asked.

'There were three mannequins when we came in,' he whispered. 'Now there's one.'

Rachel looked to the street. *Two cloaked Sentinels. They were waiting to follow the kids underground*, she thought and tapped at her console to find a map. She found a vegetation tower nearby and opened a comms link. 'Navara to escort detail, bogies on your tail. Re-route to following coordinates. Load shock rounds, take them alive.'

'Copy that. Coordinates received.'

Luke and Rachel made for the tower. They ejected their live ammunition and loaded a clip of shock bullets that delivered fifty thousand volts upon impact.

The AM soldiers escorting the two boys walked through the foyer, up an escalator to a reception area. The vegetation tower contained ten floors of hydroponic crops, growing under full spectrum lights powered by solar electricity. The crops were packed and made available for purchase in the Market Square at the rear of the building.

'I thought we were going to the underground shelters,' one of the boys said.

'I'm hungry,' the other complained.

'Rachel wants us to wait here,' one AM said distractedly while keeping an eye out for hostiles.

The other soldier saw some brief light distortion near the escalators. The steps moved, and the AM ushered the children behind the desk and took position, ready to fire on the enemy.

Luke and Rachel entered silently through a side door. A gust of cool wind followed. Rachel saw something invisible push through the splayed leaves of a fern tree.

'We're in position,' Luke reported through his comms to the soldiers. 'Hit the lights. Flash in three.'

'Copy that.'

The overhead lights went out, and the flash grenade Rachel lobbed blew. Luke fired a shock round where he thought the Sentinels were but it didn't connect. His legs were knocked out from underneath him, and he felt an invisible body pin him as soon as he hit the floor. A shot from Rachel landed in the cloaked figure's arm. It shook and became visible.

With the Sentinel still on top of him, the shock travelled into Luke. Jaw clenched, muscles twitching, he rolled the unconscious body off him. He watched helplessly as the other Sentinel decloaked and kicked Rachel from behind. Shock rounds flew overhead from the AMs guarding the kids. The Sentinel replied with a knife throw, landing the blade in one of the AMs' chests.

Rachel sweep-kicked the Raekeem, fired on her at point blank range and watched her try to rise while shaking before dropping to her side.

The boys stood up and cheered when the uninjured AM sounded the all-clear.

'We'll take these two in,' Rachel said to him. 'Call a medic for your partner and escort the kids to their parents.'

Luke dragged one unconscious Sentinel over to the other. 'Must be scouts.'

'Rache.' Lana's voice came through her comms. 'I'm back from Haze Realm. I found an outcast Raekeem Science Officer. He has intel we need. But he won't give it to us until the Council officially pledge to relocate the people of Haze Realm.'

Rachel's eyebrows rose, and she replied in a dry tone. 'When Sam and I proposed relocation to the Council, half of the members were against it. It would have taken weeks to sway their vote.'

'Oskar just gave us the ultimatum we need,' said Lana.

'Uh-huh,' Rachel said doubtfully. 'And this Science Officer of yours demanded this condition out of the kindness of his Raekeem heart.'

'What's that? You're breaking up.'

'Well played, Lana. See you soon.'

Hal stared out of the window at the enormous undercarriage of the carrier ship looming over Liberty.

Luke and Rachel arrived in the meeting room and took a seat with Lana. Oskar and all Council members were present in holographic form. They had reluctantly agreed to his demand and waited for him to speak.

'Understand this,' Oskar cautioned. 'The Raekeem cannot be bargained with. Telsta will take what he came for.'

'We were told by the survivors we're relocating that they harvest the "third eye",' said Lana. 'What does that mean?'

Oskar gave her a grave, deadpan stare. 'They must have been referring to the amygdala. Without it, one is no longer sovereign over one's own consciousness. Everything you are: your creativity, your dreams, your passion, your very will to live. That is what the Lords harvest.'

'They need our consciousness to live?' a Council member asked.

'It extends their lifetime, yes. But this invasion is not only for the harvest. Telsta has an interest in animal mutation. He needs numbers to implement his plan to develop a mutagen. He will inject animal DNA into his Sentinels and into your people. If the mutagen is of a high enough efficacy, he will take and infect as many of you as he can to build his army.'

'You served under this Lord that is attacking us,' a Council member accused. 'You developed the technology to destroy entire worlds. How can we trust–'

'I am a monster,' said Oskar. 'But I am telling you the truth. I don't know how but I developed a conscience. A trait that has been bred out of the Raekeem for over two centuries.' He gazed across his sceptical audience. 'I envy you. You have done what my people could not. You have held onto your humanity. You have protected it, developed a universal understanding for one another, and created a partnership for the purpose of not only survival but progression. You are a truly accomplished people.'

Rachel leaned forward. *Bred out of them?* She glanced at Lana, and Lana returned the same confused frown.

'Oskar,' Lana began. 'Are you saying that you… that the Raekeem–'

Oskar nodded solemnly. 'We were human.'

Chapter 15

Forest Realm

Sam directed the relocation of the Haze Realm people, with the help of the two AMs that could be spared. Every other combat unit was needed in the preparation for war against the Raekeem.

Benson and his people carried boxes from Haze Realm through the portal to the supply tent in Forest Realm. The relocation camp was set up in Chahtu and Mehra's village. Chahtu helped with the heavy lifting, and Anook worked with Jess to distribute supplies provided by the UC Aid Division. Soon, dozens of villagers arrived to offer their assistance. Sam handed out translator consoles to ensure clear communication during the relocation process.

Many families had come from the dry inland areas over the years to live closer to the coast. Before Lana had killed Galai, the Blood Demon Queen, none dared to settle in this area. The cannibal tribe had disbanded, and now there was a forest community of one hundred peaceful people.

Anook was excited to see strangers from Lana's world. He believed that every new person and family could share their skills and knowledge and be taught in hunting and farming. Together they could create a safe community.

'Would you and your brother like to join me for a meal tonight?' Anook asked Jess shyly.

Jess read the translation on her console. 'Yes, thank you.'

Hope soared in her heart. She and her brother were finally safe, far from the dangers of the city, the only life they knew.

Home Realm
Liberty

'The Raekeem are from another version of Earth?' Luke asked Oskar.

'It takes thousands of years for a species to evolve,' Lana interjected, her eyes wandering sceptically over Oskar's pale skin, pointed ears and white eyes. 'How…?'

'During early civilisation, our people warred for control of entire continents, while your people fought over borders within continents,' Oskar explained. 'Your ancestors fought civil wars and revolutions, while mine fought for world domination. This drove technological advancement to the brink of our annihilation. By the time you had your Napoleonic War, we had already developed electromagnetic matter distortion, localised void rifts, and light refraction technology that led to cloaking. We achieved nuclear-powered space flight two hundred years ago.'

Oskar shook his head grimly. 'It was then that our people formed clans. One clan, called the Raekeem, were unstoppable in battle. They took slaves after each victory. And they performed genetic experimentation on those slaves. They subjected their own people to the most successful methods of augmentation. They created Sentinels, warriors of the clan. Eventually, all of the other clans fell, and there was no one left to kill.'

He paused, sweeping his gaze over the Council. 'All efforts were directed then to developing what you call Realm travel. Those skilled in the Dark Sciences were successful in creating tears in the fabric of time and space, portals to other worlds. Our version of travel is not safe. Yours opens a protective sphere, ours a cloud of dark matter. Years of travelling through it changed our DNA. It accelerated certain physical traits, which were passed on to our children. Our aging process suffered. We even lost the ability to sleep.'

'How many worlds have the Raekeem destroyed?' Lana asked.

Oskar shrugged. 'We have been hunting, harvesting and enslaving people for generations. We truly are a plague.'

'Why were you in Haze Realm?' Rachel asked.

Oskar breathed a sigh while gazing at the floor. 'I and the other scientists were ordered to prepare for the next step in augmentation.

I argued against developing the animal mutagen. We were already monsters. Telsta wanted us to become abominations.'

He pressed his lips together. Although he had told this story to Hal before, it was no less difficult to retell. 'He assigned me to a mission with his Lead Sentinel, Feen, my brother. We were to retrieve data from Professor O'Conner on an Earth that was already dying. We found his lab. It looked to have been overrun by bandits. The Professor had been killed.'

Lana clenched her fists.

'Feen was furious, raging about the mission being "a waste of valuable time" and how it was imperative that we find another O'Conner. I didn't know what he was talking about, and he wouldn't explain. All he said was, "We are all surely doomed." He confiscated my portal device, locked me in the lab and left me there. A blessing, really. Exile meant that I would no longer be party to genocide.'

Oskar gave another sigh. 'My only regret was that I could not protect my nephew, Kordin.'

Lana remembered that name in Rowan's report. 'Kordin was one of the Sentinels who was protecting the IDBot container,' she said to Luke.

'He was following orders,' Oskar asserted. He stopped himself and thought on that. 'And so was I. But we all have a choice.' He looked to the Council members. 'I do not deserve to live. Any judgment you deem necessary to pass, I will accept.'

Hal stepped forward to plead Oskar's case. 'This man brought me up as a child with the best intentions. I have morals and values like any human, yet I was fathered by a Raekeem.'

'We have no time for judgment right now,' a Council member said. 'The time we have must be dedicated to defence.'

'You must take the fight to Telsta if you hope to survive,' Oskar advised. 'But beware, our ships are nuclear powered. Their destruction would render your cities uninhabitable.'

'What do you suggest?' asked Rachel.

'Take the brig. Fly the carrier away from your system and destroy it. I know their flight systems. And I can draw plans that will lead you to the brig.'

'How do we get into the carrier?' Lana asked.

An idea came to Rachel. 'Luke and I captured their scouts. The Raekeem will be expecting them to have found Silica's underground shelters. We have their cloaking devices.' She looked to Oskar. 'Yours makes three.'

Oskar was impressed by Rachel's bold ploy. 'I can build more cloaks.'

'You could work with Professor O'Conner at our facility on Earth,' said Rachel. She turned to Lana. 'Once disguised, you and I can get up to the carrier, set coordinates and teleport in a team.'

'It's a sound plan,' said Oskar. 'And the last tactical move Telsta would expect.'

Planet Darwin

Lincoln, Jolie, the factory staff and the new AMs emerged from the underground tunnel just as Talon arrived with the Raekeem ship she'd procured. It could only carry ten passengers, so Talon showed Jolie how to work the alien controls and Jolie took the wounded, including Sentinel Danin, to the nearest UC medical facility. She would request another transport be sent as soon as she was in outer space.

Talon watched the ship ascend and disappear into the dark clouds. The rain had eased to a drizzle, and she found a spot to sit, away from the others. She gazed out to the horizon, at the rubble that used to be the Branner Factory. There was a central fire burning, with a dark column of smoke rising from it.

Some time later, Lincoln sat down beside her and watched the sky clear. He looked to her, opened his mouth to speak.

What to say to a woman who had to fight for her life from the moment she was activated? To Lincoln's knowledge, no unit had ever been programmed to be so lethal. Talon was officially the most dangerous active AM to date. He had to consider the possible ramifications.

The wind blew Talon's pink hair across one side of her face. Lincoln watched her staring at the horizon. If for some reason Talon was to refuse orders, or if she was to go rogue, no AM soldier would be able to stop her, he thought. The only person who could have any hope against her in a fight is Lana.

He opened his mouth again, knowing this time what he must say, when Talon stood abruptly and gazed up at a transport ship breaking through the atmosphere.

Lincoln accessed his comms. 'Commander Lincoln to transport, come in.'

'We see you, Commander.'

The transport descended, rotated to face its rear door to the group of AMs, touched down and lowered the gangway. Talon and Lincoln were the last to board, and the ship set off.

Lincoln sat across from Talon. He knew he should have her reprogrammed down to a safer level of combat proficiency. But it didn't seem right. *She should be rewarded for her heroism, not demoted. She killed an entire Raekeem squad, captured their leader and survived the factory collapse. Not only that, she has saved the lives of the wounded by providing a ship.*

Lincoln decided to monitor her instead. He hoped he wouldn't come to regret it.

Aqua Sierra
Kulete City Defence Hall

Chillo watched the holographic display beaming up from the centre of the room. Kida was reporting his team's findings, having returned from reconnaissance. All sea-based warriors had been dispatched across the city to prepare for the Raekeem invasion. Those stationed in towers aimed their turrets to the surface, poised to fire.

Chillo tapped at the display to rotate the three-dimensional image of the Raekeem carrier ship while listening to his son's report.

'There are four entry points into the carrier,' said Kida. 'But our scanners detect a pulse shield that will block any assault.'

'If we calibrate our disruptor beams to match the pulse frequency, a column of our fighters should be able to slip through a temporary gap,' said Chillo.

'I and our other legged warriors can fight our way to the brig,' Kida agreed. 'Then fly the carrier away and destroy it.'

Chillo glanced over to his mother, who was pacing outside the Defence Hall doors. He had advised her to stay with her guards, out of harm's way. 'There will be hundreds of Sentinels in that ship,' he warned his son.

'We have no other plan, Father. The humans and Kiyol intend to deal with this threat in much the same way.'

'It is decided, then: you will break in, commandeer the carrier and detonate it away from our planet.'

Chillo took a moment to regard his son in this time of peril. Kida had become a man.

Amestae
Leetheria City

'Good luck, Jihna.' Ambassador Jainon took Jihna by her shoulders, and they touched their foreheads together.

'We will not fail.'

Jainon released her, and Jihna climbed onto the back of an avesti, the mount Kiyol warriors rode into battle. The tall, lanky beast squawked, and its clawed feet scratched at the stone ground. Light armour protected its feathered neck.

Jihna rode the avesti to the barracks. She looked to the pulse cannons standing by to deliver a concentrated blast that would temporarily disrupt the carrier shields. Her team would fly in on a single ship, blow their way through an entry point, land inside and fight their way to the brig.

The team of nineteen warriors watched their transport ship fly overhead and land before the barracks. The ship was armed with cannons and loaded with high intensity plasma to penetrate the carrier's hangar-bay doors.

'Our enemy wish to conquer this Realm,' Jihna called. 'We will not let them. We will fight until our last breath.'

They roared their battle cry and shook their staffs above their heads. Jihna rode her avesti up the ramp and into the loading bay, followed by her fellow warriors.

Silica
Liberty

Lana didn't have a lot of time to bring Hal up to speed as to how Home Realm became the progressive society it was or how an alliance between alien communities had been made. But she knew someone who did have the time, and he would be able to answer all of Hal's questions.

'Take a seat,' said Lana.

Hal dropped into a comfortable reclining chair in an unoccupied office. Lana closed the door and adjusted his chair so he was leaning right back.

'I've booked you in for one hour,' she said, handing him a headset. 'This is what we use to connect to the simulation program. It's probably similar to what Oskar had you learn with when you were growing up. You're going into a space where a man called Garwyn will be at your full disposal. Ask him anything you want to know.'

Hal watched Lana load a set of programs on a laptop. 'Is this really necessary?' he asked. 'Oskar ran me through every combat program. Let me help you.'

'You will.' Lana placed her hand on his shoulder. 'But first, I want you to know *why* you should help us. What it is we're fighting for.'

Hal didn't understand, but he could see that it was important to Lana.

'You'll be entering REM sleep for this,' she explained. 'One hour here is over a day where you're going.' She handed Hal a sedative and a glass of water. 'Ready?'

He swallowed the pill. 'See you in an hour.'

'This is so weird,' Rachel said, looking down at the tight, holographic rubber covering most of her body. Her skin was pale, and a long, sharp bone protruded from both of her elbows. She bared her sharp teeth in the locker room mirror and leaned back in disgust when she saw her snake tongue.

'Woah!' Lana jumped when she walked in. 'Rache? Is that you?'

'It's me.' She handed Lana a slim console. 'Oskar worked with Pete and Hutch through the night to build us more cloaks. Suit up.'

Luke entered the locker room and handed them the Raekeem comms he found on the scouts. 'They'll likely teleport you up to their carrier, but we don't know exactly where. Report in as soon as you're clear to talk.'

Rachel nodded and activated the comms link to the Raekeem carrier ship. After taking a breath to calm her nerves, she spoke. 'We have located the underground shelters.'

'Good,' a male voice answered. 'Stand by for extraction.'

Lana was ready. Her female Raekeem look was mapped over her body. She let her hair down and messed it up to appear more like them.

Luke backed away from Lana and Rachel when a black cloud swirled around them. It swallowed them both before disappearing.

They found themselves standing on a raised platform in a shadowy room. The undulating hum of electrical power was accompanied only by rapid tapping. Human operators typed and pressed at buttons on a long array of panels before them.

Lana said hello to one of them, but he ignored her. She waved her hand in front of his face. Nothing. *These guys must be slaves*, she thought. A high tone sounded, and an irritating bright light blinked in their faces. Each operator took a syringe from their breast pocket. They injected themselves in the neck. Lana grabbed the wrist of the woman closest to her before the needle went in. The others twitched for a couple of seconds before resuming their task. Lana's operator slumped onto her work station. Checking her pulse, Lana was relieved to find she had merely fallen asleep.

'We have to go,' Rachel whispered.

They walked through the only door, out onto a catwalk, and were hit with the view of a vast hangar. Pilots were rushing to attack crafts, and Sentinels were forming ranks of over one hundred units. Lana was aware of how enormous the carrier was. They were only seeing one of three hangar bays.

'Link teleport to Amestae in five,' a canned voice alerted. 'Link teleport to Aqua Sierra in ten.'

'They're reinforcements,' Lana realised out loud.

'Good for us,' said Rachel. 'Bad for our allies.'

A door slid open at the other end of the catwalk and Sentinel Kordin approached, followed by Xera and a group of six other Raekeem.

Rachel glanced at Lana to receive a quick nod, her eyes relaxed and confident.

'Where are they hiding?' Kordin asked Rachel.

'Underground, sir. We have the coordinates.'

Xera drew close to Lana, sniffing. 'You reek of human.'

'There are thousands down there,' Lana replied calmly.

Kordin turned to the group of Sentinels waiting behind him. 'Go. Transport them all to holding.'

'Lead Sentinel.' A voice came over the hangar comms. 'Report to Lord Telsta on the brig.'

Lana watched Kordin and Xera return the way they came. She was surprised to overhear Kordin cursing right up until the doors closed behind him.

One Sentinel pressed a panel on the handrail, and steps folded down from a door three metres diagonally to their right. The stairs connected to the catwalk with a clang.

Rachel tugged at Lana's arm for her to follow. They climbed the stairs to a transport room, where they assembled on a platform with the six Raekeem, and a control operator asked for coordinates. Rachel hesitated and caught Lana's "oh shit" glance. She spoke the numbers. The teleport was programmed, and all but the operator were enveloped by black tendrils.

They reappeared in front of Luke and his team of fifteen AMs, and the Raekeem immediately attacked. No weapons were drawn at such close range. Rachel and Lana decloaked and took a Sentinel each while Luke and the AMs fought the other four, taking slashes from Raekeem elbow strikes and acrobatic kicks from the leaner units among them. The Sentinels were subdued after a single minute's bout. Lana, Luke and Rachel were breathing hard after the sudden confrontation.

'Change of plans,' Rachel explained apologetically between breaths. She gestured to the six Sentinels. 'Now that we have these guys, we can return to their ship, eight of us dressed as them.'

'We have to bring civilians with us,' Lana reminded her. 'We could take them to holding just like Kordin told these jerks to. As long as they don't notice there aren't any children or elderly in the group we take…'

'We can bring soldiers disguised as civilians.' Luke caught on, wiping blood from his split lip. 'This is working out better than we'd planned.'

Chapter 16

Aqua Sierra

Ohkwai Kida swooped down through the clouds, firing pulse rounds at enemy ships in his path. He and his team couldn't find a way into the carrier under the constant assault.

Kida's father commanded a squad of thirty mobile missile launchers in the sea. They headed for the surface in a disc formation, all launchers pointed up. Chillo called 'All stop!' ten metres below the waves, and the crafts engaged stabilisers, floating level with one another as a populated circle. The crafts were powered by energy cells from the city's geothermal storage plant and could manoeuvre quickly despite a heavy payload of eight missiles per craft.

Chillo tapped at his sonar screen to confirm their position. 'Kida, clear your fighters. All launchers, first volley on my mark. Three, two, one... fire!'

All thirty fired their missiles. The gap between them and the surface of the sea was lined with bubbled trails. Kida and his squad members flew their crafts away from the Raekeem carrier, and the enemy fighters giving chase were tracked by the heat-seeking warheads that broke through the waves and shot into the air. Eighteen of the first volley exploded into the underside of the carrier shields.

The Laician aircraft had a brief window of opportunity to strike the entry points. Kida fired his shield disruptor rounds into the closest door he could find, reaching maximum proximity. It was too late to pull out when his rounds tore an oval-shaped gap in the shields. The hangar-bay doors were pelted by his continued assault and blown apart one metre before the nose of his craft, and he sailed through the gap.

Kida's craft clipped a pillar. While the ship spiralled out of control, he equipped a pulse rifle. He pulled the jettison lever on the side of his seat and the roof flew off the craft. He was shot out a second before his ship rolled over enemy fighters and buried itself in the rear wall of the hangar bay.

Kida's parachute opened, and compressed air jetted out from his seat, billowing the canopy. He escaped the flames, but flying shrapnel struck his suit and sliced his skin. He unbuckled himself and dropped out to roll across the bay floor. Sentinels opened fire while he found cover behind stacked crates.

A mercury sphere expanded to Kida's right, and eight of his fellow legged kind emerged and dispersed. A small cylinder rolled to his feet. He picked it up and threw it, but it exploded in the air, pelting his cover with shrapnel. The crates were full of holes, exposing him to enemy fire. He tumble-rolled to arrive beside one of his squad mates.

'The elevator to the ship's brig is that way,' he shouted over the shooting, and he pointed to doors on the far side of the hangar bay.

The crew member tapped at his console. 'I'll bring the next team in.'

Kida waited for reinforcements to appear on the other side of the hangar. The Raekeem were pelted with a surprise volley of fire, giving Kida and his crewmate the opportunity to run for the elevator.

Silica Raekeem Carrier

Kordin and Xera arrived at the Command level, and Lord Telsta, seated at his throne, beckoned for them to approach. He greeted them with an open smile as a human slave approached with a tray of refreshments.

Xera was startled when Kordin swatted the tray. The slave stared blankly while the glass smashed and the tray clattered on the steel floor.

'You seem upset,' Telsta said, genuinely surprised. 'Whatever is the matter?'

'Our people are dying by the hundreds because we are invading the Three Kingdoms simultaneously,' Kordin stated incredulously. 'The

Laicians have already breached one of our ships. It will be destroyed because there are no reinforcements to send to their aid!'

'Everything will go according to plan,' Telsta chided.

'Really? If a bunch of fish-people can figure out how to cut through our shields, don't you think the humans and the Kiyol will as well?'

Telsta chuckled to himself. 'You are more like your Uncle Feen than you gave him credit for, Kordin. You might have grown to admire him. Personally, I will not miss his didactic rants.'

'This campaign was doomed from the beginning,' Kordin continued, ignoring his Lord's facetious deflection. 'Can't you see we're outmatched here?'

'Calm yourself,' Telsta snapped. 'Sacrifices must be made.' He breathed a tired sigh. His next words were grave. 'These worlds hold the key to our survival… the survival of all Raekeem.'

Xera looked from Kordin to Telsta, confused. Kordin shook his head, assuming his Lord was speaking more nonsense. 'What are you talking about?'

Telsta ordered the command level to vacate, and his eyes wandered over Xera when she turned to see that all operators were leaving. She caught him staring and felt uncomfortable.

Though they were alone and the room was silent, Telsta slid to the edge of his throne, leaned forward and whispered, 'We are being hunted.'

Kordin decided to take his Lord seriously. 'By whom?'

Telsta's hands came together, and he looked away, into the unlit space to his left, as though there were ghosts lurking. 'This information is known only among the Lords and Lead Sentinels,' he said, giving Kordin and Xera a dramatic sideways glance. 'Speak of it to no one.' He stood and paced, circling them slowly. 'Six years ago, your father's Sentinels were attacked while on a routine harvesting mission. They were all killed, and a data tablet was left on your father's body. It read: "Lustitia finds the Raekeem guilty of genocide. Surrender or be destroyed."'

'Somebody called Lustitia killed my father?' Kordin asked.

'Not somebody. The Lustitians are many. We have only heard rumours, stories told among the other Lords who have encountered them in other worlds. As far as we know, Lustitia is an ancient intergalactic sect committed to justice.' Telsta rolled his eyes at the last word. 'We have not been able to learn any more about them. Any attempt to do so has alerted them to our whereabouts.' He tapped at the console on his throne's armrest and brought up holographic images of five Raekeem Lords. Telsta's face was among them. 'They have killed four of my fellow highborn.' As he spoke, four of the Lords' profiles blinked red and faded to black. 'Only I remain.'

Xera's brow furrowed. 'And the fleets they commanded?'

'Destroyed.' Telsta pressed his lips together, sympathising with Xera when she gasped.

Kordin shook his head in disbelief. 'How can the Lustitians destroy entire Raekeem fleets?'

'They possess warp technology.' Telsta brought up a holo-video, which showed the stars spreading as though stuck on the surface of an expanding bubble. The invisible sphere shrank, and the stars realigned. A white and gold vessel shed its cloaking field. Aerodynamic, teardrop shaped, with a saucer section wedged in its middle, the Lustitian ship drew closer before firing pulsing white missiles. 'They warp into firing range in a single bound. This fleet was hunted and ambushed.'

Xera stared, wide-eyed, from Kordin to her Lord. 'How can we possibly defend against them?'

'That is why I summoned you.' Telsta gave Xera a reassuring smile, proud that his Sentinel had not suggested surrender. 'We have evaded the Lustitians thus far by travelling between alternate worlds. But they have been tracking us.'

'How?' Kordin asked.

'Your Uncle Oskar believed they have the ability to identify trace signatures in the residual rifts that our portal travel creates. They can determine which Parallel Universe we enter and open their own portal to it. Once we find what we came for, we will make our stand.'

He brought up a new holo-image of a man in his early sixties. Xera didn't understand why her Lord had displayed it. 'A human?'

'His work,' Telsta corrected, gazing at the image of Professor Peter O'Conner. 'Scouts have located him and are awaiting your arrival. This man holds the key. The key to confronting those who seek to wipe us out. Retrieve him, and we may stand a chance.'

Amestae

The Kiyol transport carrying Jihna and her team flew at the Raekeem carrier. Blasts from their cannons pounded the enemy's shields, disabling them long enough for Jihna's transport to fly through. Smaller manned turrets positioned along the rooftops of the city provided cover fire, taking down enemy fighter crafts swarming the sky.

Jihna's transport blew in the bay doors with a final volley of cannon fire and landed on the runway. The ramp came down, and the Kiyol warriors rushed out to engage the enemy.

Jihna's avesti chomped a Sentinel and kicked another in the chest, sending him flying. Making a run for the elevators, she called to her fellow warriors to follow. They blasted their rifle staffs at the incoming enemy units. She dismounted and arrived with four others in the elevator while the remaining six stayed behind to fight. A sweeping look over her team bolstered her pride, for none of them were badly wounded. They were ready, weapons poised, eyes focused on the doors. The elevator shot up to the brig level, arriving in seconds. The doors opened, and the group of warriors followed a dark, empty corridor, stepping lightly to avoid detection.

They reached the door to the brig. Jihna accessed the briefing package on her console, which Luke Palmer had sent all entry teams. It showed that the room was oval-shaped, the perimeter lined with operators at computer stations. Information from the outcast Sentinel, Oskar, advised caution, as the control system would enter lockdown at the first sign of brig infiltration, preventing them from flying the ship away from Amestae.

Jihna whispered orders to her warriors, pointing out the consoles they were to destroy before any of the operators could initiate lockdown. They all nodded in confirmation and followed her stealthily into the brig. Each aimed at a console and fired their staff, destroying the alarm system. The enslaved operators remained seated, staring blankly at the sparking workstations before them. None tried to stop Jihna when she moved to the central control machine and lifted the pilot out of his chair like he was a child. She was about to access the control interface when a plasma blast struck her side, knocking her to the floor. Sentinels burst into the brig and shot down two other Kiyol.

Jihna clenched her teeth, held her wound with one hand and tapped at the controls with the other. She followed the directions on her wrist console. The thrusters' icon flashed a symbol that translated to

"Engaged", and she issued a transmission ordering all Raekeem fighter ships to return to hangar bays. She glanced at the slave woman sprawled like a lifeless doll beside her and then to the others sitting, staring blankly ahead, plasma fire flying past their heads. She programmed a teleport and sent them all to the training hall in Leetheria City.

Kiyol citizens of Amestae watched from below when the colossal ship rose into the clouds, followed by a swarm of fighter ships returning through the bay doors as ordered. The crowd cheered as the enemy ship flew into space.

Silica

The armoury of the Liberty Security building was busy with AM soldiers equipping pistols, concealing them beneath civilian clothes.

Hal arrived, having finished his simulation session with Garwyn. He found a vacant gear locker and suited up. Once armed, he stood out of the way and waited for orders.

'We're going in cloaked to look like Sentinels,' Lana said when she walked over to Hal. She strapped a console to his wrist and activated it.

Hal looked down at his holographic appearance and turned around when Lana asked him to while she made sure the Raekeem skin looked real.

'You're good,' she said. 'Follow our lead.' She checked her comms as a text message came through, and she turned to Rachel. 'The ship at Amestae is clear. Jihna is engaging self-destruct. Kida's team have control of their carrier and are leaving Aqua Sierra.'

'Good.' Rachel faced the AMs, ready and waiting. 'Now it's our turn.'

'Hoorah!' the team shouted.

Rachel used her Raekeem comms to report to the carrier. 'Prisoners ready for transport. Sending coordinates.'

Two black clouds swirled from the floor. One engulfed the AMs dressed as civilians. and the other took everyone posing as Sentinels.

Lana blinked through the dark matter as it dispersed and saw the civilian team in a cylinder-shaped holding cell. It was capped with a thick disc of glass. Two Raekeem guards were standing on it, looking down to inspect the new arrivals. She ascended the stairs to join them.

'All I know is Lead Sentinel Feen went after Kordin and didn't come back,' one of the guards said. 'Now Kordin is Lead.'

'Where are the children?' the other guard asked when Lana arrived between them.

'We have orders to put them in a separate cell,' she replied nonchalantly. 'Any word from our other carriers?'

'They're lost,' he said, unable to hide his unease. 'The aliens on Aqua Sierra and Amestae broke through the shields. The humans could attack at any moment, and their allies are free to aid them. We should've gassed them and the Kiyol as soon as we arrived.'

'And we should have dumped our entire waste containment load on the sea-people,' the other Sentinel added. 'Thousands of gallon drums of toxic material would've wiped them out.'

'Woulda, coulda, shoulda,' Lana chimed in, and then grunted when they eyed her suspiciously. 'Do you think Telsta will order a retreat?'

'He has a plan,' the first Sentinel replied confidently. 'Kordin and Xera were sent to retrieve a human who has information we need.'

Lana became still. 'What human?'

'Some scientist,' he said.

Lana glanced up at the half-spheres attached to the ceiling, guessing they were cameras. She looked to Hal and Rachel when they arrived behind her and raised her eyes quickly to warn them they were being watched.

Hal took aim with a Raekeem blaster at the same time as Rachel, and they each shot a camera. Lana chopped one Sentinel at the base of his neck, turned, and roundhouse-kicked the other before he could pull his blaster. They both fell, unconscious. Rachel found a console and released the AMs below.

'I have to alert Renee,' said Lana, tapping at her comms. Her eyes narrowed when her console read "Not Responding". 'They were talking about abducting the Professor.' She disengaged her Raekeem cloak to reveal black leggings, an orange tank top and leather boots.

'Oskar said the Raekeem were in Haze Realm to find that version of Professor O'Conner,' Rachel said.

'They probably have him by now,' said Hal. 'They're going to make him develop the mutagen Oskar was talking about.'

Rachel was standing beside Hal when Lana bent over to tighten her boot laces.

'They need him alive,' said Rachel. She flicked a finger under Hal's chin to close his mouth. 'Later. Head on a swivel.'

Hal's eyes shot up from Lana's butt.

'Lana, you and Hal go and find where they're holding Pete,' Rachel ordered. 'The rest of us will take the brig. Let's move.'

Chapter 17

Lincoln arrived at the prison in Liberty. He and two other AMs escorted Danin, the Sentinel Talon had captured, to the cells in the east wing. While walking the corridor to the security checkpoint, he recognised an inmate assigned to cleaning. The inmate looked up briefly and continued to mop the floor. Lincoln told the escort to check Danin in and approached him.

'Mr Conroy.'

Skin sagged beneath the old man's eyes. The face Dr Kindred had surgically grafted to his skull was now pale, wrinkled, and drooping. The nerves connected to his skin tissue had gradually numbed. Conroy's mask was failing.

'I hear the invaders destroyed Branner's Factory,' Conroy taunted, creases bunching around his mouth when he smirked at Lincoln. 'You'll be overrun in days, Commander.' He nodded to Danin. 'Send him back with your terms of surrender.'

Lincoln gave Conroy a frank smile. 'That is just the kind of advice I would expect from a war criminal. If the Raekeem take control of this city, you will be stripped, probed and experimented on in a lab, like every other human.'

Conroy pressed his lips together and hung his head like a disgruntled child. He pushed the mop across the floor in the circles he'd maintained along the corridor. Lincoln walked away, and Conroy paused, placed his other hand on the handle and waited for his limbs to stop shaking.

Inmates in the west wing called out and cursed at Danin as he was escorted to his cell. He entered the three-by-five-metre room. He glanced at the cot and the toilet in the corner. The barred door was sliding shut, and he turned and stopped it. The guards took batons from their belts and ordered him to step back. Danin locked eyes on an inmate watching him from the cell opposite.

Jericho Williams was sitting up in his bed, looking over a book titled *Masters of War*. He held the Sentinel's gaze, took the weight of the book with his prosthetic hand and dog-eared the page with his other. The bedsprings squeaked when he moved to the edge and stood up.

Danin bared his teeth at the guards while they slid the cell door open to push him back. The novel Jericho held was thick and heavy, and when he'd lifted it to shoulder height, he threw it down hard so that it hit the concrete floor with a loud bang.

The two AMs turned, putting themselves between Danin and the perceived threat. Though Danin's wrists were bound in front, his ankles were not. He used the cell bar struts to lift himself up. He swung and kicked the guards in the back of the head. They fell to the floor while he staggered to the nearest exit, his wounds causing him pain.

Jericho leaned against his cell door, casually scratching his chin with his prosthetic fingers. An alarm sounded, and moments later, gunfire erupted in the direction Danin had fled.

Talon sat in a mobile AM servicing truck parked outside the prison with Jolie and three other new units, who were waiting for their programming. Jolie was running protocol tests via Talon's wireless link to her console.

'There's a lot of work to be done here,' she said while she re-tied her ponytail, which had become tousled during the escape from the Branner Factory. 'Standard directives, vocal repair… this'll take some time.' She glanced up at Talon's pink hair and smelt the faint odour of battery fluid. 'And I'm afraid you're stuck with that colour.' She read the data from the assessment under her breath. 'Morality protocols are running…'

The truck doors were open, and Talon was sitting in the sunlight. She gazed out at the swaying trees. The spring leaves were bright yellow in the afternoon sun. She turned back to look upon the AMs seated in the shadow of the truck interior. They were staring blankly ahead. They hadn't received any skills or personality programming. They were just machines waiting for a purpose.

The van comms speaker beeped, and Lincoln spoke rapidly. 'All units, secure the perimeter. The Raekeem Sentinel has escaped the east wing. Target is armed. Proceed with caution.'

Talon jumped out of the truck.

'Woah, hey, we're not done here,' Jolie exclaimed.

Talon held her hand out while looking toward the prison car park, judging where Danin might emerge.

'Our security units can deal with–'

Talon pointed impatiently at the side-arm in Jolie's thigh holster.

Jolie pulled out the gun and handed it over. 'Fine. Go get him.'

Danin broke a window and jumped out of the first floor, landing deftly on the roof of a car. He spotted Talon and fired blindly at her while running for cover.

A line of holes pushed through the bonnet of the car Danin hid behind. Talon fired again, closer to the mark. Boots pounded the bitumen, echoing against the side of the admin building. Danin knew he would be cut down the moment he tried to run. And he would be recaptured if he stayed.

Still crouched, Danin turned the pistol on himself. He slid the barrel over his tongue and against the roof of his mouth. With his finger not yet on the trigger, he froze when he felt a hand clasp over his. His eyes darted to the machine woman crouching silently beside him. She grasped the gun rail before he could stop her. She released it after adjusting its aim, so it was aligned with the top of Danin's skull.

Talon stood slowly while Danin watched her from the ground. Her blank expression said nothing, until a subtle nod dropped her fringe across her eye.

Lincoln arrived at the front of the car. He lowered his gun when he saw what was about to happen. 'Wait, stop–'

Danin pulled the trigger.

Lincoln swore and thumped the hood of the car. His eyes wandered from the black splatter over Talon's stomach to the gun in her hand.

'Why didn't you stop him?' he demanded.

Talon met Lincoln's questioning stare. She looked at the AMs, at their clean uniforms. These soldiers were untested, fresh from training.

They'd been assigned to the correctional facility and would be assigned to a dozen other places over their decades of service.

'At ease,' Lincoln said to his units. 'Holster your weapons.' He watched Talon, now questioning his decision to keep her level of combat programming.

Talon knew the AMs saw her as a threat. She raised her gun, watched their synthetic jaw muscles twitch and their eyes turn to their Commander. And she set it down on the car.

Lincoln took a step toward her and stopped when she gave him a look of warning.

She turned around and started walking.

Lincoln made no attempt to stop her. All AMs were built with a tracking device. He knew he could find Talon again. But he wasn't sure if that would be a good idea.

Hal and Lana made their way through dark corridors aboard the Raekeem carrier ship. For the last hundred metres of the labyrinth of stairwells, ramps and elevators, they hadn't encountered a single guard or locked door. The ship seemed to have been added onto in some parts, remodelled and extended in others.

'What's your augmentation?' Lana whispered to Hal.

'Fast healing.'

'Good to know.'

Lana pulled him back around the corner when she saw a door open to their left. They waited while a number of Sentinels jogged out. Another group could be heard approaching from the corridor Hal and Lana had come from. They quickly slipped through the open door, and Hal found a panel to close it behind them.

'What's the plan once we find your Professor?' Hal asked.

'We teleport him somewhere safe and go up to help Rachel.' Lana tapped at her console and found that it wasn't working. 'There must be electromagnetic interference nearby.'

Hal peered through the dim light. Deep shelves either side of him stretched metres into the dark. He could smell the excrement of war-dogs. It was trodden across the floor.

Lana followed him to the end of the room, and they climbed the stairs to a catwalk. They looked down to a large, open-topped cage ahead, where they could hear barking and growling. It held six well-fed war-dogs, twice the size of those seen in Haze Realm. The dogs were leaping, trying to reach something underneath the catwalk. A woman screamed.

Hal set his rifle down, climbed over the rail and was horrified as he saw a man and a woman hanging hogtied, just out of reach of the war-dogs. 'Two of your people,' he said, climbing back up, and he ran up the catwalk with Lana.

Lana swung over and hung herself crouched. Recognising them, she yelled out, 'Brad, Renee, hold on!'

'Shoot them!' Renee shouted.

One of the war-dogs leapt and snapped its jaws, taking strips off Brad's camouflage pants. Another came closer still but yelped when Lana shot it in the side of the head.

Hal pulled his knife and cut Renee free. He quickly sheathed it and took her weight. She reached for the catwalk to climb up and felt a violent pull.

Hal saw the terror in Renee's eyes when she was ripped away from him. A war-dog had locked its teeth on her belt and was pulling her down.

'Renee!' Brad shouted.

She felt bones break in her ribcage and right shoulder when her body hit the cage's metal floor. Through blurred vision, she saw the dog that had brought her down fend off the others, stopping them from taking its prize.

Lana cut Brad's wrist ties once he could take his own weight on a support rail, and handed him the knife. While helping him climb up onto the catwalk, she saw Hal staring down at the pit full of beasts and called out, 'Hal, no!'

He threw his arms wide and dropped from the rail.

Hot saliva dripped over Renee's face when she rolled onto her back to face the war-dog standing over her. She blacked out as its jaws opened wide over her throat.

Hal landed on the dog's shoulders, and it fell sideways. He drove his knife through the base of its skull and pushed the palm of his hand down on the end of the handle until the beast was limp. Another tackled him to the floor. Now on his back, Hal caught the beast by the corners of its mouth, stretching its gums into a manic grin. It drove its head forward. Hal's grip slipped for a millisecond, and then he caught the dog's fur either side of its head. It gnashed its teeth inches from his face. He pulled it down, raised one knee under its jaw, slid his fingers over its eyes and snout, and locked his elbows to his sides. The dog tried to push forward again, to twist free, and when it found that it could only escape by pulling back, Hal let go and kicked it hard at the base of its jaw. Blood sprayed over the other beasts when its severed tongue flew out of its mouth.

Brad and Lana dropped from the catwalk. They each pinned one beast, and Brad used Lana's knife to cut the throat of his while Lana fired a forty-five millimetre round between her thighs into her dog's skull. She looked up to see Brad shoulder-charge one that was stalking toward Renee. He collided with enough force to lift it and pin it to the bars of the cage. Lana shouted and threw her side-arm to him. He caught it and fired twice under the dog's jaw.

Teeth sank into Hal's forearm. He turned to deliver a heavy fist into the eye of the beast that caught him. It let go, and Hal rolled away as another dog leapt to attack him.

A tone sounded from hidden speakers above the cage. A barred door rose beside Brad, and all of the remaining dogs loped out, obediently ignoring their prey.

Brad lifted Renee from the floor and made a break for the opening. 'Come on!' he called over his shoulder. Once he was through, the bars came down. Hal and Lana arrived too late, and they tried to lift the door.

'Can you teleport?' Brad asked.

'Signal's jammed,' said Lana, backing up to see the height of the cage. The bars were horizontal with no footholds. There was no way to climb it. 'Get Renee out of here.'

She flinched when a plasma blast hit the cage. Brad tossed her gun through the bars to Hal before he disappeared into the shadows, carrying his partner.

'Let them go.'

A voice came from the catwalk above. Lord Telsta leaned on the rail, bringing his face into the light. He smiled his sharp teeth at his captives.

Lana drew her axe, but she was hit by a blast that came down from the shadows. It was an electrical stun, which her armour couldn't withstand. Hal caught her when she fell. He fired up at the catwalk, the bullet ricocheted, and he took a stun blast to the chest.

Kordin returned his blaster to his hip holster. One of the two guards with him received a report through their comms. 'Sir, you are needed below.'

Kordin's eyes narrowed at Lord Telsta, who stood with Xera further up the catwalk. Telsta had asked her to join him to watch the humans fight the war-dogs. Now Telsta's arm was around her waist, and his hand was sliding over her buttocks.

Kordin pushed past the guards, and their hands gripped their holstered blasters when he marched toward Telsta.

'Xera and I are needed below,' Kordin said. 'We will report to you once testing is ready.'

'See that the Professor does not expire before the extraction is complete,' Telsta replied. 'We need everything.'

Xera turned to leave with Kordin, and she felt her Lord's hold on her tighten.

'Join me in my chambers, my dear.' Telsta looked over Xera's shoulder and gave his Lead Sentinel a dismissive chin rise and a knowing smirk.

Although her heart was thumping in her chest, Xera was able to remain composed while Telsta ushered her along the catwalk.

Kordin's fists clenched. He was aware of the guards behind him, and he didn't care. He would cut Telsta down before they could fire on him.

But Xera. They would kill her as well.

Kordin swallowed back his anger. 'Wait!' he blurted out.

Telsta stopped and turned. 'Kordin, you are beginning to sully the mood.'

Kordin realised the smirk his Lord gave him was impersonal. Telsta clearly had no idea of the bond he and Xera shared. 'A quick word with Xera, my Lord,' he requested evenly.

'Do not delay, my dear.' Telsta's words were both polite and threatening. He released Xera and continued down the stairs while the two guards lingered.

Xera watched her Lord disappear. Kordin arrived at her side. He took her hand and spoke close to her. 'We can leave right now.'

Xera leaned against the rail and looked down at the male human and the female lying over him. Kordin couldn't understand how she could be so calm. 'Xera, I can get us out,' he insisted and pressed his lips against her head while his eyes grew hot and his jaw clenched. He felt his anger coil around what love he had inside of him. It tightened in his belly, in his chest.

A glaze had formed over Xera's eyes, which was not the beginning of tears but a turning. Her beauty was lit, penumbral, by a single light beaming up from her feet. She pressed her hand gently down onto Kordin's and wiped him away.

'I must do this.'

She left him and was escorted down the stairs from the catwalk by Telsta's guards.

Kordin gripped the rail. He doubled over as though he had been kicked in the stomach. He groaned and came back up, baring his teeth, and let out a guttural roar that echoed against the walls. He stormed across the catwalk to a service elevator and took it down to the laboratory.

Scientists were monitoring rows of large capsules when he arrived. Many of his fellow Sentinels slept inside them. Beside each one was an open vat of black, viscous fluid. The environmental controls were set to eighty per cent humidity for the cultures in each vat to grow. The entire deck had been dedicated to developing the mutagen, Telsta's answer to the Lustitian threat.

Kordin arrived at the bay where Peter O'Conner was strapped to a table leaning at a forty-five-degree angle.

'How are his vitals?' he asked the medical officer assigned to retrieve the necessary information from O'Conner's brain.

She pressed a gloved hand against her chest, startled. 'Lead Sentinel, I'm so glad you came. I was afraid we might lose him before you had a chance to question–'

'His vitals,' Kordin repeated impatiently.

'Fading, but we will have all our Lord needs in just a moment.' The officer wiped beads of sweat from her brow and returned her attention to the data flow on a screen. A tone sounded. She turned off a machine that had been humming and left Kordin alone with O'Conner.

Kordin watched the remaining war-dogs from the cage being led into capsules of their own. He was glad these scientists had the good sense to test the Warden mutagen on them before ruining any of his fellow Sentinels.

'Kordin, my boy,' the old man croaked. His eyelids quivered. 'I thought it would be my bastard brother, Feen, standing over me in my final moments. Fate has been kind for once.'

Kordin's eyes narrowed while he tried to discern the Raekeem cloak that perfectly masked the man's body. 'Who are you?'

'It's me, boy. It's your uncle Oskar.'

Chapter 18

The Kiyol families who'd been evacuated into the tunnels re-emerged. They cheered Jihna and the other warriors upon their return via teleport to the city. Though her side was burnt and a rib was broken, she raised a fist high. The people roared triumphantly, and the other warriors helped Jihna seek medical attention. They had been summoned to a feast at the city hall.

Later, when they entered through the tall doors of the city hall, Jihna and her fellow warriors were greeted with applause from community leaders and senior members from the highest positions in the Kiyol home world. They were led to the dining hall and received another standing ovation.

'We are honoured,' Jihna said, once they were all seated. 'The threat is almost over.'

'We have had no word from the humans for some time now,' one of the community leaders stated solemnly.

'Should their attack fail…' another started.

'We cannot let the Raekeem take Silica as a foothold,' Jihna stated firmly. 'We must dispatch ships to aid them.'

'The humans should have followed our lead,' a young Kiyolo commented in a patronising tone. The many gold wristbands that adorned his arm clinked when he waved his hand flippantly. 'An air assault was the obvious course of action.'

Jihna stood abruptly from the dining table, teeth clenched from the pain in her side.

The Kiyolo speaking flinched despite Jihna's short stature. His eyes fell on the waxed trophy hanging from her belt. He swallowed, recognising it as a human hand. Stories had been told over the years and now he knew them to be true. Jihna had in fact severed and kept the hand of their enemy, Colonel Jericho Williams.

'Rachel Navara's infiltration tactic was designed to subvert the need for a battle over the city,' Jihna stated equably while staring down the Kiyolo who had spoken out of turn.

Ambassador Jainon stood. 'New information regarding the carrier occupying Silica's airspace has come to light. We now know why the Raekeem did not engage the humans with aircrafts as they did us and the Laicians.'

Jainon shared Jihna's confidence in the humans and their military abilities. And she was proud of how fearless a warrior Jihna had become. 'My colleagues and I have been working with Luke Palmer's surveillance team. We calibrated an x-ray scan powerful enough to penetrate their shield. We have a complete layout of the ship decks.'

'What did you find?' Jihna asked.

'The ship above Liberty is an altered version of the other carriers. Scans show that the entire keel carries a complement of over five thousand pods. That carrier is designed to deploy an invasion force.'

Rachel and her team were fighting their way to the brig. Plasma blasts lit the corridor when the Raekeem defending their station fired back. One of the AMs fell, and Rachel dragged him behind cover.

'Pull back,' she ordered. 'We'll try to lure them in.'

She retreated with her team and leaned against the corridor wall while a throbbing pain erupted in the front of her head. 'We can thin them out.' She tried to ignore the aching and focus on the task at hand. 'Split up,' she ordered and pointed to the two doors either side of them. 'Crossfire.'

Rachel called through her comms, 'Luke, come in. Luke, are you there?'

There was no response, so she reset the link to Lana. 'Lana, have you found the Professor?'

Rachel's voice woke Lana. She lifted her head from Hal's lap and wiped her eyes. 'Not yet,' she replied.

She heard the metal door to the cage rising and turned to see two beasts enter, one after the other. These were more muscular than the other war-dogs. Their hairless skin was smooth and dark except for a ridge of black hair that ran along their spines. Lana spotted the damaged right eye of the closest dog. *They've been altered. More.*

Hal rose with a gasp and froze when he saw the dogs.

Lana slowly moved to her feet.

The sudden drop of the cage door startled the dogs. They turned their attention to Lana, her axe head scraping on the metal floor as she picked it up. They bared their teeth and growled.

Hal raised his gun and fired at the one-eyed dog. Its head twitched when the bullet bounced off its skin.

'Shit.'

'Yup.' Lana saw that both of them were wearing steel collars with a light that glowed red. Each had purple vials attached.

Hal shoved Lana to help her break into a run and sped off to the opposite side of the cage. The two dogs parted, bounding after their prey. Hal dove forward and rolled when the one-eyed war-dog jumped and snapped its jaws. Its body slammed sideways, and the cage shook.

Lana jumped against the wall before pushing off into a cartwheel flip. The female dog flew straight into the metal bars, and Lana landed and rolled backward across the muck-covered floor. The dog recovered from the collision and pounced at Lana. She armoured her skin before its claws slashed her ribs. It struggled to find purchase on her, and she rolled onto her stomach in an attempt to scramble away. She cried out when its jaws closed over her right leg. Its teeth slid off her thigh, unable to penetrate her flesh. She rolled again, using her momentum to hammer her axe across the side of the dog's head, knocking it sideways.

She felt Hal's arms slip under her armpits, and he lifted her to her feet. The two of them made it to the door, turned, and pushed away from each other in time to avoid both dogs pouncing at once. The door buckled and the dogs slid backward through the muck. Hal leaned against the bars to create an opening for Lana. She slipped through, used the notch in her axe head to hook the door, and pulled with all her strength.

Hal took off his flak vest and fed himself through the gap Lana made for him.

A second later, the door clanged when the dogs pounced. Their collars flashed, and Hal and Lana heard what sounded like trigger clicks. Purple liquid syphoned from the vials on their collars.

The lights above flickered as though the power was cutting out. The dogs howled in pain, fighting the effects of the dose of mutagen. Their muscles grew and their bones lengthened as their cell growth accelerated exponentially. Their limbs stretched and their paws sprouted fingers. The female dog stood upright, arching her back to reveal a toned human-like abdomen and chest. Her hind legs grew longer and larger, and her shoulders widened to become anatomically human. She lurched against the cage and revealed sharp fangs when she roared. Her long black hair met with the mane that ran the length of her spine to her tail.

Lana tugged at Hal's arm and they ran. Clanging echoed behind them as she followed Hal through the corridor. One last bang, and the cage bars hit the floor.

Lana was breathing heavily, her boots slipping in dog faeces. Sensor-activated elevator doors opened to her left. Hal's arm came around her waist, and he pulled her into the compartment. Blood sprayed across her face after a black arm crossed the door and slashed claws across Hal's chest. Lana wiped her eyes to see two glowing yellow rings in the dark, growing closer. The beast lunged into the elevator. She pushed away from the back wall, swung, and drove her axe into its open mouth. It reeled back with a hollow scream, flicking black blood, and collided with the other beast.

The doors closed and Hal slid against the compartment wall, clutching his chest. Lana tapped repeatedly at the next floor up, hoping to go up to Rachel, but the elevator compartment wouldn't move. She crouched to inspect Hal's wound. 'You're okay. It's not deep.'

Hal winced at the stinging pain, took Lana by her shoulders and turned her. He'd seen the female dog maul her and was relieved to find that she wasn't bleeding.

'I'm fine,' Lana said, even though her muscles ached. She flinched at the jarring force of the beasts throwing their bodies against the doors.

'It'll hold.'

As soon as Hal said that, there was a deafening bang and the doors bent inward.

Lana found a ring pull in the floor and swung the latch open. They stared down at the depth of the shaft. The Wardens slammed into the door again, creating a gap wide enough for one of them to jam their nose through and draw in the scent of their prey.

Hal lowered himself through the floor after Lana. Red lights lit the shaft as they descended. Lana stepped from the service ladder onto the ledge of the next set of doors and pressed her fingers into the rubber pads. Hal arrived beside her, and together they forced it open. They were met with hot air and a sickly mix of chemicals. The room they climbed into was illuminated by dim lights beaming up from the floor. Vats of purple liquid bubbled. The walls either side of them were partitioned enclosures containing various reptiles and arachnids. There were also aquariums for piranhas and larger aquatic predators.

Lana approached a tall one that appeared to be empty. She looked up and saw bats hanging from the top. Her shoulder pressed into Hal's back, and she turned to find him staring down at two Raekeem Sentinels lying unconscious on a bed beside one another. One male, one female. Their heads were shaved, with a dozen probes stuck to their skulls. Cords led to a computer that measured their brain function. The monitor above them read "Transfer Complete".

Hal and Lana crept through automatic doors to a large room. Raekeem scientists in black lab coats monitored Sentinels housed in capsules. Lana saw Kordin. He was talking to a patient on a bed, but she couldn't see who it was. She and Hal followed the curve of the outer deck wall where the room wasn't lit.

'Why did you take his place?' they heard Kordin say.

'I will not be responsible for O'Conner's death,' the man on the table replied. 'Not again.'

Hal recognised the voice and moved out of the shadows to approach the man who'd raised him. Lana dashed at Kordin and took his holstered blaster before he could react.

'Everybody out!' she yelled at the scientists working nearby.

Oskar took hold of Kordin's arm. 'You have to stop this invasion.'

'You killed the Professor who created me?' Hal asked Oskar.

'I'm sorry, Hal. I couldn't let Feen take him.' Oskar coughed and wheezed and took in a deep breath. 'Lana, your Professor is safe. What you've seen here could've been much worse had they taken him instead of me. In their hands, Peter's work would've created something much more powerful.'

Kordin wiped Oskar's weak grip from his wrist. He glanced from Hal to Lana, back to his dying uncle. 'As much as it pains me to see my fellow soldiers being changed into monsters,' he reasoned, 'Telsta's Warden program is our only defence against the Lustitians.' He looked to Lana, who was poised to shoot him. 'This is why we have invaded your worlds. We are here to make up numbers. Without a Warden army, we will be destroyed.'

'So be it!' Oskar thumped the bed. 'Can't you see what we have become?' The sudden exertion caused him considerable pain. 'We should have fought to retain what humanity we still have.' He clenched his teeth, his neck muscles straining. 'I tried to stop this... this madness!'

'Madness?' Kordin retorted. 'Uncle, we are Raekeem. We are born of madness!'

'We are born of *them!*' Oskar shouted, extending an open hand to Hal and Lana. He stared openly at his nephew, willing him to understand. 'The Raekeem exist only because of what we are: human! We keep bonds, like what you and Xera have. We mate, instead of growing our people in labs, because of our human ancestry.' Oskar took Kordin's arm again. 'Kordin, do not turn these people into monsters. Do not let them suffer the same fate our ancestors forced upon us!'

Kordin gazed across the room to the pods containing his fellow Raekeem. By now, they had been exposed to enough of the mutagen to become Wardens. Hundreds had undergone the process and were awaiting deployment. 'It can't be stopped,' he murmured.

Lana raised her gun to Kordin's head. 'Order your Sentinels to leave the brig.'

'This ship is not like the others your allies destroyed,' he said, glaring back at her. 'There is no self-destruct. The shields are powered by a dedicated core. It cannot be penetrated.' As he spoke, he realised the genius and the insanity of his Lord's plan. 'Telsta has already programmed the cloud teleport relay. We will deploy over the Earth city of San Francisco, over Kulete on Aqua Sierra, and it will terminate over Leetheria on Amestae. The Warden mutagen has been weaponised. If they bite or cut you, your people will be turned.'

Hal looked down at his chest wound, but didn't say anything.

Lana was shaking her head in disbelief. 'No ship can teleport to three different star systems in—'

'We use the cloud teleport to harvest planet cores,' Kordin stated flatly. 'It is our source of power.' He paused, realising it was another stroke of genius that Telsta or one of the other Lords must have devised. 'The resulting sun explosion… masks trace signatures of our exit travel. It is why the Lustitians have not been able to find us.'

The monitoring equipment connected to Oskar started beeping loudly. Kordin turned to his uncle and watched the old man's eyes roll back.

'I haven't much time,' Oskar breathed. 'Where is Xera? I want to say goodbye to her.'

Kordin's expression softened. He forgot that during the stories his uncle had read to him as a child, he had sat cross-legged on the floor, in Oskar's quarters, beside Xera. Kordin would let her hold the bird figurine while they listened.

'She followed you everywhere when you were children.' Oskar saw his nephew's melancholy expression turn to pain. 'What is it, boy?'

Kordin's jaw muscles twitched, and he did not answer immediately. 'Telsta has taken her to his chambers.'

Oskar became momentarily alert. His eyes grew wide, and he searched the darkness above him. The veins in his neck bulged. With great effort, he raised himself to sit upright. He took his nephew by the arm, this time roughly, and squeezed. 'She means to avenge her mother.'

Kordin gritted his teeth. 'Telsta killed Xera's mother?'

'She cannot fight him alone.'

The conviction in Oskar's eyes gave Kordin new strength. The anger he had felt when he'd let Xera slip away from him returned. 'Goodbye, Uncle.' He squeezed Oskar's hand.

Lowering her gun, Lana allowed Kordin to leave. 'Wait.' She armoured her skin and handed him the side-arm.

Kordin gave her a neutral nod and walked out.

'Hal.' Oskar reached for the man he had raised. 'I'm sorry I lied to you.' His body was shaking, and he lay back to rest his head. 'Brad and Renee were taken, are they–'

'We found them,' said Lana. She placed her hand on Hal's shoulder and left him and Oskar to talk while she guarded the door to the lab.

Hal leaned close, watching Oskar fade in and out of consciousness.

'Telsta has a secret lair,' Oskar said, his voice faint. 'It is the secret to his longevity. I tried to find it… to destroy it… end this madness. Kordin must find the lair.' He could feel himself slipping. 'You are strong, Hal. You're going to be alright.'

Lana watched from a distance. Her fingers crept over her mouth, and she felt a tear roll down her cheek.

Hal was leaning over Oskar, holding his hand. 'Dad,' he said.

'Son.'

Oskar's face wrinkled when he smiled, and he closed his eyes.

Chapter 19

'You want to please your Lord.'

The last length of Xera's uniform coiled in a heap around her ankles.

Telsta stepped back to admire her naked form and gestured like a director waiting for his actor to say her line.

'I want to please my Lord,' Xera whispered obediently. She watched him move around his bed, lighting ornate oil lamps. They looked like the ones from a book Oskar used to read her and Kordin. Rubbing the lamp released a spirit that could grant wishes. Xera approached one while Telsta disrobed and stroked it with her fingers.

'Make yourself comfortable, my dear,' he said, gesturing to the king-sized bed.

The mattress had been raised to a comfortable sitting height for Telsta. Xera had to hop up in order to climb onto the bed. When she arrived at the head, she lay down and steeled herself. The air was humid, and she could feel the sheet sticking to her skin.

Two Sentinels hung Telsta's robe on his stand, and he arrived naked beside her.

The sheet bunched in Xera's closing fists while Telsta's wandering hand caressed her body. She gritted her teeth and stared beyond him when he moved on top of her. An unnatural surface under his skin pressed against her breast. She guessed it to be a device that monitored his heart.

Telsta thrust himself into her with a grunt.

Xera's nails dug into her palms.

'What is it?' Telsta stopped and slapped Xera's cheek. 'You said you wanted to please me.'

'Send them out,' said Xera with a glance to Telsta's guards.

Telsta waved the two Sentinels away and they left immediately. He watched the door close, then felt Xera take hold of him. She rolled Telsta and mounted him.

Feigning enjoyment, Xera placed her Lord's hands on her hips, leaned down, turned his head and licked his neck. With her palm pinning Telsta's face, Xera opened her jaw wide. Her sharp teeth plunged into his flesh, tearing veins, nerves and muscle. She jerked her head back, ripping out a mouthful of Telsta's neck.

He kicked and struggled, gurgling blood.

Xera spat in his face and backed off him while he clutched at his fatal wound. A tone and a flashing red light were emitting from his chest implant. Xera knelt at his kicking feet, watching her Lord bleed out.

Black tendrils snaked from the lamps and circled the bed. Both he and Xera were ensnared and lifted into zero gravity.

Xera fell from the height of the ceiling, bounced, and rolled against something that felt rough and sticky against her skin. One of the lamps hit the floor. Flames climbed the sheets. Viscous ooze was dripping down her back, and she scrambled to the end of the bed.

She looked over her shoulder, and her eyes widened. The serpent monster she had been told of and had feared as a child was bearing down on her. It screeched, and she weaved, too late, screaming when its teeth cut her shoulder. It plunged its head into the bed, ploughing through the mattress until it hit the metal floor. It twisted violently, flicking Xera with its tail. The blow threw her across the room and into the far wall.

Xera hit the ground and stayed there, her body too broken to move. She saw the monster burst out of the bottom end of the bed, throwing shreds of padding. It swivelled to the door when one of the guards came staggering backward into the room, clutching his throat. Kordin stepped in and was tail-whipped to the floor.

Lying on his side, Kordin pulled his side-arm and fired on the monster twice before it knocked his blaster out of his hand. He rose and weaved around the serpent's mouth when it tried to take hold of him. Its tail whipped his legs out from under him, spinning him one hundred and eighty degrees in mid-air. He came down on his hip, and before he could get up, the serpent latched its teeth over his shoulder and lifted him high.

With his jaw clenched, fighting intense pain, Kordin reached with his free arm and found the sword sheathed at his back. The serpent's slime oozed over the blade as he pulled it free. He pushed it past his neck and plunged the entire length of the blade into the serpent's mouth.

The monster released Kordin, gurgled, and spat blood. He took up his blaster and fired into its head. It fell to the ground, writhing and whipping its tail. Kordin stood over it and continued firing until it stopped moving.

He peered through the smoke and found Xera lying on her side, eyes glazed. He thought the worst when he saw her covered in so much blood. Lifting her gently, he carried her out, lurching by the body of the other guard he'd killed to reach Telsta's chamber.

Kordin's broken rib made every move excruciating. He slowed and dropped to one knee and looked down at Xera, unconscious now. Black drops dabbed her forehead from his shoulder wound. *Get up.* And with a groan, he did, but staggered against the wall. Sliding a few steps, he pushed off and continued on, lurching further down the corridor until he reached a wall console where he programmed a localised teleport to the nearest medical room. A black cloud took him and Xera, placing them a deck below in a well-lit room.

Kordin set Xera down on a table. An auto-scan machine came down from a panel in the ceiling and panned over her body, producing the results on a console screen at the end of the bed: two broken ribs, lacerations, broken collarbone, shattered knee. Kordin tapped confirmations on each recommended procedure, typed in his ID code for authorisation, and the automated treatment began.

Machine arms descended on Xera from above. Kordin pushed a lock of hair away from her face and watched her. He felt as though he might pass out, and he opened a cabinet and found healing injection serums. When he turned around, one of the machine arms deviated from Xera and injected a localised anaesthetic into the flesh and muscle covering his broken rib. Kordin braced himself while the arm cut into him, resetting and sealing his rib. It stitched him back up in seconds and returned to Xera's procedure.

Kordin found the main console in the room and tapped at the communications screen, opening a ship-wide channel.

'This is Lead Sentinel Kordin. The Warden project is underway, and the teleportation sequence will commence. By order of Lord Telsta, all personnel must proceed to the main hangar for evacuation. All ships will receive rendezvous coordinates. Leave your posts and evacuate immediately.'

Hal and Lana were on their way to the brig when they heard Kordin's announcement. They had programmed a cloud portal to get to the upper deck. Halfway up the corridor leading to the brig, Hal was spotted by an AM unit.

'Friendlies incoming,' she reported.

Lana was relieved to see Rachel and the rest of her team emerge from two adjacent rooms.

'Are you alright?' Rachel asked, looking Hal and Lana up and down. Their clothes were torn, and they were covered in filth from the war-dog arena.

'We're okay,' Lana said.

'Good. The brig is clear, we're about to try and fly this thing out… Where's Pete?'

'Professor O'Conner wasn't taken,' Hal reported. 'My fath– Oskar took his place. They probed his brain for the information they needed to make the Warden mutagen. They've been making genetically altered Sentinels.'

'We need explosives,' said Lana. 'A uranium core, something. Kordin said there's no self-destruct.'

'Helm controls aren't responding,' an AM called out from the flight deck in the brig.

'Our comms aren't working either,' said Rachel. She leaned against the console desk, suddenly feeling ill. 'Even if we get a ballistics crew teleported in… we're directly above Liberty. How are we going to move the ship into outer space?'

'We have to evacuate the city,' said Lana. She noticed Rachel's weary speech and could see she was struggling to stay upright. 'Rache, are you alright?'

'The wreckage would level Liberty,' said Rachel, trying to think of an alternative.

'Telsta is going to use the Wardens to infect millions,' said Hal. 'The ship has been programmed to deploy Wardens on Earth, Aqua Sierra and Amestae.'

Rachel wiped clammy hair away from her brow, her hand shaking. 'How many?'

'A thousand per drop,' Lana guessed. 'Maybe less on Aqua Sierra. Infecting Laicians wouldn't be as useful to Telsta.'

'I can't… I won't destroy Liberty.' Rachel's last words were slurred.

'Rachel!' Lana caught her just as she slid off the desk. She lowered Rachel to the floor and pressed the back of her hand against her forehead. 'She's burning up. Rache, can you hear me?' Lana opened her eyelids and saw no responsive movement. She ordered the nearest soldier to find a working console and program a cloud teleport to the surface.

'Hal,' she said. 'I need you to locate the main power source. I'll start the evacuation and bring explosives when I can.'

'Got it.'

Hal watched black tendrils swallow Lana and Rachel and disappear with them. He was about to leave when an AM alerted him to an approaching Sentinel. They raised their weapons at Kordin.

Kordin stood at the entrance to the brig with his hands away from his sides. 'I can show you where the main power source is. But it won't do any good. By now, every Warden will have been transferred to the ejection pods in the keel. The keel will separate when the teleport sequence begins.'

Hal nodded slowly, taking in Kordin's torn and bloodied uniform. 'Did you save her?'

'She's alive.'

'Good. Take us to the keel.'

Down on the surface, an ambulance had arrived at Lana's location, and she rode with Rachel toward the nearest hospital.

'Right here is fine,' Lana called to the driver. Though Rachel was still unconscious, she leaned down, kissed Rachel on the forehead and whispered, 'You're going to be fine. See you soon.'

The ambulance stopped at the UC security building. Lana disembarked and ran to the entrance. The AMs on guard duty stopped her for an arm tap to make sure she wasn't a cloaked Sentinel. They let her through with a nod.

Luke and Jihna were reviewing their plans to defend Liberty against invasion. Jihna saw Lana through the translucent holo-display of the ship and alerted Luke.

'Lana, we've been trying to get through to you,' he said. 'What's the situation up there?'

Lana tapped the holo console to bring up Earth, Aqua Sierra and Amestae in sequence. Lincoln and Jolie entered the room, right before Lana began explaining that a new breed of Raekeem soldiers would be deployed at three different cities.

Luke's eyes slowly stared down to the floor. He could see no alternative that would save the city. 'We'll gather as many explosives as possible. Has Rachel located its power source?'

Lana glanced from Luke to Jolie. 'Rachel's being taken to hospital.'

'What happened?' Luke asked.

'She collapsed. It could have something to do with the medication she's been taking. It's supposed to suppress her Mitochondrial Memories.'

'Teleport me to Liberty Hospital,' said Jolie. 'I'll be needed there anyway.'

Luke programmed a teleport. 'It's fortunate in a way that San Francisco is their target. The city has an earthquake protocol system in place.'

Jolie took Lana's arm gently. 'I'll call you if Rachel's condition changes.'

'Thank you.'

Jihna was receiving intel on the warden carrier. 'My people may have a way to penetrate the carrier shields to allow teleportation,' she said. 'We could fire a pulse cannon similar to what we used against the ship that entered our space. I must go and supervise transport.'

'Thank you for helping us, Jihna,' said Lana.

'Of course. I hope Rachel will recover soon.'

Lana watched the Kiyola warrior leave. She turned to Luke. 'Is Pete alright? We saw Brad and Renee up there. They'd been abducted with Oskar.'

'I haven't heard from Pete, but we received word from Brad a moment ago. He's heading back to the Hub with a security team now.'

Lana began to pace, checking her comms for a message. 'There has to be a way to disable the teleport sequence.' She paused. 'Contact Charlie. He's a programming genius.'

'Of course. I'll have a unit escort him here.'

Lana checked her comms again. No word from Jolie.

Gently, Luke placed his hand on her shoulder. 'She'll be alright.'

Lana held herself, arms crossed, trying to stop her hands from shaking. Her eyes were watering, watching the far corner of the room. 'She… she just fell.' She couldn't stop seeing Rachel limp and unconscious. Rachel had always been her strength to draw on. She felt like running to her, holding her until the threat of invasion went away.

'Lana, we can do this,' said Luke. 'We can stop them.'

Lana remembered the fight against Sabre Company. The conflict against a reactionary militant force bred here, in Home Realm. Now this, an invading force bent on assimilating entire populations of people in order to fight their ultimate enemy.

'After Sabre Company,' she murmured, 'I thought the fighting, the conflict, was over. Will it ever end?'

Luke was staring at the planning table. He turned back to Lana, and met her searching gaze, but he didn't have an answer.

A nurse checked the monitor beside Rachel and hooked her data pad onto the foot of the bed before leaving. The emergency ward was busy, and he was needed elsewhere.

Rachel's eyes darted back and forth beneath her eyelids. She was somewhere else, and it wasn't the sound of footsteps, beeping monitors and low voices that she heard. It was shouting, distant explosions and machine-gun fire.

What Rachel saw was a battle on the Golden Gate Bridge. And she was in it

Smoke billowed from a burning car, obscuring her vision. She turned and saw Lana lying on her back, taking cover behind a fallen AM. She was hugging an assault rifle to her chest, and she was breathing hard. After rising to fire her weapon at an unseen target, she dropped back down and called to somebody further back. It was Hal. He confirmed Lana's order before leaning out behind an overturned bus to provide cover fire. His volley pelted a Raekeem Warden but did not stop it. The altered Raekeem soldiers seemed to have arrived unarmed but were taking weapons from the AMs they had beaten down.

Rachel looked up to see a UC hover jet flying outside the bridge's suspension cables. She turned and stared out at San Francisco Bay.

Columns of smoke rose to her left. Rachel judged by the devastation that the Wardens had been deployed over Sausalito and were trying to cross the Golden Gate Bridge.

Rachel heard a girl scream and strained her eyes to see through the car wrecks and drifting embers. With a gasp, she saw a teenager limping along the middle of the bridge, calling out for help. A low rumble was building, shaking the road. Rachel's eyes grew wide when the approaching mass of Wardens came into clear view, just metres behind the girl.

They were a horde. Hundreds of muscular men and women, their skin black, running down the bridge at speed. Their eyes shone, slanted inward. They were gene-spliced with a dozen different animals, and they roared as they charged.

Rachel ran toward the girl. The gap quickly closed between the child and the monsters behind her. Rachel's feet pelted the road. She leaned forward, giving every bit of power to her legs, pushing to cover the remaining metres between herself and the injured girl.

The girl extended her arm, tears streaming down her face. She cried out, pleading for Rachel to save her.

Rachel took her hand and felt grit from the road in her palm. The thundering feet of the Warden army pounded all around them. The girl was ripped away from Rachel, her cry drowned out by the sound of the horde.

Rachel woke screaming. Her hands clawed away the bedsheet, and she rolled and became tangled in the cords connected to her wrist and temples. She fell to the floor, her gown soaked in sweat, her chest heaving. A nurse rushed in and helped her to her feet, urging her to calm down.

'They're coming!'

Jolie arrived and assisted the nurse in restraining Rachel. 'Breathe. Just breathe.'

Rachel stopped struggling and stared about the room. She tried to allow her heart to settle, breathing out long and sucking in as much air as she could. 'Where am I?'

'Liberty Hospital,' said Jolie. 'Lana said you collapsed.'

'We have to get to San Francisco.'

'We know about the invasion, the three locations,' Jolie assured her. 'They're working on a way to blow up the Raekeem carrier before it can leave.'

'It won't work,' said Rachel. 'I was there, Jolie. I saw them.'

Jolie checked her pulse. Rachel's heart was racing, as though she had been running. 'Slow your breathing, Rache. Wh-what are you saying?'

Rachel stared up at her friend. 'They're coming. And we can't stop them.'

Chapter 20

Brad entered the Portal Hub with a security team. There were bullet holes and burn marks along the walls of the main corridor, from when AMs had tried to hold back invading Sentinels. He heard banging from the locker room and called out to the Professor.

'I'm in here, Brad.'

Brad let Pete out of the locker and saw the bruise on his forehead. 'Come on. Let's get you some ice.' He guided Pete to the kitchen. 'We were hoping you'd escaped to Forest Realm with Hutch.'

'Oskar and I couldn't get to the portal room,' Pete said, holding his sore neck. 'We hid in here when we saw you and Renee get taken. Damn fool must have knocked me out and stuffed me in the locker.'

They arrived in the kitchen, and Pete thanked Brad when he handed him an icy pole from the freezer. 'He must have changed to look like me and let them take him.' Pete winced as he pressed the plastic-wrapped raspberry ice against his head wound. 'Did we get him back?'

The two were interrupted when Brad's comm beeped and a priority message came through from UC Security HQ.

'Everybody in the San Francisco area has been advised not to enter the city,' said Brad. 'All roads have been made into exits.'

'Why? What's happening?'

'I don't know,' he said. 'I've been out of the loop since Renee and I were captured.'

The Portal Hub alert system sounded an incoming portal, and Hutch's voice came over the comms speaker. 'Pete, I hope you're there, buddy. We've gathered an armed team and are ready to come in guns blazing.'

Pete followed Brad to the portal room. He hit the comms receiver on the wall. 'All clear, Hutch. Come on back.' He saw Brad checking his comms, deep concern on his face. 'Is Renee–'

'Unconscious.'

'You should go,' said Pete. 'Be there when she wakes up.'

Hutch emerged from the mercury sphere that expanded over the platform. He stepped down from the ramp and clapped his hand on Pete's shoulder. 'Glad to see you're alright. How the heck did you get away from them?'

'Oskar switched places with me.'

'Brave man,' said Hutch. 'I've read the report Luke sent us. We need to start rolling out jetpacks immediately. If it comes to a battle against Wardens, our forces are going to need an edge.'

Pete looked in the direction of the workshop where he and Hutch had assembled the jetpack prototype. 'We need more production. A factory.'

'A friend of mine has one in Osaka,' Hutch suggested.

'Make the call.'

Carrier above Liberty

Hal and Kordin descended an elevator shaft via a service ladder and approached stairs to the keel, which were built into the inner hull of the ship. The AMs followed behind them, their footfalls echoing a rhythm to the hiss of steam pipes and the hum of hidden generators. After twenty metres of gradual descent, they came to a solid metal door.

Kordin tried the access panel, but his code was denied. 'We have to cut through.'

'Teleport,' Hal suggested.

'No. Inhibiters were installed on the inside.'

Hal's comms beeped and Lana's voice came through, fading in and out with grainy interference. 'Hal… the power source?'

'We're at the door,' he said. 'We need equipment to cut through.'

'Copy that. Stand by.'

'Did you kill him?' Hal asked Kordin.

'I killed the serpent,' he replied. 'There was no sign of Telsta.'

Comms interference echoed against the walls of the narrow stairway. 'The Kiyol… fire a pulse into the carrier shield,' Lana advised. 'Give me an opening to teleport in. Firing. Brace for impact.'

The walls of the corridor shook. A brief light flashed, and Lana appeared, wearing a backpack full of ballistics equipment. She set down a lancing torch and a gas canister. Her comms beeped, and Lincoln's voice came through.

'Lana, the disruptor blast has interrupted the carrier's computer security system. Charlie says he can hack the brig navigation controls. We're sending him up there.'

'He'll need a translator,' Kordin offered.

Lana ordered one of the AMs to go with him. 'Teleport all of the slaves you have to the surface. The animals in their cages too.'

Kordin gave her a questioning look.

'Do it.'

The soldiers had already begun cutting through the door to the keel.

'He has fresh scars,' Hal told Lana, nodding to where Kordin had left. 'The near-fatal kind. I think he almost died trying to save his lady friend. They're… more human than I thought.'

'I'm yet to be convinced.' Lana pulled Hal's shirt up to examine where he had been slashed by the Warden. His skin tissue had already closed over the lacerations, leaving three long scars. There were signs of previous injury on the left of his abdomen. Lana was shocked to find a healed bullet entry wound.

'This'll take a while,' said Hal, squinting away from the bright flame cutting the door. He noticed that Lana had had a chance to clean up and change her clothes. 'I saw a washroom on our way down here. Cover me while I clean up?'

'Sure. Let's be quick, though. Those two Wardens we lost could be anywhere.'

They climbed the stairs, and Lana asked Hal about his scars. He told her about the raiding gangs that roamed Haze Realm's city. He'd encountered them on patrol and fought to get away. There had been times he couldn't return to Oskar and the others at the lab in case he was being followed. So he'd spent days hiding until the raiders lost interest.

'One time, I had to pretend to be one of the Mutated,' said Hal. 'I was connecting extension cables to an underground generator. I hooked it up to the lab. It'd rained heavily that morning, so the stormwater current was raging. There I was, hanging right above it. The second I finished the connection, I lost my grip on the pipe! I fell. The current took me a city block away from where I was before I could grab hold of a ladder. I climbed to the surface…'

It was a narrow street, and the yellow haze was thick. Hal could hear the Mutated. Dragging feet, gasping shrieks. Some whimpered and moaned. A cool breeze thinned the haze, and Hal found himself completely surrounded. There were over thirty men and women standing and staggering about him. One woman came close, walking slowly, eyes wandering along the road. Her hair was blonde and matted. Her tattered silk shirt hung from her shoulders. Her skirt was torn and muddied.

Hal kept his head down. The woman bumped into him, looked up with shallow, sunken eyes, and let out a sharp rasp that sounded like "sorry". Hal saw a clearing in the direction she was headed and decided to follow. He studied her movements and mimicked her lopsided gait. Left shoulder dropped, one foot turned inward and dragging, right arm limp. Hal weaved between two men, bumped into a short woman and let out the same rasping noise he had received from the woman he was following.

A few more metres through the crowd, Hal was shoved to the ground. A large Mutated man dropped on his chest and clawed at his neck. Hal punched him, took a fistful of his hair and pulled him sideways. This caught the attention of the others, and high shrieks sounded all around. The slow and aimless were jostled awake. They followed the surge of bodies to Hal and his attacker and threw themselves into the fray.

Hal got to his knees and crawled. A dozen Mutated climbed over him and leapt onto the large man. He could hear tearing fabric and screaming as the fallen man was torn limb from limb.

Lana stood listening to Hal recount his experience. She found a towel while he undressed and what looked like Raekeem gym clothes: slacks and a tank top. She couldn't begin to comprehend how perilous his life must have been. She wanted to know more.

Hot water hissed and jetted down Hal's back, washing away blood and grime. One light shone on him in an otherwise dark room. He was done scrubbing and thanked Lana for the towel and clothes. He dressed and tensed when Lana stood close to him, reaching her fingers to press on his temples.

'Tell me how you escaped the Mutated,' she said. 'I want to see.'

'I made it to the clearing,' Hal started, and he immediately felt some kind of flow emanating from his mind into Lana's. 'Hunters found me…'

Hal crawled through the haze toward a creaking sound and found himself in a playground. The sound was a swing. It was her, the woman he followed earlier. Her head was resting against the chain and her legs swung limp, her bare feet dragging in the dirt. She swung herself gently, humming a sad tune Hal didn't recognise.

Hal's pace slowed. The woman looked up. Her eyes wandered to something behind Hal, and her humming stopped. He turned to see two men approaching with rifles. One raised his gun, and Hal's shout was muted by the shot. He whipped back around and saw the woman fall. Her legs flew up, and her body landed in the dirt.

The chain links clinked. The seat twisted and swayed. Hal felt tugging at his arm and heard the men shouting for him to run. The ground was vibrating, and a horde of thirty Mutated came running through the haze.

'I followed the hunters into a building, and we escaped through a basement tunnel.' Hal shrugged and took Lana's hands. 'That's it.' She was looking at him as if she had never really seen him until now. 'You saw?'

Lana broke eye contact. 'They'll be through the door soon.'

They returned to the stairs and descended to the keel.

'Why did you jump?' Lana asked. 'At the cage. When Renee fell.'

Hal felt something on the back of his hand. He shined the torch and saw that the veins beneath his skin were pronounced. His blood looked purple.

'Is she alright?' Hal asked, deflecting her question.

'She's stable.'

Their footsteps echoed against the narrow walls while they descended. The hiss of the lancing torch could be heard below.

'I never knew my parents,' said Lana. 'But I think what they would want… what every parent wants for their children is for them to experience more than just survival.' She looked at Hal, encouragingly. 'More than fear.'

Hal gazed at the walls that seemed to narrow and meet in a monolithic void. He stopped and turned to meet Lana's watchful eyes.

'I know it might not feel like it right now,' she said, trying to read Hal's despondent expression. 'The fighting never seems to stop. But anything there is to face here we can face together.'

Lana took Hal's hand and felt his muscles tense. His skin was hot and sweaty, and he was beginning to shake.

Lana saw purple coursing beneath Hal's skin. And his eyes were ink black.

Chapter 21

'There,' said Rachel, pointing at the airspace above Sausalito. 'Right there.' The holographic projection beaming up from the table lit the tip of her finger blue.

'So they miscalculated, or they knew we'd evacuate everyone through Sausalito,' Lincoln speculated. 'Either way, we'll deploy along the bay and install turrets on the mountain. What weaponry did the Wardens have?'

'They'll arrive unarmed.'

'Rache, I think you should sit this one out,' Jolie recommended.

Rachel's head jerked back as though she smelt something foul. 'Sit… What? No.'

'We need you here,' said Lincoln, respecting Jolie's advice. 'You'll have all the coverage you need to guide us through this invasion.'

'Fine,' Rachel conceded, after a huff.

'Commander,' a communications officer called from his terminal. 'Dr Bryant has set the Silica carrier on a course for outer space. Lana and her team have breached the keel and are ready to plant explosives.'

Lincoln tapped at the table comms console. 'Lana, I want all of you off that ship as soon as you're done.'

'Copy that.' Lana closed her comms and helped Hal to his feet. 'Are you sure you're alright?'

'I think so.' He had been sitting, leaning against the wall at the bottom of the stairs before the door to the keel. The blue of his eyes had returned, and the purple in his veins had receded.

Kordin had returned to the keel after helping Charlie hack the ship systems. 'The mutagen has entered your bloodstream,' he informed Hal. 'You are infected.'

'Thanks for stating the obvious,' Lana said impatiently. 'Is there an antidote?'

He shook his head.

Hal stared at the floor. 'I'm going to become one of them?'

Kordin pressed his finger upward against Hal's eyebrow without warning and peered at him closely. He couldn't understand why the mutagen hadn't taken Hal over completely.

'Hey, easy,' said Lana. 'He's not one of your lab rats.'

'The mutagen is designed to rewrite host DNA,' said Kordin, ignoring Lana's remark. 'Your body is either fighting the mutagen or adapting to it.'

'Lana, if I turn…' Hal started.

'You won't.' She placed her hand on Hal's shoulder. 'You were engineered to adapt.'

They followed Kordin into the keel with the AMs. Dim lights flickered over walkways between egg-shaped pods.

Lana ran her hand along the smooth surface of the first pod. 'What is this… Titanium?'

Kordin nodded. 'Your explosives will not penetrate.'

'Charlie couldn't program self-destruct?' Hal asked.

'We were locked out of the system before he could. And the navigation controls allowed us minimal speed.' Kordin felt that he was no longer of use. The humans were doomed, and there was nothing he could do to help them. It was time for him to leave.

'Can we release the pods now?' Lana asked. 'Let them drift in outer space?'

'I'll look for a manual disengage.' He knew full well no such mechanism was installed. 'Set your explosives. The blast will destroy the power source,' he lied.

Lana nodded to the AMs, and they split off, planting bombs beginning at the first ring of pods. Lana walked along the rows, shining her torch down each length. The keel was completely full.

She paused when her flashlight shone over what she thought was a mane of black hair. She flicked it back and saw nothing. Tapping at her console, she accessed the thermal readout that detected every living organism in the keel. Warden signatures didn't read due to the titanium shells shielding their presence. But she counted two more life signs than there were supposed to be.

Before she could speak into her comms, she heard a yell and a body fall. Muzzles flashed ten metres to her right, echoing gunfire against the low ceiling. She paced to the centre of the keel and issued an order. 'There are two Wardens hunting us. Overwatch at my position.'

Hal glanced at the ceiling on his way to Lana. He shone his torch up to reveal metal rods spaced a few metres apart, lining the entire roof of the keel. There were hundreds of electrical cables connected between them.

Hal stilled when he heard heavy breathing close by. He pressed his back against a pod, a second before a female Warden crept out from the aisle in front of him and sniffed the air. Her ears twitched at the sound of an approaching AM. Hal stepped out to fire, but the soldier was whipped away, and the Warden disappeared.

Rachel's voice came through Lana's comms. 'Lana, I have an idea.'

She listened while sweeping her torchlight along the pod aisles, aiming her gun down each row. None of the AMs had made it to her. Neither had Hal. Lana had to watch her own back.

'Open a portal at the opposite end of the keel and set it for outer space,' Rachel instructed. 'Make it as big as your Shifter can handle. The carrier will move through the portal. Everything that passes through will be taken from the ship into space.'

'On it.'

Lana froze when she heard rasping breath behind her. She spun around, armoured her skin and threw a roundhouse kick. Her boot struck the Warden's head and it staggered against a pod. It roared at Lana, throwing saliva at her chest.

Lana saw the murderous grin her axe had given the beast back in the elevator. Its gums were cut right back to the jawbone. Lana hopped, tucked her knees to her chest in mid-air and kicked the Warden's left knee, causing it to fall on its side.

Throwing herself onto the Warden's chest, Lana pinned its shoulders with her knees. Its claws raked Lana's thighs, ripped through her leggings and squeaked along her armoured skin.

When the Warden roared, Lana drove the barrel of her gun into its mouth and fired three times. She ran for the edge of the keel, in the direction the carrier was travelling, while tapping at her console to program a portal.

The male Warden saw the body of its mate from atop a pod and roared at Lana. It landed behind her with a loud clang. She was still thirty metres from the keel perimeter. She kept running. The Warden's claws scraped the metal, pelting the floor as it bounded after her.

Hal saw Lana running and the beast closing on her. He leaned into a sprint between the pods, leapt, and squared his shoulders for a side-on collision. The impact of muscle on muscle was jarring, and both Hal and the Warden rolled across the floor. The beast sprang back to its feet. It wrapped both hands around Hal's neck and raised him high. Hal snatched a combat knife from his belt and tried to stab the pit of the Warden's arm. The blade tip couldn't penetrate its black skin.

Lana glanced over her shoulder and stopped when she saw Hal being choked to death. She drew her axe, turned, and threw it hard. It hurtled through the dim light and slammed into the back of the Warden's skull, causing it to cough a gout of saliva into Hal's face. It threw Hal into a pod and turned its attention to her. She was running, but there was no light ahead, and she crashed into the far wall.

Lana whirled around and gasped. The beast was racing in for the kill. She tapped a final command while it leapt at her with outstretched arms. The portal opened a centimetre from her nose.

Outside the carrier, the Warden flew through the exit portal and into the vacuum of space.

Lana reopened her eyes and breathed. The ship was moving through the mercury sphere, which was close to the floor. It intercepted a pod and swallowed it whole. Lana tapped at her console to expand the portal to its maximum size, and she watched the perfect curve cut along the titanium capsules like a lance. Everything was being taken into outer space.

An alarm tone sounded. 'Hull breach,' a canned voice warned. 'Containment field initiated.'

Lana ran down the aisle, careful to avoid the portal on her way past. She picked up and sheathed her axe, and found Hal unconscious, bleeding from his head. She tried to kneel down beside him, but something pulled at her hip. An invisible force lifted her from the floor. She unbuckled her axe, and it flew out of its sheath. It hit the roof above with a loud thrum. She fell to the floor beside Hal and a deep bass vibration battered her ears. Sparks above caused her to look up, and she saw electricity forking across the roof of the keel.

Lana tried to program a teleport to Silica. The command screen read "Error". Electromagnetic interference was preventing their escape.

The shiny, rippling ball of quicksilver was drifting closer. Lana dragged Hal away as it scooped up the floor, sinking deeper and deeper until only its top was visible. It disappeared a half metre from Lana's feet when the magnetic build-up shut it down.

Clanging roared down the aisles, and Lana saw the egg-cup shapes holding each capsule retract. Black tendrils whipped across the roof, darkening the light sparking from the rods. A boom sounded from above, and the entire keel shook. Inky clouds consumed all light until Lana could see nothing.

The thundering of metal and raw electrical power quietened. Lana could hear her own rapid breathing. Her eyes searched for any point of reference. The floor fell away from her, and she felt Hal's body float against her. The zero gravity lasted seconds before metallic clattering sounded and a deep bass rumbled again.

Hal and Lana dropped to the floor, and she felt the keel come to a shuddering halt, causing her and Hal to slide against a pod. She picked herself up and was blinded by a sudden rush of daylight. Silhouettes of hundreds of pods appeared before sinking down through their egg cups. Light shone up from the holes left gaping in the base of the keel, spotlighting the roof. The portal had tunnelled through the keel and taken over thirty Warden pods before the teleport was complete. The keel's thrusters were losing their fight against Earth's gravitational pull.

Lana felt Hal arrive beside her, and he braced himself against the nearest hole. They stared down at the vertiginous scene below. Warden pods were raining down on boats in the bay, crashing through solar-panelled roofs of homes and businesses, pounding the roads, crushing cars on the street.

'Sausalito,' Lana murmured. 'We have to get down there.' She found and sheathed her axe, and reset a teleport command with a nod toward the Golden Gate Bridge. 'The lab is close. I'll get us to the armoury.'

They braced themselves against an impact explosion. Two more cannon shells hammered against the hull of the keel. Artillery had been positioned ahead of the invasion and had opened fire as soon as the keel had appeared over Sausalito.

Hal saw electricity surging across the ceiling. The same throbbing bass that vibrated through the hull before was building again.

'Get us out now,' he said. 'It's teleporting to the Laician home world.'

Lana opened a portal to the Hub, and Hal followed her in.

The Warden that had lunged at Lana and travelled through the portal was frozen solid, drifting with its arms outstretched. Subtle glowing lines tracked it. The lasers manipulated the space around the creature, creating a gravitational pull. Bay doors opened to a bright interior, and the Warden disappeared inside.

Stars rippled over the hulking shape of the cloaked Lustitian ship as it moved within firing range of Telsta's carrier.

Kordin entered Lord Telsta's fire-blackened chambers, shining the light from his wrist console across the room. He went to the charred serpent carcass lying against the wall and pulled his sword out of its mouth.

'It's not him.'

Kordin heard Xera's quiet voice and turned to see her standing behind him. She wore the black slacks and singlet that the medical robots gave to her.

'It took his place,' she said, tearing the bottom of her singlet and using the strip of cloth to tie her thick mane into a ponytail.

Kordin sheathed his sword. 'This was your plan all along.' He watched Xera crouch beside the serpent and tear a scale from its body.

'Light.'

'You could have been killed,' he said, shining his torch as requested. 'You should have told me.'

Xera studied the carcass while Kordin tapped his comms and ordered the ship waiting for them in the hangar to prepare for flight. The pilot responded quickly. 'Sir, there is an energy signature in the area. Maybe a cloaked ship.'

'Teleport us aboard immediately.'

Xera and Kordin emerged from a cloud teleport on the brig of their craft, and it flew out of the hangar. It had travelled only ten kilometres when four torpedoes were fired from the empty space ahead. Their trajectory was high, and they sailed over Kordin's ship. The torpedoes ripped through the shields of the carrier and into the hull. It exploded, the shockwave causing Kordin's ship to tumble out of control. The hull shuddered. A fire started on the instruments in the cockpit, and the ship systems engaged water vapour jets to extinguish the blaze.

'Report,' Kordin ordered.

'Shields at eight per cent,' a crew member replied. 'Stabilisers engaged. Power is back online.'

'Get us out of here.'

The crew member pushed the thrust control forward. The ship vibrated and the hull shook.

'Why aren't we moving?' Kordin barked.

'Something's holding us, sir.'

Xera looked out of the forward windows to see a large, chromed vessel decloaking. It drew close and stopped.

'Raekeem vessel.' A voice came over the ship comms. 'Prepare to be transported.'

Chapter 22

The surface of the ocean glimmered in the sunlight. The wind was calm, and the few clouds in the sky drifted slowly.

Chillo's marine crafts travelled in a line of seven beneath the sea. Kida commanded another seven heading in the opposite direction, twenty metres below the surface, opening between them a vast net made of processed seaweed. Seaweed was used for all building projects in Aqua Sierra, produced in a variety of tensile strength and elastic grades. This weed net stretched to cover an area half the size of a football field.

Chillo and Kida positioned the net directly above Kulete City. Motion-sensor mines were housed on its every intersecting line. When triggered, the mines would each jettison a propelled plasma charge that could track a target. These would create a pocket of compounded pressure that could expand with enough force to punch a hole through an armoured enemy ship.

Jihna captained a battle cruiser in Aqua Sierra airspace. Its pulse cannon was ready to fire on the Raekeem keel as soon as it arrived. She watched the monitors, which were fixed on the sea above Kulete City.

'Captain.' A comms operator broke the silence in the brig. 'We've received word from our scout in Silica. The Raekeem carrier there has been destroyed. And an unidentified interstellar drive energy signature was detected on an intercept vector to Earth.'

Jihna looked up from the monitors. The operator seemed confused after reading the next report. 'An abandoned Raekeem cruiser was found in the vicinity.'

'Forward that report to Commander Lincoln,' Jihna ordered.

An alert signalled the arrival of the Warden keel.

Jihna watched the main viewer zooming in on the flat-topped, disc-shaped craft emerging from a mass of swirling black.

'Pods are being deployed,' said the pilot.

She tapped on the monitors to isolate an area of the keel that was already damaged. 'Target that hull breach. Fire when ready.'

'All crafts detach,' Chillo ordered. 'Ascend ten metres.'

All fourteen tow lines connected to the fleet remained taut while each craft jettisoned a buoy from its rear. The buoy propellers activated, churning the water. The vast net of mines was held in place, ready for the descending pods.

Chillo's forces rose to form a perimeter above the net. The nose of each craft tilted, and they took aim at the hundreds of pods raining down toward the sea.

Chillo waited, watching the silhouettes grow larger against the bright impact blasts slamming the keel above, as Jihna's battle cruiser continued its bombardment.

'Fire at will,' he ordered.

The first volley of fourteen torpedoes snaked through the light. Eight pods were ruptured and torn apart. Over a dozen slipped through the explosions. Mines were jettisoned from the net. The first reached its target, and a soundless bubble expanded and retracted in the blink of an eye. The pod caved in on itself, crushing the Warden inside.

The keel was taking intense blasts to its top as Jihna's battle cruiser flew over it. Explosions ruptured it from inside. The bombs that Lana's team had laid were detonating. It lost thrust control and began to dip toward the sea. A moment later, an eruption in the centre of the craft sent an impact through the entire structure, blowing pods and hunks of the ship across the ocean.

Portal Hub
San Francisco

'You saw the future?' Lana exclaimed.

There was a pause on Rachel's end of the comms connection. 'Yes, and it's not good. Take the time you need to grab what hits the hardest. The pods haven't opened yet. And our forces are on their way to the bridge. Rache out.'

'How are you feeling?' Lana asked Hal. She had taken a blood sample from his arm. There were no AM medics available to diagnose his mutagen infection, and she felt a sample had to be tested as soon as possible to determine if he was going to change and become infectious.

'Good,' Hal replied. 'You?'

When Lana met his concerned gaze while pressing a bandaid over the hole in his vein, she felt her cheeks grow hot. She quickly averted her eyes, annoyed that her attraction to him was surfacing at a time of crisis. 'I need to sit down,' she admitted. Her legs and hips were sore from the fight and from being tossed about in the Warden craft.

She sat on a cushioned chair and couldn't believe how good it felt to be off her feet. *Hopefully, Jolie can find a way to purge the mutagen from Hal's body*, she thought while programming a small teleport to send his blood to Jolie.

'Have you ever been hurt?' Hal asked, noting Lana's shredded leggings hanging over a chair. She had changed into a fresh pair.

Lana tilted her head at his loaded question. He coughed, his throat still sore after being strangled by the Warden. 'Physically.'

'I've had a lot of muscle injuries,' she said. 'My armour only gives me a thin layer of protection. And I've been caught unawares.' She pulled her leggings down to reveal a three-centimetre scar on her right hip.

'Knife fight?'

'Cyclist.' Lana raised herself from the oh-so-comfortable chair and walked with Hal to the armoury. 'Happened last year, out running on the bridge. I joined the bike lane without looking. The guy who hit me felt responsible, bought me dinner. We saw each other for a while.'

They entered the armoury and each took belts and straps to equip side-arms and ammo.

'Still together?' Hal asked, clipping on his utility belt.

'Nope.' Lana bit her bottom lip and shrugged, like the outcome couldn't have been helped. 'He knew who I am, what I do, what I can do. Then he found out what I can't do.'

'He found out you don't age,' Hal guessed.

'Yup.' Lana put a P90 aside as her primary weapon and strapped on her thigh holster. She scanned the row of side-arms for something that might penetrate Warden skin. 'What about you? Was there anyone–' She stopped and waved a hand. 'I'm sorry, that's none of my business.'

'No one,' said Hal.

Lana's posture straightened, and she turned to Hal. She couldn't read his blank expression. 'Never?'

'There were women I liked,' said Hal with a shrug. 'None of them liked me.' He chose a combat shotgun. *Single-shot rounds should at least stun a Warden*, he thought. *And a head shot would kill.*

'Not even the women on Benson's guard detail?' Lana asked. 'They seemed okay.'

'We used to trade a lot, hang out. But they were into "talkers",' Hal said.

'Extraverts, you mean.' Lana scoffed. 'If women read the data we've collected over the years, they would never date the charismatic type. Ever.'

Hal was confused. 'Really? In my world, the saying goes "watch out for the quiet ones", like they're dangerous or something.'

'Anyone who perpetuates that social myth is doing more harm and definitely no good.' Lana brought up a video feed to monitor the situation outside. AMs were getting everyone off the bridge and erecting barricades to prepare for the Warden assault.

'When Rache and I go to different Realms, we access the international database, if there is one,' Lana explained. 'We've made over a dozen successful hacks.' She tapped her console to bring up a window beside the camera feed and scrolled down the page until she found *Psychological and Criminal Statistical Data.* 'The data we collected shows that ninety per cent of all psychopaths are charismatic people. More than half of that percentage are married or married with children.'

'Huh.' Hal's brow furrowed. 'That makes "watch out for the quiet ones" sound like…'

'Bullshit,' Lana prompted. 'Correct. Which makes it a saying most likely invented by a…?'

'Psychopath.'

Lana tipped her hand. 'Or a serial killer.'

Hal pulled on a pair of gloves and decided to change the subject. 'The future Rachel saw… do you think we can actually change it? I mean, what if the future is pre-determined no matter what?'

Lana found .44 magnum rounds and loaded them into a Raging Bull revolver. 'Hal, if there's anything I've learned during my years of Realm travel…' She spun the six-round cylinder. 'It's that the future doesn't exist' – she flicked her wrist, sending it in behind the barrel with a satisfying metallic click – 'until we make it.'

Unity Building

Lincoln monitored a holo-display of the Golden Gate Bridge while maintaining contact through comms with his soldiers, ordering formations and feeding them intel.

Rachel approached a window that gave her a view of the bridge. She could see smoke rising from buildings that had been struck by the pods and debris from the carrier.

Pete arrived beside her and sighed with relief. 'The keel has been destroyed. The Laicians have the aquatic Wardens under control.'

She nodded without turning away from the devastation outside.

'Rachel, I'm sorry. What's happening to you… it's my fault.'

She looked at him as though she didn't understand his apology. 'We were both aware there might be side effects. You couldn't have known the medication would make me see the future.'

'I spoke to colleagues of mine at the Academy of Science,' he said. 'Their theory is that your consciousness was transferred forward to some other temporal plane. A plane essentially in situ, linked as a likely future, based on the course our world is on.'

Rachel gave Pete a "Translation?" look.

'They think you saw what might happen.'

'*Did* happen,' Rachel corrected him, pointing a finger to the scene outside. 'I saw them hit Sausalito. They're going to storm the bridge.'

Hal and Lana teleported to the halfway point of the Golden Gate Bridge. AM troops were firing from behind a truck parked at an angle across both lanes. Bullets flew at them from Wardens, armed after taking up assault rifles from AMs they struck down on the Sausalito end.

Lana took point, moving swift and low. Hal followed her from cover to cover. She pulled the pin on a grenade and threw it at the group of Wardens heading the pack. As soon as it exploded, she, Hal, and the AMs rose from cover and opened fire on those still standing.

Lana sprayed a volley at the next line of Wardens, who were hurdling their fallen. She dropped three with her P90, but they advanced so quickly she was soon shooting them at point blank range. She ducked under a claw swipe, shouldered her rifle, pulled out her axe and rose with a hammering uppercut. Her attacker's head rose from the impact, and it was knocked sideways by the Warden stampeding behind it. Lana rolled onto a car bonnet to avoid the beast charging her. She lunged and hooked another Warden's neck with her axe. Its roar was cut short when she used her momentum to slam its head into a car boot. She landed on her feet, tucked, and shielded her face against a shower of bullets. Every round ripped through her tank top, and she gritted her teeth while they bounced off her armoured skin and clinked onto the bitumen. She pulled out her revolver, hopped, slid across the bonnet of another car, kicked a Warden in the face and shot another in the forehead.

Hal stepped into a side-kick, landing the heel of his boot on a Warden's chest, aimed his gun and shot it down. He charged and spear-tackled another that had just vaulted over an SUV. Its DNA had been spliced with a mandrill's, and it was ferocious.

They collided. While turning in mid-air, Hal used it as a shield against a volley of bullets. He spotted the muzzle flash, raised his shotgun and sent a slug into the gun-wielding beast's head. The second passed and gravity took him and the mandrill down hard.

It rolled on top of Hal, its jaw open wide, revealing a set of long teeth. Its primal roar threw saliva into Hal's face. He managed to raise his shotgun in time to stop it from biting down on his throat. Reaching a finger to the trigger, Hal could only manage to drop the barrel beside the mandrill's face. He fired a deafening shot, causing its head to jerk away. He ejected the shell, aimed at its head and fired again.

Hundreds of Wardens, creations of various genetic splices, continued to charge along the bridge. And they were crowding ever thicker. Their manic thirst for violence, to break free of the herd and get their kill, escalated from shoving one another aside to clawing, biting and bashing.

Lincoln came through on the shared comms. 'Hal, Lana, pull back. Aerial reinforcements incoming.'

Lana pressed her back against Hal's. They were surrounded. They fired on every Warden that attacked but weren't able to get a head shot every time. Each Warden that took a nonfatal hit was only momentarily stunned.

Hal looked up and saw six AMs, each wearing a jetpack. They slowed as they descended, firing their assault rifles. Hal pulled Lana behind a car. Lines of armour-piercing rounds pelted the Wardens on the road. Lana felt Hal's hand pressing at her back, urging her to run for cover further up the bridge. Another six AMs swooped between the bridge cables and assumed assault formation. They fired rocket launchers into the Warden horde. Cars and trucks exploded. Wardens were blown off the bridge, thrown into the cables and crushed under wreckage.

The jetpack AMs came in waves, firing on the Wardens in groups of six, and then returning to a reload bay positioned on the San Francisco side of the bridge.

One soldier broke formation and hovered beside the bridge cables when he spotted a civilian at the end of the bridge the Wardens were coming from. A teenage girl looked to be waking from being knocked unconscious. The front of her car was buried into the back of a van. The roofs of both vehicles had been squashed by the horde. She crawled out, hugging the twisted passenger door.

'Civilian sighted,' the AM reported. 'Moving to inter–'

There was an earsplitting screech as a Warden dropped on top of him, swung him and crushed his head into the bridge pillar. The Warden was spliced with bat DNA, and the claws that protruded from its wings were imbedded in the soldier. It kicked the AM, sending him into the path of a loose rocket, then beat the air with its large wingspan and escaped the explosion.

'Jetpack. Now!' Lana shouted to the nearest AM. The soldier promptly descended, touched down beside her, released his harness and unlatched the carbon chest plate.

'I'm out!' Hal shouted, after his shotgun clicked empty. He took the barrel with both hands and swung the butt into the side of a charging Warden's head.

Lana called to Hal and tossed her revolver to him. He caught it in time to turn and fire on an approaching Warden.

The AM held the jetpack while Lana fed one arm through the harness, then the other, taking the ten-kilogram weight of the pack on her shoulders. With the straps pulled tight and the armour plate clamped over her chest, she listened to the soldier's brief instructions while watching the bat Warden fly away from the bridge and toward the city.

Chapter 23

Unity Building

Lincoln was coordinating his ground forces. The aerial units were more successful with their assault but they were exposed to gunfire and winged beasts. The Wardens were pushing further up the bridge. *We can't stop them*, he realised.

'Sir,' an operator called from the other side of the room. 'Sensors have picked up the energy signature the Kiyol reported. An unidentified vessel has entered our airspace.'

The room went quiet. Lincoln paced over to the operator's console. 'Another Raekeem carrier?'

'Full spectrum sweep does not identify the craft as Raekeem. They're hailing us.' The operator rolled back on his chair to a comms specialist working behind him. 'Do you have the frequency?'

'Locked in,' she reported. 'Receiving now.'

'…Captain Valhez of the Lustitian Enforcer. Please respond.'

'This is Commander Lincoln,' he said, speaking with authority. 'You have entered our airspace without authorisation. State your intentions.'

The AM guards in the room pulled their side-arms, and Lincoln spun around, snatching his own pistol from its holster. He aimed at the closest of multiple shimmering figures phasing into the centre of the room. Three men and a woman appeared.

One of the men stepped forward. He had an olive complexion, and his grey head and facial hair were perfectly maintained. His white and yellow uniform was double breasted, with three small silver dots pressed into his collar. When he spoke, his tone was forthright, and his accent was Latin American.

'My apologies for entering unauthorised, Commander,' he said and offered his white-gloved hand to Lincoln. 'I am Captain Valhez.'

Lincoln holstered his gun and shook the Captain's hand. *These people can enter our solar system undetected*, he thought. Testing their combat ability would only make this bad situation even worse.

Valhez glanced around at the guns pointed at him and his crew members. 'We don't have a lot of time,' he said, locking candid eyes on Lincoln's. 'The further these creatures spread, the harder it will be to stop them.'

'Stand down,' Lincoln ordered his soldiers. 'Captain, this city will be overrun within the hour. If you have suggestions, I am all ears.'

'This is Kim, my Science Officer.' Valhez nodded to the woman behind him, and she approached with a digital pad. A holographic display beamed up from it.

'After recovering the Warden your people ejected into space, I was able to isolate the mutagen genome signature,' said Kim. She looked to be of Korean descent, in her twenties, wearing rimless glasses. 'We can now use our photon particle ray to sweep the bridge, targeting any life form that carries the mutagen.'

'Have you used this ray before?' Professor O'Conner asked. He was standing next to Rachel, and he folded his arms sceptically when Kim hesitated. 'You've tested it?'

'Only on Raekeem DNA,' Kim admitted. 'We have successfully removed Sentinels from dense populations while they have mimicked people. The ray will work.'

Rachel immediately thought of Hal. Lana said he had been attacked by a Warden and now had the mutagen in his body. She'd opened her mouth to speak when the bat Warden crashed through a window and flew across the ceiling of the command room.

Lincoln and his AMs opened fire, and the Warden flew directly at Professor O'Conner. Rachel pushed him aside and took a blow to the head from the beast's wing. She fell, unconscious, to the floor.

Lincoln pulled Kim and Valhez to safety. 'Do it,' he said. 'Fire the particle ray.'

Valhez nodded to Kim, and she teleported out of the room. The other two Lustitians shot at the beast's wings with white-hot bolts. It ploughed into the carpeted floor, rose, and hit one of the Lustitian guards sideways into a loadbearing pillar.

Lana flew through the broken window, turning sharply to intercept the bat. She cut the jetpack's engine a second before impact, rolled in mid-air and slammed into the Warden, using the weight of her pack. She and the beast crashed through partition walls, computer screens and office chairs.

Lana slid to the far wall and rolled onto her stomach with an aching groan. The Warden recovered, arched its back and let out an ear-piercing screech. Everyone dropped to their knees and held their heads.

Lana forced herself to her feet, hit the jet ignition button in the palm of her hand and flew toward the bat. She cut the engine, rotated her body and drop-kicked it in the chest. The beast fell at Captain Valhez's feet. He held his gun to its forehead and fired twice.

The wind was blowing in through the broken window, and the battle on the Golden Gate Bridge could be heard in the distance. Kim's voice came through Valhez's comms. 'Firing particle ray. Stand by.'

Lana helped Rachel to her feet. 'Are you okay?' She pulled a chair over and sat Rachel down.

'No… stop,' Rachel stammered. 'Stop the ray.' She was dazed, barely able to open her eyes.

'Who are these people?' Lana asked Pete when he arrived beside her. 'What ray?' She looked to Lincoln and Valhez. They were gazing out at the bridge. A red hue shot across the sky and over Sausalito.

'They're Lustitians,' said Pete. 'Their ray will eliminate the Wardens.' He gave Lana an uncertain look. 'Any living thing containing the Warden mutagen will–'

Lana grabbed Pete's arm roughly. 'The ray is targeting the mutagen?'

Valhez approached. 'I assure you, none of your people will be–'

'Shut it off!' Lana shouted at him and turned to Lincoln. 'Hal was infected. He has the mutagen in his blood.'

'We'll be overrun,' Lincoln argued. 'We have to stop them now.'

Lana pushed through the AMs standing in her way. She dove out the broken window, engaged her jetpack thrusters and flew toward the bridge. In the far distance, she could see the particle ray sweeping slowly across Sausalito, culling all of the Wardens in the bay town. She tried to contact Hal through comms, but he didn't respond.

Hal was running, ducking, weaving, and dodging through the fray of Wardens and flying bullets. The teenager was trapped, hiding beside her car not twenty metres away, and he was fighting to reach her.

A muscular Warden spliced with gorilla DNA set its eyes on Hal. Its knuckles drummed the road as it gained momentum. It shouldered a station wagon, causing its rear end to skid aside.

The gorilla met Hal with a chest slam that sent him flying into the windscreen of a van. He hit the road and looked up in time to avoid its downward fists. He drove his elbow up under its jaw, and it staggered back.

When Hal stood, he saw black coursing through his veins. The outside of his vision was pulsing red. He side-kicked an approaching Warden and deflected a claw swipe from another. He took a firm hold of that Warden's skull and head-butted it.

The mutagen was making Hal stronger, faster. He was fuming with rage, and he was using it.

When Hal arrived at the woman's car, a Warden with four arms dropped down from the bridge cables onto the roof, crushing the car pillar down to the door. It pounced at Hal, and he caught it by the throat, swung it over his head and released it as he jumped to complete a three-sixty spin and kicked its gut. It crashed through a bus window, tumbled over the seats and smashed through the opposite window.

The young woman ran around her car and cried out a warning to Hal. Two Wardens pinned him against the driver's-side door. They struck him in the face and stomach. He leaned on them and growled through his teeth, drooling blood as he walked backward up the side of the car, bent his knees, braced himself in a vertical squat and pushed away with all the strength in his legs, sending the car skidding sideways into the road barrier. He threw the two Wardens, who tumbled into a group of approaching beasts. He returned to the woman and knocked a Warden reaching for her down with a heavy left cross. She screamed when more of them advanced on her.

'Stay down,' Hal told her. And he jumped, rotated his body over her and landed a blow to the head of the first in range. He landed, turned again and roundhouse-kicked one to his side. He hopped and kicked against another Warden, pushed away on the impact to the beast's abdomen, and completed another aerial spin over the girl to deliver two consecutive blows to others as they arrived.

A circle of fallen Wardens was forming around the young woman, as Hal knocked each one down when they attacked.

Lana arrived overhead with two jetpack AMs she'd ordered to follow her. The soldiers fired on the beasts, and Lana swooped down to Hal's side. In his berserk state, he turned and raised his fist at Lana. His eyes widened when he saw her, and he took a step back.

Lana removed her jetpack. She nodded to the red particle ray that had now swept onto the bridge. 'That ray is going to kill you if it reaches us!' She held out the pack for him to put on.

The ray was approaching fast and beamed wide across the bay, vanishing any Wardens that had made it into the water. It was going to sweep the bridge in seconds. The Wardens running through the red light were disappearing just ten metres away from him.

'Lana, the girl. Protect her until the ray has passed,' Hal said, feeding one arm into the pack's harness while Lana held it. The two of them were knocked down by charging Wardens trying to escape the ray. The pack was thrown, and it clattered under the bus.

Lana got to her knees and stood in time to armour her skin before a Warden raked its claws down her chest. She swung her elbow across its jaw, back-handed its face, turned her shoulders and buried her armoured fist in its temple, dropping it like a sack of meat.

A wall of red light was pushing at Hal's back. He punched and shouldered his way through a pack of Wardens to get to Lana. He was wedged between two beasts, reaching with one arm.

Lana's eyes watered at the sight of the empty red light coming for Hal. Only the bridge and the abandoned cars remained in its wake. She reached out and took Hal's hand. The Wardens holding him were lit scarlet, and Hal fell forward. Lana grabbed him with both hands and pulled. The red beamed over them, shining through Hal until he became intangible.

Lana stared into his wide eyes.

Hal vanished.

The thundering vibration of Wardens running on the bridge stopped.

The wind blew through Lana's hair as she sank to her knees. Her shoulders trembled. Tears streaked her dirt-covered face. She sat and stared into her empty hands.

In the following hours, medical staff began to triage the wounded, and emergency crews cleared the debris and commenced building repairs.

Science Officer Kim completed a sensor sweep on board the Lustitian ship docked beside the Unity Building. 'No life forms carrying the mutagen have been detected. The particle ray was successful.'

Pete and Rachel listened to the report as it came to Captain Valhez. They stood on the command floor where the bat had attacked.

'Lord Telsta is the only Raekeem unaccounted for,' Valhez said with a furrowed brow.

'Lana said the Lead Sentinel was cooperating after we took the carrier,' said Rachel. 'He may know where Telsta fled.'

'Is she alright?' Pete asked.

'She was banged up pretty bad.' Rachel's voice wavered. 'Hal's gone.'

'I can't believe that,' said Lana.

Everyone turned to see her holding the left side of her ribs.

'Lana, you shouldn't be up,' said Rachel.

'I'm done resting. I want to speak to whoever designed the ray.'

Valhez spoke into his comms. 'Officer Kim, please report to the transport room. Valhez to transport. Bring myself and three others in my proximity aboard.'

'Copy. Transporting now.'

A bright, golden light beamed through each of them, and they were transported onto a platform inside the Lustitian ship.

'Interrogation of Kordin and his crew has not yet yielded results,' Valhez said to Rachel.

She and Pete looked around the white walls and the polished white console stations.

'Let me speak with him,' said Lana.

'What makes you think he'll talk to you?' Valhez asked, gesturing for them to follow him out of the room.

'Everybody wants something,' she replied bluntly, barely taking in the ship and these new powerful people. She met the Captain's expectant gaze. 'Do you want Telsta or not?'

Valhez stopped abruptly and spoke as though he were addressing the slow child in the class. 'Kordin and the Raekeem he served with are responsible for the abduction – and, in many cases, the extermination – of millions of innocents across hundreds of worlds. You cannot offer him freedom.'

'Your courts will sentence them all to death,' Lana said, unflinching. 'Kordin knows that. Spare Sentinel Xera. Kordin will talk.'

Valhez flashed Lana a warning glare.

'You said I can't offer *him* freedom,' she said.

Officer Kim arrived before Valhez could respond. He instead ordered her to give Lana any information she needed on the particle ray.

'Of course.' Kim nodded. 'This way, ma'am.'

'Wait.' Valhez held up his hand when Kim and Lana started walking. 'Why would Kordin cooperate if I spared only her?'

Lana turned side on. 'She is all he has left. He would die for her.'

Chapter 24

Odd things about the interior of the Lustitian ship became apparent to Lana. There was a lack of any discernible smell – everything was spotless and white – and apart from shape, due to the saucer-like configuration of the ship, every interior was identical. She entered Kim's science lab and found herself looking back the way they'd came. It was as though she'd walked through a rotating set.

Kim had been explaining particle ray technology. Lana got the gist and was convinced Hal had not been killed by it.

'Lana, I am deeply sorry that our weapon was the cause of–'

'From what you've told me, the ray didn't necessarily kill the Wardens. It took targeted matter, the Warden mutagen, out of our Realm. Where did that matter go?'

'Into the Ether,' Kim replied without explanation.

Lana opened her hands expectantly. 'Is that a figure of speech or is it an actual place?'

'It is a place where no life form can survive.'

Lana became animated, raising her voice. 'How do you know that? Have you been there? Is the Ether out in space? Where is it?'

Kim waited for Lana to take a breath. 'I'll show you.' She accessed a video file on the computer console in front of her. 'We had the same questions you have. So we exposed water to the ray, water containing particles that would be transported into the Ether. By containing the water in a force field, we were able to insert a receiving rod and essentially probe the Ether. We received no atmospheric data. There is nothing there.'

'But there's light,' Lana said, pointing to the screen. 'That's not nothing.'

The two of them watched the footage. It brightened then became dim once more before fading to black. The same thing happened again after a few minutes. Sometimes there were flickers of shadowy white or orange light, but it would always fade to black.

'Slow it down.'

Kim and Lana turned to see Rachel standing behind them.

'I got bored listening to Lincoln and your Captain's blossoming bromance.'

Lana peered at the screen while Kim tapped at the footage options. The light began to take longer to fade, and a blue hue became visible. And beneath the blue came green. There were shifting shapes. White was coursing across the blue.

'Clouds,' Lana exclaimed. She jabbed her finger at the screen. 'It's an atmosphere. Kim, play it frame by frame.'

Lana's eyes were wide with anticipation, searching the screen for any distinguishable detail. 'There,' she said, pointing to the bottom of the screen. 'Trees.' The frozen image was blurred, but she could make out treetops and branches.

Kim couldn't believe what she was seeing. 'Our particle ray has sent the Wardens to another world. There could be inhabitants of the Ether who we've endangered.'

Lana turned to Kim, waving her hands at herself. 'Ray me. Send me there.'

'I can reprogram the particle ray,' Kim agreed, but she hesitated and looked from the screen to Lana's excited expression. 'You would need the same particle frequency to get back.'

'Can you build a ray gun?' Lana asked, grasping at any solution she could think of.

'Let me speak with my colleagues,' said Kim. 'We'll have something for you within the hour.'

Lana took Kim's arm when she made to leave. 'It wasn't your fault. Your Captain, all due respect, obviously wanted a blanket solution. You did as he ordered.'

Kim nodded appreciatively, though she still felt guilty.

'Looks peaceful enough,' Lana said to Rachel. 'But hundreds of Wardens were sent there with Hal.'

Rachel had been counting the number of the day-night cycles on the screen. Her eyebrows rose when she finished a rough calculation in her head. 'By their time, Hal has been there for more than three weeks already.'

'We need to work fast,' said Lana. Her comms beeped and she stepped away to check the caller ID.

'Kida, hello. How are things on your end?'

'The Wardens have been defeated,' Kida reported. 'I have been told the threat is gone in your world as well. Who are these people who helped you?'

'They call themselves Lustitians,' Lana replied distractedly. 'Kida, I'm going to have to call–'

'You must be quite relieved,' Kida stammered. 'Lana, I'd like you to… I mean, I would like to invite you…' He let out a frustrated sigh. 'We are having a victory celebration, and I would like you to come.'

'I can't.'

'Oh.'

Lana pressed the heel of her palm into her forehead. 'I mean… thank you for inviting me. But there's something I have to do.'

'I understand,' said Kida. 'Maybe another time, if you'd like to… as your people say, "get a bite to eat"…'

Lana recalled the time she had joined Kida for a meal in Kulete City. She wore a transparent film that covered her body.

Kida tried to fill the awkward silence. 'Is that not the correct expression?'

'Kida, you're a genius. I'll call you back.' Lana closed her comms and turned to Rachel. 'The Laicians have technology that allows us to eat and drink underwater.'

'The second skin.' Rachel nodded.

Kim returned from speaking with her colleagues. 'Second skin?'

Lana was jittery, her eyes wide with anticipation.

Rachel cocked her head at Lana. 'I'm not sure where you're going with this. The second skin is a membrane,' she explained to Kim. 'It lines your body in a transparent film and allows you to push food or drink into your mouth without getting a lungful of water.'

Kim's eyes immediately widened like Lana's. She pointed to the screen. 'That footage is taken from a receiving rod because we couldn't send a drone.'

Rachel looked from Lana to Kim, starting to feel left out. The two women were excited by a train of thought that she had in no way boarded. 'You poked the Ether?'

'Yes,' Kim said, liking Rachel's way of putting it. 'We can't teleport there because we need coordinates. So we "poked" and could only keep the rod there for about an hour before it was severed.'

'The Kiyol developed the ability to travel between alternate timelines,' Lana informed Kim. 'They use a Shifter. It's a mobile device that opens portals, big or small, depending on your power source. The Kiyol and the Laicians may be able to help us develop a portal that can open inside the second skin and expand it.'

'That would allow us to pass through the portal into Ether Realm,' said Rachel, catching on to their plan.

'The portal wouldn't need coordinates.' Lana shrugged. 'Shoot it with the particle ray, the ray hits the membrane and takes it to Ether Realm with the portal riding along inside.'

'That's brilliant,' said Kim. 'My team can build you an inversion pulse emitter. We can calibrate the ray to take the second skin if the Laicians can give me a complete breakdown of the membrane composition. The maximum delay before the ray would take you and the pulse emitter would be approximately two seconds. In theory, you'll be taken to the exact location where Hal and the Wardens were sent.'

'Fire the ray gun, step in, gone.' Lana raised her palms. 'Piece'a cake.'

Chapter 25

Lincoln followed Valhez to the holding deck of the ship. The number of guards and surveillance cameras covering every corridor seemed satisfactory. An airlock led to the cell block. Lincoln counted over twenty two-by-three-metre cells. *The entire block must be modular, so it can be detached from the ship and connected to some kind of prison port. Perhaps a space station.*

Valhez pressed a button on a wall and the cell doors became transparent. This revealed two Raekeem to a cell, except for Kordin, who was alone. He was seated, staring ahead, and when Valhez pressed the button again, he looked up. Lincoln guessed that a second layer had been removed that allowed two-way visibility.

'Sentinel Kordin, I am Captain Valhez. This is Commander Lincoln of Earth.'

'Do you know where Telsta is?' Lincoln asked.

Kordin ignored the question. 'What is our sentence?'

'Due to your numbers, our mandate requires us to attempt rehabilitation,' Valhez explained, trying to sound compassionate. 'One of you will be selected. If no progress has been made within ten days—'

Kordin stood abruptly. 'Free Xera, my second in command, and I will help you find Telsta.'

'Fine. Start talking.'

Kordin looked the Captain up and down, unimpressed. *Pompous fool.* 'We all thought Telsta had the ability to transform into a serpent. Nobody dared challenge him for fear of bringing forth the monster. I suspected he was not transforming but switching places with a creature that was held somewhere else.' He faced Valhez and glared proudly. 'I killed the serpent. Someone, somewhere, must have been feeding it all these years. That is where Telsta is hiding.'

'Where should we look?' Lincoln asked.

Kordin pressed his lips together, reluctant to help someone else hunt the Lord he hated so much. 'I will give Xera all of the access codes I've committed to memory. All teleportations from the ship were logged. She can start there.'

Lincoln spoke to Valhez once they left the cell block. 'This mandate of yours…'

'It does not apply to this situation,' Valhez said coldly.

'Then they'll all be executed.'

Though Valhez did not detect any judgment in the Commander's tone, he felt it necessary to clarify his position. 'You must understand; the Raekeem are widely known for the devastating acts they have committed. They are feared and hated by entire worlds. Sparing the life of even one of them would make us appear weak in the eyes of the galactic community.'

Lincoln's comms beeped an emergency transmission.

'Commander, we have a situation. The maximum security prison has been breached. The inmates are… Sir, they're gone.'

The neural inhibitor on Xera's left temple would only allow her to walk and speak. She was escorted out of holding to the situation room. Technicians looked up from their computers and watched her while she was guided to a chair by two armed guards.

Kim entered the room, reading the briefing Valhez had forwarded to her. She took a seat at the table next to Xera, set her data pad down and assessed the Sentinel's composure.

Xera's white eyes were blank, staring at the far side of the room. Her jaw was set, and her posture was straight.

Kim saw a muscle twitch in Xera's left bicep that indicated discomfort, possibly from injury. She tapped through files on her pad to bring up the results of Xera's medical exam. Her brow furrowed when she read the report. The list of detected surgical procedures performed on this woman's body was horrifying.

Kim looked up at Xera, opened her mouth to speak and paused. She couldn't address somebody reduced to a doll state, enemy or not.

'Remove the inhibitor,' Kim ordered the guards.

They hesitated. 'Ma'am, Captain Valhez—'

'Do it.'

Xera's eyes flicked to Kim. *What kind of fool would present a captured enemy an opportunity for escape?* Xera thought. *It must be a trick. Are these self-righteous crusaders even capable of decept—*

'We are here to hunt down their Lord,' Kim said sternly when the guards looked at each other. 'This prisoner is the key to finding him. I need her functioning at her natural capacity. Remove the inhibitor.'

One of the guards did so while the other drew his weapon.

There were three others in the room, technicians, and they all backed away, staring wide-eyed in fear of the violence that could ensue.

Xera rolled her neck, then her shoulders, glancing to the exit and to the guards.

'Everybody out,' Kim ordered.

'Ma'am—'

'Now.'

Once the room was clear, Kim spoke to Xera in an even, respectful tone. 'We need your help to find Lord Telsta. If you agree to cooperate—'

Xera stood abruptly and walked to the door, speaking over her shoulder. 'Do you not value your life, Lustitian?'

'We will grant you probationary release once we have found Telsta,' Kim continued, without faltering. 'You will be watched, but you will be free to—'

'I will kill him.' Xera turned and took a step toward Kim, giving her an unnerving glare. 'I will find him and I will kill him.'

Kim glanced at the data on her pad listing Xera's most recent injuries. 'He did this to you.'

Xera took the chair in one hand and swung it before Kim could blink. It hit the wall, and Xera screamed through clenched teeth, 'He did this to *her!*'

The guards rushed in.

'Everything's fine,' Kim told them calmly. 'Wait outside.'

Xera glared after the guards until they were gone. Her eyes darted back to Kim when she spoke.

'Go on,' she said and held Xera's gaze with an open expression. She waited and listened.

Xera's next words were no less angry. 'He killed her,' she spat between her sharp, set teeth. 'And I failed to avenge her.' Her chest was heaving, tears spilling down her cheeks. She turned away. Her voice was barely audible. 'I failed you, Mother.'

Kim could see plainly that Xera was both enraged and broken. She placed a hand on Xera's trembling shoulder.

'We will find him, Xera,' she promised. 'You will have justice.'

Xera wiped her eyes and gave Kim an uneasy sideways glance. After all the worlds of people the Raekeem had destroyed, Xera couldn't have anticipated any gesture of compassion, least of all from a Lustitian.

Xera wiped Kim's hand off her shoulder and raised her chin, remembering that her fellow Raekeem were locked away not far from where she stood. 'All of my people will be executed.'

Kim could not lie. She could not tell Xera that Captain Valhez might somehow show leniency.

'What of Kordin?' Xera asked. 'If he cooperates—'

'He will stand trial with the others,' Kim said.

Xera's shoulders dropped in defeat. Though she felt some shame in breaking down in front of her captor, she also felt that she had nothing left to lose.

'May I see him?'

'Of course.' Kim ushered her to the door and ordered the guards to escort Xera to Kordin's cell.

Once they left, Kim picked the chair up from the floor and saw four claw marks torn through the upholstery. She let out a long breath and held her hands together to keep them from shaking.

Lincoln's eyes darted from one frame of video footage on his data tablet to the next. Black tendrils expanded into every cell in the Silica-based prison. They consumed the inmate in each room, contracted, and disappeared in an instant, leaving no trace of the occupant.

Standing outside Kordin's cell, Lincoln showed him the footage. He had no reaction to the abduction.

'Tell me what you know about this.'

Kordin looked at him blankly. 'I was not made aware of this operation. Telsta must have planned it in secret.'

Xera arrived with her guard escort. Lincoln observed the silent look of devotion she and Kordin exchanged, and he actually felt sympathy for them. In a strange way, their separation made Lincoln think of his and Jolie's situation. He walked away to give them their privacy.

A torrent of supressed and unresolved issues surfaced in Lincoln's machine mind. *Sooner or later, people are going to start asking questions. Jolie and I could be together among trusted friends: Rachel, Lana. But if word spread, the public – human and machine alike – might question the status of Automated Machines, our rights as citizens, our function as units manufactured to serve. Jolie and I should stop seeing each other. That would be the responsible thing to do. But that's not fair. We've fought and bled for the Universal Community. We deserve to live as—*

'Monsters in love.'

Lincoln's focus returned and he looked to Valhez. 'Pardon?'

The Captain nodded to Xera, her forehead pressed against Kordin's cell window. He was doing the same from the other side, whispering to her.

'I recommend we put both of them to the task of finding Telsta,' said Lincoln.

'That would be an unnecessary risk, Commander.'

'Release them into my custody,' Lincoln insisted respectfully. 'Let them have their final hours.'

Valhez raised one eyebrow, turned back to consider the couple and let out a patient sigh. 'Fine.' He walked away to speak to the guards.

Lincoln approached Xera. 'You two are coming with me to the site of the abduction. Raekeem technology has been found: capacitors that were cloaked right up until the teleportation occurred.'

'Kordin is to be pardoned as well?' Xera asked. Her hopes were instantly diminished when she saw Lincoln's bottom lip rise and his jaw clench.

Kordin glanced over Lincoln's shoulder to Valhez. 'These self-righteous sycophants seek justice only to maintain their image.' His judging eyes went to the cells holding his fellow Sentinels. 'The Lustitians will execute us so they can tell those who survived our invasions that the monster has been slain.'

Chapter 26

Peter O'Conner arrived in the portal room with Rachel. They found Lana at a table covered with survival items, camping gear and packaged food.

'Rachel told me what you're going to do,' Pete started, watching Lana fill her backpack.

Lana heard concern in the old man's tone and looked up. 'Hal needs my help.'

'Do you have everything you need?'

'I can only take what I can carry,' Lana replied. 'This will have to do.'

Rachel wished she could go with Lana. But it was too dangerous to send two people at once. 'Kim delivered this while you were finding supplies,' she said and handed Lana a case.

'She did it,' Lana said in hushed anticipation. She opened the case, took the ray gun out of its foam indent and turned it in her hands. She doubted Lustitians had followed 1960s sci-fi art and movies and yet the design was exactly from that era.

'Kim said it opens particle portals,' said Rachel. 'She called it a PP gun because it opens two portals at once: one you enter and another you exit.'

Lana smirked. '*Ray gun* sounds less urinary.'

'This is no time for jokes,' Pete cautioned. 'There may be more dangers than Wardens where you're going, Lana. You're not entering another version of our world. You could be entering another plane of existence. The rules of physics may not apply there. Physical matter–'

'I get it,' said Lana. 'Freaky dangers abound.'

'Expect anything and everything,' Pete continued. 'It could be any season, any type of weather. And however unlikely, you should know that what early cultures called demons, and what we call ghosts and apparitions, are all well documented, could in fact be real, and would therefore all come from somewhere… maybe where you're going.'

'Really?' Rachel gave Pete a disapproving look.

'Great,' said Lana. 'Ghosts and demons.' She sighed and raised her chin when an optimistic thought occurred to her. 'Well, at least that tropical lemonade… flavour thing isn't likely to happen.'

Pete took a long, patient breath while pinching the bridge of his nose. 'Entropic Cascade Failure.'

'You don't have to go right now,' said Rachel. 'If you're not ready–'

'Hal has been lost to us for days.' Lana did a last check over: food, water, ammo, first-aid kit. 'For him, that's months. He had no weapon, no supplies, nothing. I'm ready, Rache.' She changed her stance to strike an action pose, aiming her ray gun. 'Time to make PPs.'

'Oh, grow up,' said Pete, and he walked out of the room.

Lana burst out laughing, doubled over, and wheezed. A stifled snort escaped Rachel's lips.

Lana wiped tears from her eyes. 'Have you told Sam?'

Rachel shook her head. 'I don't want to worry her.'

'You have to tell her, Rache,' Lana insisted while strapping on a thigh holster to accommodate her ray gun. 'She needs to know what you're going through. I mean, come on. You can see the freakin' future.'

'Take this,' Pete interrupted, returning with a jetpack. 'I've linked the controls to your console. You can cover more ground.'

'Thanks, Professor.' Lana hefted the pack over her shoulder and stepped up onto the portal platform.

'Contact us as soon as you can,' Rachel said. 'Kim told me you can use the menu screen on top of the gun to open comms to us.'

Lana aimed her ray gun at the floor and pulled the trigger. She was enveloped by rippling mercury. Two seconds later, the portal flashed red, and it vanished in a blink.

Bright light blinded Lana and she dropped five feet from mid-air into snow. She found herself sliding down the side of a steep gradient, between pine trees a metre either side of her. Glare from the snow made it difficult to see. When a cliff edge came into view, Lana gasped and dug her heels in to try and reduce her speed. She unbuckled and shed her rucksack. While feeding both arms through the jetpack straps, she felt her body jettison over the edge of the cliff. She was upside down, staring wide-eyed at a forest and a river, a fatal fall below. She clipped the final strap over her chest, threw her arms wide and reoriented her body so her feet pointed at the cliff-face rushing away behind her.

The river was approaching, thirty meters below her, when the jetpack engine hummed to life. Lana hit the thrusters, sending her forward at a sharp horizontal angle across the water's surface. She was drenched when she dipped too low, skimming the water. She skirted the embankment and tucked her chin to avoid a face full of pine needles, but the pack struck a solid branch.

Lana rolled, flicking through reeds, before she could reorient herself. Tilting her head and arching her back gave her the ascent she needed to rise above the timber line.

She tapped at her wrist console, found the control menu and adjusted the power output. Now levelled out in an upright position, she swore when she spotted her backpack. It had burst, and her survival gear was strewn downstream.

When her eyes adjusted to take in the horizon, Lana saw snow-capped mountains and rivers forking between the forest. There were no structures. No signs of human life. But she could hear elk-like calls and could see a distant murmuration of what she assumed were starlings. Their ever-changing pattern of dipping and whirling flight mesmerised her.

The jetpack groaned. Lana's stomach was turned by the sudden inertial two-metre drop. The thrusters restabilised, and she decided now would be a good time to make a gradual descent to the embankment. Her feet touched down, and she breathed a sigh of relief at the sight of jagged rocks, which she would've hit earlier had Pete not given her the option of flight.

Lana pulled her ray gun and tapped a menu screen on top of it, opening comms to the Portal Hub.

'Rachel, Pete. I've arrived and I'm safe.'

The whisper of wind through the trees and the babble of the river did little to settle Lana's nerves. She let out a long, apprehensive sigh and walked downstream to retrieve her gear.

Liberty
Maximum Security Prison

Kordin and Xera had been given street clothes so they didn't cause alarm in public. Xera had taken more persuading but settled for tight, elastic materials. Predictably, all black.

Xera was walking the corridors with her escort when she stopped abruptly at a cell to her right. The comms device she was given sounded a tone.

'That was Danin's cell,' said Lincoln.

Xera entered. Danin's scent wasn't strong. He must have only stood inside for a minute before making his move. She followed her nose through doors to a corridor of meeting rooms.

Kordin was with Lincoln in the surveillance room, watching the footage of Danin's escape. There had been a loud noise, and the guards had spun around to see what it was. Danin ran to where Xera was now, shot at a window, clawed away the steel mesh and leapt out.

Kordin returned his attention to Xera. She looked like she'd found something inside a meeting room.

'A cleaner was used in here,' she said.

'All rooms and cells are sanitised weekly,' Lincoln told her.

Xera shook her head. 'Raekeem chemicals. Used to clean away blood. He was here.'

'He teleported in,' Lincoln said to Kordin. 'Do you have that on record?'

Kordin had been given link access to his ship computer. He checked the teleport log on the wrist console Lincoln had given him.

'There is no record of anyone coming here. Telsta may have used an algorithm that tracked his teleportation signature and erased each log after it was made.'

'Jericho was in that room,' Lincoln remembered out loud. 'He's a high-profile inmate. He was interviewed there recently.'

Xera crouched and ran her index finger along the corner of the wall. 'Carapace,' she said after inspecting the residue closely. She took in the scent and stood abruptly. 'He showed him.'

Lincoln glanced at Kordin. 'What does she mean?'

Kordin's jaw muscles twitched while he watched Xera standing motionless. 'Telsta showed your high-profile inmate his serpent form. Suffice to say, the two of them have an understanding.'

Ether Realm

Lana made camp, having spent the remaining light retrieving her gear. Hours passed and she could not sleep. She had been so eager to find Hal, she hadn't thought about how long it could take. How long she would have to go without company. Without a single soul to talk to.

Lana tucked in her chin and hugged her knees. A scurrying in the woods caused her to jump and stare into the darkness. *Where are the Wardens?* she asked herself. *They could be out there, watching.* She shook her head and tried to think practically. *They would have moved on from here.*

She yearned for morning. And when she finally did sleep, she did not wake again until the sun shone light through the trees. The warmth on her face was pleasant, and she rose feeling not only optimistic but adventurous. She walked to the stream to wash her face and fill a bottle of water. It tested safe, according to a scan she completed using her console.

Something caught her eye from across the stream. It was staggered writing. Large white letters were scrawled across the flat surfaces of the rocks facing the stream.

"Head south", Lana read. There was a break, and the last three letters spelled "Hal".

Lana ran back to her gear, pocketed, strapped and tied everything she could carry, and returned to the stream. The jetpack hummed to life, and she rose above the treetops to get the lay of the land. Her console displayed a sonar map of the area. She set a beacon in the south, leaned forward and hit the thrust. Nothing happened. She descended and took the pack off to assess the damage. Her collision with the pine branch had busted the fuselage. *Probably not safe to fly. Probably not smart to go rocketing over land, attracting the attention of possible hostiles, either.*

Marks on a tree caught Lana's attention. The riverbank rocks grinded under her feet when she ran to it. Hal had carved out an arrow pointing left. She stepped into the forest and saw another marked tree and another further ahead. Her heart raced, and she moved quickly, watching out for more of Hal's signs.

Chapter 27

Lana hiked all day through the cold and undulating rise and fall of wooded land. She stopped to eat a protein bar and to drink the last of the water she collected from the stream.

While resting, Lana admired the enormous trees. They were tall like redwoods, many over three metres wide. Her eyes snapped to a female figure walking along the forest floor. The last light of day obscured Lana in shadow, affording her the opportunity to approach undetected. She crouched and peered through the brush to try and discern whether the woman was armed.

Her wrist console screen lit up. She was about to turn it off when she read a notification she didn't understand. "Unknown language. Translation one hundred per cent." The woman ahead hadn't spoken. *Why—*

A twig snapped under Lana's knee. She froze.

'Show yourself,' the woman called out in English. 'I am unarmed.' Lana guessed by her young voice that she was aged around twenty. Her accent sounded Baltic.

Lana stepped cautiously into the light with her hands held away from her sides.

'Who are you?' the woman asked.

'My name is Lana. I—'

Her eyes widened, and she stared, open mouthed, when the young woman moved closer. She was a humanoid version of a red panda. Her fur was reddish brown with a white streak running from her snout to her hairline. But she had hair like a human's, chestnut coloured, hanging loose to her shoulders.

'I am Miri,' she said.

Norse embroidery was stitched into the long panel of what looked like wool between her legs. She was petite with strong arms, like a tennis player. *They probably don't play tennis here*, Lana thought. *Archer, maybe.*

Miri studied Lana's strange clothing. 'You have entered my people's territory, Lana. Why?'

'I'm…' Lana wiped her wet fringe away from her eyes. *Am I losing it? This girl looks exactly like the stuffed toy I've slept with since I was a kid!* 'I'm looking for my friend, Hal. Have you seen a human passing through here?'

Miri's brown eyes softened. She raised her narrow chin and nodded. Lana's hopes rose.

'He led a group,' said Miri. 'Not human.'

He led the Wardens through here?

'Can you tell me which way they went?'

Miri read the tired, desperate emotion in Lana's voice and in her eyes.

'I will tell you what I know. Follow me.' A log leaned against a nearby tree, and Miri took hold of a branch sticking out of it and pulled. The log was a camouflaged door to an opening in the two-metre-wide tree.

Miri stepped in and motioned for Lana to follow. She closed the door once they were both inside the pitch-black space, then tugged twice on a rope. This signalled what Lana guessed to be a pulley system operated by somebody above them.

Light crept into the elevating compartment, and Miri caught Lana staring. She raised her eyebrows expectantly.

'Sorry. I've never seen anyone like you,' Lana said. 'I am not from this world.'

'When did you arrive?'

'Yesterday.'

Miri nodded slowly. 'This will be a lot for you to take in. My people are Fyrst Born. You are human?'

'Yes.'

The wooden cage in which they were ascending arrived at a rope bridge. Miri walked out across it and raised her hand to her right then to her left. Lana only saw the archers for a split second before they disappeared from view. The tree-mounted huts they were posted in were well camouflaged.

Miri opened a door to the adjoining tree, and Lana followed her into a wool-carpeted room where braziers were glowing, creating a subtle orange hue against the carved walls. Wood smoke rose up and out of louvred windows. Two female humanoid red pandas were seated at a table, sharing a bowl of what looked like spiced dry mushrooms. They stood, each dropping a hand to a short sword sheathed at their side.

'Stand down,' Miri ordered and kept walking to a door on the opposite side of the room. The guards resumed their game, the object of which appeared to be placing clay pieces to make their symbols join a sequence with the others already placed. Lana stopped briefly to see that the markings on the pieces were very similar to Germanic from the runic alphabet. Though experiencing this new culture was indeed a lot for her to process, their tree dwelling, its warmth and woody aroma, created a cosy atmosphere.

Miri beckoned for her to follow. 'I'll take you to my sister's tree and find you a bed.'

'You said you would tell me what you know,' Lana protested.

'You cannot act on news of your "Hal" without rest and then food,' she insisted. 'Come.'

Home Realm
Liberty
Maximum Security Prison

Kim entered the surveillance room. Lincoln turned and raised an expectant eyebrow at her.

'Spectral analysis confirms that the mass teleportation was not triggered remotely,' she reported. 'Someone teleported in, activated the sequence, and was taken along with all of the inmates.'

'The prisoners will most likely be confined and processed for mutation,' Kordin said.

'How long until they're turned into Wardens?' Lincoln asked.

'A day at the most.'

'My people have heard of Telsta switching places with a creature…' Kim paused and tapped at her pad. 'But our sources couldn't determine its species or where it came from. If there is any physical trace of it, we could run a search for planets containing that life form.'

'Can you trace its origin from a sample?' Kordin asked. 'Xera found one just now. And I killed the serpent. Its body was destroyed along with our carrier, but my sword–'

'We have your weapons locked in our armoury,' said Kim. And she turned to Lincoln. 'I'll get to work on testing and contact you once we have a trace. Have you received word from Lana?'

'I'm out of the loop on that,' Lincoln said with a quizzical look. 'I'm surprised your Captain directed you to help her. I assumed the Raekeem would be your people's top priority here.'

'Part of our mandate requires us to support law enforcement in each solar system we travel to,' Kim explained. 'The Captain has chosen to recruit Lana.'

'You want to deputise Lana?' Lincoln's posture straightened in surprise.

'He will give you the full details of his proposal,' Kim replied distractedly after a text transmission beeped on her pad. 'Apologies, Commander. I'm needed aboard my ship.'

'Does Professor O'Conner keep biological samples from the worlds your people have travelled to?' Kordin asked Lincoln.

Lincoln gave him a considering look. 'You think Telsta hid his serpent in a Realm, not a different planet.'

'Yes. O'Conner may be able to search his database of Realms for that biological signature.' Kordin mirrored Lincoln's studying gaze. 'One of the Raekeem Lords built machines like you and programmed them to maintain ship systems. They proved more reliable than human slaves. I have a point to make,' he said, raising a hand when Lincoln's brow furrowed in offence. 'Though Telsta was pressured by his fellow Lords to follow suit, he forbade it.'

'Alright, I'll bite. Why?'

'After harvesting their essence, a human's remaining brain functions make them a safe tool to use. Telsta believed the other Lords were unwittingly harbouring automatons with developmental potential.' Kordin's gaze turned to Xera. 'Telsta fears what he cannot control… trusts what he *can* control.' He made a fist tightly. 'When we find him' – his teeth clenched – 'we will use that trust against him.'

Ether Realm

Lana woke to the smell of porridge and, through waking eyes, peered around the storage room. It was warmly lit by an iron brazier. The walls were shelved, holding jars of flour, oats, dried berries and grain. Lana rose from her cot of woollen blankets and stretched, feeling refreshed after her long sleep. She was rolling her neck when she thought she saw the sheet hanging from the ceiling move. It was the door to the kitchen.

Lana had hung all of her clothes on a pole mounted below the ceiling to dry overnight. She reached on her tiptoes to collect her underwear.

'Come away from there,' Miri hissed from the kitchen.

Lana saw a red panda girl peeking from behind the sheet. She gave the girl a smile before she scurried away.

Once dressed, Lana greeted the young girl, Miri and another adult Fyrst Born, joining them at a table in the dining room.

'My niece has never seen a human before,' Miri explained apologetically.

She introduced her older sister, a woman with grey flecks through her red fur, who looked up from her berry-coloured porridge. 'Welcome to our home.'

'I will show you where your friend was headed after we eat,' said Miri, pushing a bowl to Lana. She moved a plate of berries, picked fresh that morning, closer as well.

'Thank you. I don't know how I can repay you.'

'Well…' Miri's sister started, with a hopeful look, but in a frustrated tone. 'We have a problem you could–'

'This is not her world, sister,' Miri interjected. 'We cannot involve her.'

'Please.' Lana glanced openly between the two sisters. 'How can I help?'

'We trade with humans on the other side of the valley,' Miri's sister explained. 'We have a two-day window this month to meet them on the road that skirts the river.'

'We always take the path from the edge of our forest,' Miri added. She used her bowl as their forest and ran her nail across the table to the plate of berries. Lana thought it curious that her nail did not mark the wood or make a sound when she drew the map.

'We travel a road through Tundra Country,' Miri continued. 'Down to the river road. It is the only way.'

Miri's sister clenched her fists. 'A tribe of deformed creatures have taken control of the Tundra road. We cannot pass unless we pay their "taxes".' She huffed. 'We will not pay.'

Reading a look in her younger sister's eyes that begged compassion, she pressed her lips together and returned her gaze to Lana. 'True, they are surviving harsh conditions. This makes them desperate. It is only a matter of time before they invade our forest.'

'In what way are they deformed?' Lana asked, her suspicions growing.

'They are mostly human in form,' said Miri and looked down at her arms. 'One I saw had more arms than two.' She touched her nose. 'Another had an ugly snout.'

Lana supposed that the Wardens were stripped of their mutagen and those who survived kept their animal-gene-spliced forms.

'And these are the ones who were travelling with Hal?' she asked.

Miri nodded. 'We didn't stop them because none of them seemed to know they were walking beneath an entire village of Fyrst Born. They were unarmed, destitute. We let them go.' She looked to her sister, who had drawn an arm around her teenage daughter's shoulders. 'Had we known they would become so hostile…'

'How many?'

'Our scouts counted about fifty,' Miri's sister answered.

This number surprised Lana. She'd seen hundreds of Wardens taken by the particle ray.

'I'll speak with them,' she decided.

Miri's brow furrowed. 'Lana, these are dangerous people. We captured one of their scouts two days ago–'

'She tried to kill herself,' Miri's sister exclaimed. 'Why would they assume we would resort to torture?'

Lana caught Miri's niece dropping extra berries into her porridge while her mother wasn't looking before spooning a serve too big for her mouth. She pushed it between her lips, chomping and dribbling her breakfast down her chin.

'Did the scout say anything?' Lana queried.

Miri shook her head. 'She refuses to speak.'

'Tell me your terms,' Lana said confidently. 'I'll negotiate on your behalf.'

'Thank you.' Miri's sister planted her elbows on the table, clasped her hands together and rested her chin on them. 'We must call a meeting with the elders.'

Miri found a quill, a pot of ink and a sheet of rough paper for her sister to begin writing. Then she left to speak with the Fyrst Born elders of the forest.

Home Realm
San Francisco
Portal Hub

'Rachel, Pete…'

Pete hurried up to the communications deck and hit the receiver. 'Lana, are you alright?' He waited for a response. 'Lana, if you can hear me, we've received word from Captain–'

'I've arrived and I'm safe.'

Pete realised there was a delay in the communication relay between Home Realm and Ether Realm.

'I'm glad you're alright, Lana,' he said. 'We're going to send in backup. As you know, that can only be one person. We'll wait until you send us coordinates and confirm that someone else can enter. Pete out.'

Rachel arrived at the communications deck. 'Was that Lana? Is she alright?'

'She's safe. I told her we can send help.'

'Good… good.' Rachel breathed a sigh of relief. 'Lincoln is here. He wants us to search our database for–'

Lincoln entered the deck, followed by Sentinels Kordin and Xera. Pete saw them, pulled a handgun from a holster concealed beneath the desk and aimed it at Kordin.

'Woah, woah!' Rachel stood in front of Kordin.

'Pete, it's okay,' said Lincoln. 'They're helping us.'

Pete glared at Kordin. 'What did you do to Oskar?'

Kordin stepped in front of Rachel, a foot from Pete's gun. 'My uncle was subjected to an intense memory purge. It killed him.'

Pete lowered the weapon, but his expression was no less stern. 'He was a good man.' He returned the gun to the holster and spoke past Kordin. 'What can I do for you, Commander?'

Everybody was able to breathe again, and Lincoln sat next to Pete. 'We have a lead on Telsta. He switched places with a serpent creature.' He set a test tube down on the console. 'Xera found this residue in a room where Telsta met with Jericho Williams. Kim is working on a bigger sample. She'll be in contact with you.'

Pete raised an eyebrow at Lincoln. 'Telsta's creature killed Jericho Williams?'

'He was alive when he was taken.'

'Taken to be assimilated along with the other inmates, I assume,' said Pete with an unkind glance at Kordin and Xera.

'Telsta may have used his serpent to convince Jericho that he was a power worth joining,' said Lincoln.

'No,' Kordin said bluntly. 'Telsta would have given your inmates a choice. Not to join him but to serve. Serve or die.'

'Pete.' Lincoln glanced at the test tube. 'If you can trace the serpent's origin, we can find Telsta, Jericho. All of them.'

Pete held the sample of carapace scales floating in cloudy, viscous liquid up to the light. 'I'll see what I can do.' He looked back at Lincoln. 'I need to send someone to help Lana. Rachel shouldn't go in her condition. Who is your best operative?'

Lincoln tucked his chin and raised an eyebrow at Pete. 'You don't trust Valhez to send–'

'It's *Lana*.'

Lincoln considered the fatherly concern in Pete's furrowed brow. 'I'll bring you my best soldier.'

Chapter 28

Ether Realm

The meeting concerning negotiations with the Tundra tribe – whom Lana knew to be the Raekeem – took all afternoon and all night. Periods of recess gave the elders time to rest. During that time, the warriors among the Fyrst Born discussed the possibility of a violent outcome. Miri's sister feared retaliation, arguing that the Tundra tribe would see the proposal as a threat. Lana decided it was time to tell them all exactly who these hostile people were. While explaining the conflict between humans and the Raekeem, Lana could see in the warriors' eyes that peace may not be achievable. Yet to her astonishment, the Fyrst Born insisted that the proposal of a treaty go ahead as planned.

'Thank you for informing us of their propensity for violence,' said Miri. 'However, we wish to give the Raekeem an alternative rather than an ultimatum. We will provide assistance in relocating them from the Tundra to grasslands in the west, near the coast.'

Lana was in awe of these people. Their compassion and willingness to help a potential enemy equalled their dedication to protecting their own people.

'How will you communicate this in written form?' she asked Miri. 'Have you studied their language?'

Miri ushered Lana to the table where a slender Fyrst Born was adding the final touches to the peace accord. Lana was impressed by the woman's illustrations. Though simple and stylised, the many frames' portrayal of gatherings, partnership and relocation was perfectly clear.

It had been an exhausting process, planning for possible outcomes and putting security measures in place, including evacuation of the children and the infirm. All of this was going through Lana's mind while she bedded down. Her head had just touched her pillow when her Shifter console alerted her to a received transmission. It was converted to text, and when she read it, her heart was warmed by Professor O'Conner's words. She missed everybody from Home Realm, and she wondered how their hunt for Telsta was faring.

Miri knocked on the wall outside. 'Lana? May I speak with you?'

'Of course. Come in.'

Miri entered and sat beside Lana.

'This must be a very unsettling time for you,' Lana offered. 'I'm going to do everything I can to make this work.'

'Thank you.' Miri tried to smile, but she was obviously anxious. Her hands were clasped, each kneading the other. 'We only use weapons for hunting. And we only train to fight because of the threat of less peaceful settlements and their constant warring. Most of them leave us alone. But these people in the Tundra… they see us as prey.'

Lana tilted her head. 'I'm not sure what you mean.'

'We evolved the ability to emit electrical signals,' Miri continued. 'When our signal reaches the brain of any creature, it interacts with the neural pathways that influence sensory perception.'

Lana raised her chin and let out a long, 'Ooh. You were speaking literally. They actually *see* you as prey.'

Lana also realised how it was possible for her translator to have achieved one hundred per cent accuracy before Miri had spoken a single word. It received her electrical signals like a kind of cheat sheet.

'So,' Lana queried further, 'the way I see you now…'

'Is not my true form,' Miri prompted. 'It is a defence mechanism we can use once our brains are fully developed. Our signal basically tells your brain to see us as whatever you perceive as nonthreatening. Comforting, even.'

'You're not red pandas?' Lana said, disappointed.

'I don't know what that is.'

Lana reached her hand over Miri's thigh and paused. 'Do you mind?'

Miri shook her head, and Lana gently patted her soft fur coat.

'You feel like the animal I see you as,' said Lana.

'Right now, your brain is refusing to interpret what you are physically feeling as anything other than a "red panda".' Miri straightened her posture and flicked her hair back to give a better view of her appearance. 'Close your eyes for a moment. Concentrate. When you open them again… try to look through me.'

Lana closed her eyes.

'We look like you. Our skin is painted in decoration according to the season. The clothes you have seen are what we wear.'

'I've seen dozens of your people, but so far, no males,' Lana commented, her eyes still closed. 'Do they live apart from you?'

'All Fyrst Born are what your people call feminine in nature.'

Lana opened her eyes and tried staring through Miri. She began to blur. 'All of you? How do you reproduce?' Lana allowed her eyes to wander over Miri, starting with her bare legs and feet. She didn't see fur but smooth freckled flesh, painted with intricate white flowing patterns.

'Only a third of us are born with one reproductive organ. The majority of us—'

'Huh?' Lana met Miri's pensive brown eyes. She found herself unable to disengage, and a kind of warmth kindled in her chest she had never in her life known before.

A lock of Miri's chestnut hair swung across her left cheek when she asked, 'Are you okay?'

She was no longer the red panda she had appeared to be only moments earlier.

'The majority of us have both sex organs,' Miri continued. 'Here, I can show you.'

Lana quickly slapped her hand down on Miri's crotch, in an attempt to stop her from lifting her sash, then slid back upon feeling Miri's reaction to her touch. She was embarrassed and no less so when she stumbled her next words. 'You have both parts?'

Miri's freckled cheeks blushed. 'Is this not common among your species?'

'It's, it's…' Lana stammered, struggling to regain her composure. 'It's uncommon.' She decided to change the subject. 'It's freezing out there. How do your people wear so little?' she asked, gesturing to Miri's lack of upper body clothing.

'We normally wear wool in the cold,' said Miri, crossing one leg over the other. 'I did not have time to don my coat when I stepped out to intercept you the other day.'

Lana noticed that Miri had become shy since their brief physical contact. 'You knew I was coming.'

'Our scouts spotted you. I volunteered to make contact.' Miri nodded to a woollen piece hanging by the doorway. She dared not stand to retrieve it for Lana. 'That one is yours. For your journey.'

Lana had assumed that the grey and white length of wool hanging by the door was a blanket. When she stood and took it down from its hook, she saw that it was a half-length coat. It was surprisingly light. 'Miri, this is… beautiful. Thank you.'

Miri began to relax and resume eye contact with Lana. 'The wool is shorn from the Mountain Folk. Their heads and torsos are human, but their lower bodies are four-legged and hoofed.'

'You're kidding.' Lana let out an exasperated laugh. 'First you tell me you can control how people see you. Then you tell me you're fully equipped. Now you're telling me there are *centaurs* in this Realm?' She raised her hand apologetically. 'Sorry, I'm just a little overwhelmed.'

Miri's bottom lip pushed up and she nodded. 'I should let you rest.' She stood to leave.

'No. Stay,' said Lana. 'Please.' She sat down with Miri and returned the conversation to its narrative flow. 'The centaurs shear each other's coats?'

Miri turned her head to one side. 'I do not know centaurs. But yes. They make and trade the finest winter clothing.'

Lana and Miri talked for another hour, asking questions about each other's species. Lana explained the normal growth process for a human and was surprised to learn from Miri that Fyrst Born grew to bodily adulthood quite rapidly. This explained the seemingly teenage girl's behaviour, stuffing porridge into her mouth like a child. Miri also described the long span of time Fyrst Born young were allowed to be children and how play was a sacred, life-long skill, never to be discouraged.

Lana wanted to know if the Fyrst Born used their ability to appear more formidable against their attackers.

'We can display ourselves as demons,' Miri replied casually.

'Wow,' Lana exclaimed. 'Okay, show me your game face.'

She saw that Miri didn't understand, so she made her own look of intimidation – leaning forward, shoulders squared, brow furrowed, teeth bared – and she growled.

Miri laughed. She looked away for a moment and rolled her neck and shoulders to loosen her muscles.

Lana jumped when Miri turned back. Her eyes were glowing fiery orange. Her body paint was stone-black on her now marble-red skin, and she bared tiger-like teeth.

Miri grinned and returned to her true form. 'Unfortunately, this does not work on the Raekeem. If their past was half as violent as you described, it makes sense now why they see us as prey.'

'They must have seen horrors we can only imagine,' Lana agreed. 'But they don't scare me. It'll be my honour to help your people.'

Miri looked Lana up and down. 'I see now why he loved you so.'

'Excuse me?'

'Your friend, Hal, passed through our village many times. Alone at first, then after many months, he came with a wolf woman.'

'He went back to the waterfall where he arrived,' Lana said wistfully. 'He's been waiting for me.'

Miri's expression changed from hopeful to despondent. 'It seemed that way for a time, but Lana, I think he and—' She watched Lana staring off, clearly thinking about Hal. She placed her hand on Lana's, hoping to reach her.

Lana drew back her hand to yawn and stretch. 'I'm sorry, I must be tuckered. What were you saying?'

'I will bring clothes for you in the morning,' Miri answered impassively. 'You don't want to look conspicuous.' She stood and turned to give Lana a smile before she slipped through the cloth doorway. 'Sleep well, Lana.'

'Good night.'

Chapter 29

Home Realm
San Francisco
Portal Hub

Pete ran a search in the Realm database that flagged samples taken from worlds scouted by their land rover, samples that closely matched the serpent scales. The little robot was used during Earth's early space exploration. It worked fine, and Pete bought it for a fraction of what it had cost to build back in the day. One of the hundreds of Realms the rover was sent to could be the world Telsta was hiding in. The amount of morphological data coming through was too much for Pete to analyse by himself, so he called Sam for assistance.

Rachel was waiting in the portal room for her. The mercury sphere expanded, and Sam stepped out. She opened her arms in time to receive Rachel, and they embraced each other.

'You're okay?' Sam held Rachel's shoulders at arms-length, looking her over.

Rachel hesitated. 'I have to tell you something…'

Sam listened with growing concern while Rachel explained what happened: her collapsing after the skirmish aboard the Raekeem carrier ship and being admitted to hospital, where she had a vision of the future.

'So you somehow… transferred your consciousness forward to some other temporal plane,' Sam speculated. 'To the future.'

'A possible future,' Rachel added.

'And you think it has something to do with the medication my dad gave you for your Mitochondrial Memory?'

'I don't know.' Rachel shrugged. 'Maybe there's no way of stopping my brain from tapping into either the past or the future.'

'I'll work with Dad to find a way to dampen the effects,' Sam offered. She saw her father appear at the door to the portal room. 'Hey, Dad.' She approached and gave him a hug. 'You must feel popular. Every time a new enemy attacks us, they want to kidnap you.'

Pete sighed ruefully. He didn't tell Sam that had he been taken, he would have been pumped full of drugs and had his mind purged. He wouldn't have fared any better than Oskar.

'Any promising pings on the sample trace?' Sam asked.

'The intra and interspecific variations are being processed,' he said. 'If your mother were here, we'd have this done in half the time.'

'Mum was the most efficient taxonomist in the biology community,' Sam agreed.

'But with your skills,' Pete said, optimistically, 'I'm sure we'll find a match soon.' He looked to Rachel. 'You told her. Good.'

'It wasn't your fault, Dad. You couldn't have known that Rachel's meds would have such a wildly adverse effect.'

'Come on,' said Rachel, ushering them both to the command level. 'I'm no taxidermist, but surely there's something I can do to help.'

'Taxonomist,' Sam corrected.

'Whatever,' Rachel huffed.

Silica
Desert outside Liberty

The Cheney Fracking fields had been cleared of all mining machinery, buildings and vehicles. Plans for residential and commercial expansion were at the pre-utility phase. So Talon had the land to herself, where she worked on the Raekeem craft she'd procured after the destruction of the Branner Factory. She had located and liberated it from a UC Security impound bay.

The salt wind blew over her. The bright light of the welding torch reflected off her protective goggles. Once she'd finished installing the final high-powered magnet, she rolled under the left wing and made her way around to the loading bay door. Her retrofit would enable the craft to attach itself to any metal surface. Although the magnets were powerful enough to support the weight of the ship in an inverted position in planet surface gravity, she planned to use the upgrade to travel attached to larger ships and enter other regions of space undetected.

After running translation software, Talon was able to study every file on the ship computer relating to specs, functionality, maintenance and repair. She found that she had been very lucky to attain this ship.

It was an impressive design, equipped not only with forward cannons and cloaking but also with very unique shielding. The wings could extend, fan out and close over the craft. The wing tips would meet at the nose, creating an inverted bowl shape. And when the shielding completed this shape, an electromagnetic charge was emitted across the wing array. The charge created an external barrier which could deflect energy blasts.

When Talon had activated the shield, and she had seen its magnificent ingenuity in action, she had decided to call her ship the Black Heron.

The ship was equipped with an infirmary and bunk beds, as well as a toilet and shower. The armoury was a wall on the left side of the loading bay, which had stored Raekeem weapons until the ship had been fleeced by UC security.

After washing the grime of mechanical oil off herself, Talon dressed in gym clothes she found in a drawer. The proximity alarm sounded, and she heard the sentry turret on top of her ship rotate.

Talon stepped outside to find Lincoln standing twenty metres away. She hit the "cease fire" command and the turret resumed sentry, ready to fire on any other intruders.

Lincoln approached with his hands away from his sides, palms facing Talon.

'I'm alone,' he called. 'And I have a favour to ask.'

Lincoln received an "out with it" head movement from Talon, so he closed the gap between them at an even pace. He glanced to the setting sun, shielding his eyes from salt picked up by the cool wind. 'I need your expertise.'

Talon moved to block Lincoln's path to the loading bay ramp.

He stopped and spoke reassuringly. 'I'm not here for your ship. You procured it, so it's yours. My friend Lana is in a dangerous place. She needs backup.'

Everybody in the Universal Community knew who Lana was. Talon had had little time to catch up on recent history, but what she had learned was enough to impress her. Lana, Rachel, and Lincoln too. These people were heroes.

Talon had no real plans for the future. Her immediate goal was to avoid being enlisted like all of the other AMs were, to avoid being made to serve.

She appreciated Lincoln treating her like an equal. He came alone with a request, an offer – as Talon saw it – of purpose. Right now, she didn't know what hers was. She looked at Lincoln and nodded.

'Excellent.' Lincoln tapped out a message on his wrist comms device. 'I'll have units make sure your ship is safe while you're gone, which probably won't be long. I'm told time moves a lot quicker where Lana is. How soon can you be ready to–'

Talon tapped through two command menus on a slim Raekeem remote control.

Lincoln's eyebrows rose while he watched the Black Heron transform. The wings extended, swung around to meet its nose and locked into place to create its impenetrable shield.

'Outstanding,' he said. 'Let's go.'

Ether Realm

Miri guided Lana to the edge of the forest, to a path that would lead her to the Tundra. Miri wished her luck and returned to her people to continue preparations in the event of a bad outcome. With the peace accord in her backpack, Lana continued her long hike through the valley and into the Tundra land.

Soon, she found herself very much alone. Lana had been in Ether Realm for four days and still had not found any real evidence that Hal was alive.

The sun dipped below the tree line, and the trail ahead became too difficult to see, forcing Lana to make camp. She found a clearing by a stream running along the valley floor. She collected twigs and fallen branches for a fire and then tied twine at shin height between the trees surrounding her. Miri had given her shells, once homes to what she imagined were quite large, slimy creatures. She tied them as per Miri's instruction, so the shells would make enough sound to wake her were anything to trip on the twine. Lana thought it was sweet of Miri to be so concerned. She thought a lot about the Fyrst Born and wanted to know more about them.

Lana found comfort in the thought of backup. She had replied to Professor O'Conner's offer the previous night and had given him the coordinates of the broken jetpack she'd left in the forest, so if whoever was sent in could fix it, they could use it to catch up with her on the Tundra trail. Calculating coordinates relative to Lana's point of entry was easy because her wrist console had been tracking her all the way from the cliff she'd fallen from. She'd activated a transponder on the jetpack before leaving it, and it was linked to her wrist console. Whoever arrived in the forest would be able to link their console to the transponder, thereby automatically connecting to Lana's location. And initiating that link was going to send an alert to Lana's console, letting her know that backup was on its way.

Lana woke in the dimness of early morning light to the sound of shells clinking together. The sound came again, this time from the opposite side of her camp. A hooded figure reached down, grabbed her sleeping bag and pulled it away, right before a second intruder pounced. He landed on top of the bunched ferns Lana had arranged under her sleeping bag in the shape of a body. The two Raekeem men looked at each other, perplexed.

Though fog had enveloped her camp, Lana could see clearly enough to watch from up in a tree. Another man stepped over the twine perimeter. He looked around for any sign of their prey. Lana remained hidden on her bed of leafed branches that she'd laid across the thick limbs of the tree above her camp. The intruders searched the surrounding area for some time. When they finally decided to leave, Lana climbed down and followed through the bushes. There were two Raekeem men and a woman as well. They looked dirty and malnourished.

After following them out of the fog, down a dirt path, Lana lost sight of one of them. The other two continued on, walking at a casual pace. Lana froze at the sound of footfalls before being spear-tackled from her left and pinned to the ground.

'Off her!' a woman shouted. She shoved the man away from Lana. He glared at his attacker, another female Raekeem, and bared two fat teeth that were thick like tusks. Lana saw that he had a pig snout as well.

'We have been searching for you for days,' he said to the woman, and added in an accusatory tone, 'We were beginning to think you had deserted us. If you have sided with Hal, you are dead to us. Molren is our leader now.'

'I would not abandon my people, you fool,' the woman retorted. 'I made camp when the weather turned sour.'

'By the sound of your voice, you have taken ill. Do not slow us down, woman.' He called out to the others, then jabbed a stubby finger at Lana. 'Hold her while I fetch the rope.'

As soon as he was gone, the Raekeem woman flashed brown eyes at Lana, before changing them back to white.

'Miri?' Lana whispered.

'I thought you could use some help,' she said quietly. 'This is the form of the scout we captured.'

Miri's hair was long, black and tousled. She was thin like the others, her skin pale.

Lana stood and turned her back to Miri so she could take hold of her arms.

'The ugly one said your friend, Hal, was once their leader,' Miri whispered.

'I hope he's–' Lana paused when she heard the other Raekeem approaching. 'Let me go!' she shouted at Miri.

The three Raekeem arrived, and Lana's wrists were bound.

The pig-faced one demanded a scouting report from Miri. She told them that the "Wood Folk", as the Raekeem called the Fyrst Born, were well armed with ranged weapons, and that it would be foolish to provoke them. One of Lana's captors muttered something under her breath. The others grunted agreement, hung their heads and marched in silence.

Miri trailed behind, holding Lana's restraints. She whispered that it would take several hours to reach the Raekeem camp.

Lana asked her what the Raekeem woman had said.

'Better to fight than die of starvation,' Miri answered.

Chapter 30

Lana's captors spied a three-tent camp ahead and quickened their pace, forcing Miri to react as well. One Raekeem woman was on watch outside the camp, and she ran to gather the others. Eight people formed two defensive lines.

The pig-faced man stopped a few metres away from them and shouted, 'You were banished from the Tundra! Leave!'

Lana saw that these Raekeem were also malnourished. She gasped when she heard a man reply in a tone that commanded authority.

'Do not threaten us, Hog,' said Hal. 'We've stopped to gather our strength.' He saw Lana staring at him, and he strode toward her, bearded and weathered, hardly believing his eyes.

Hog stepped into Hal's path, puffed his chest and bared his teeth. Hal head-butted him without hesitation and Hog fell into the mud.

The other Raekeem rushed at each other. Hal shouted and opened his arms between them before they could clash. 'This is between me and him!'

Miri realised she was lingering at the back and dashed in to lift Hog from the muck. Hog shook her off and spat at Hal's feet.

'You are a dead man,' he seethed, and he glared at Hal's party of outcasts. 'Molren will have your heads!'

Hal took hold of Lana's arm before she could be pulled away. 'She stays with me.'

Hog stopped and turned slowly, reaching for a knife sheathed on his lower back.

'No,' she whispered, giving Hal a warning look and a shake of her head. 'I'll be fine. Someone is coming from Home Realm as backup.

Take your group to the Wood Folk. Tell them I sent you.' She received a tug at the rope that bound her wrists and Miri shoved her from behind.

Hog was last to move on. He and Hal stared death into each other's eyes.

Hog's party walked for another two hours through arid land before finally arriving at the Tundra camp. Guards stood at the beginning of two staggered rows of tepee-style tents. Lana counted ten. Some were patchworks of stitched hide and others were hemp-tied bark. Lana was taken to the biggest tent, which was roped to keep its tall conical shape stable. Hog tripped her to her knees in front of a heavyset Raekeem man seated at a wooden throne.

'Lord Molren,' said Hog, and bowed. 'We bring a prisoner. And I must report that Hal and his band of traitor scum are camped not far from here. I will leave with more warriors at once to–'

'You will leave them be,' Molren commanded. The new leader of the Raekeem had DNA spliced with a lion's, complete with a prominent black mane, and when he spoke, he revealed large sharp teeth.

'Hal spoke with this human,' said Hog. 'I believe she is a spy.'

Molren leaned on a wooden staff and gazed down at Lana. 'You know Hal?'

'I know of him,' she said, thinking up a story on the spot. 'Word has spread of Hal and his savages. How he has tamed them.'

'You lie!' Hog spat.

'My land is between the Forest and the Mountain Folk's,' Lana continued. 'We are all allied.' Her last word was a threat.

Alarm erupted among the Raekeem that had begun crowding into the tent.

Molren thumped the ground with his staff, quelling the unrest. 'And you are here to gauge our strength? You and your allies plan to attack us?'

'On the contrary, I am here on behalf of the Fyrst Born, the Wood Folk, as you call them. They do not take kindly to your taxes.' Lana turned and glared at Hog. 'Instead of simply wiping you out...' She resumed eye contact with Molren. 'The Fyrst Born offer peace. You can't farm here, and there is little to hunt. The allied lands thrive on partnership. Become our ally. Thrive with us.'

More of the Raekeem had gathered outside the tent. Arguments for and against Lana's offer began, and Miri slipped away to speak out among them.

'I want to hunt game,' she said behind one group, and moved on to infiltrate another. 'How can we survive without crops?' she complained. 'How can we hope to rear children?'

Voices were raised in agreement with Miri's words. The Raekeem became rowdy, calling out their concerns for the future.

'Enough!' Molren shouted. His eyes wandered around the now full tent and to the crowd pressing in from outside. 'For generations, it has been the Raekeem way to serve our Lord, to travel through space to plentiful worlds, to take what we need in order to survive.'

Molren stood from his throne and slowly walked through the crowd. 'You chose me over Hal because you want to live like Raekeem! To fight like Raekeem!'

The crowd responded to his shout with approving roars, as Molren made his way outside the tent to a slab of rock.

'You want to take what you need!' he hollered, driving their captive momentum.

Hog raised his arms with his fellow warriors, enthralled by their leader.

'You will die for your Lord!' Molren continued. 'You will serve as Raekeem have for generations!'

Lana and Miri exchanged a look of defeat. But when Lana returned her gaze to Molren, she saw that he had led his mate, a short woman with a strong build, out of the tent. Molren helped her climb onto the rock podium and stepped up beside her.

'Answer me this, then, my Raekeem…' Molren raised his voice louder, his deep tone thumping every chest in the audience. 'When your Lord has taken you to all lands… when you have killed the last of the humans, the Wood Folk, the Mountain Folk… when you have taken everything they have…'

Molren drew a lungful of air and lion-roared at his people. 'What then?'

The Raekeem were stunned into silence.

Molren lifted his mate's shirt to reveal she was pregnant. He had roared so harshly that his next words were hoarse. 'What future does my child have… when there is nothing left for you to take?'

Miri wiped a tear from her cheek. She found herself in awe of a creature whom only moments earlier presented enormous threat. Her hand found Lana's of its own accord.

Lana glanced down at her touch. She gasped in alarm. Miri's painted skin emerged, and her hair turned brown.

The wave of emotion had caused Miri to revert back to her true form. The Raekeem men and women standing close took several steps back, causing those behind to stumble.

Hog looked in the direction of the commotion and drew his knife. 'Seize them!'

Miri and Lana were grabbed. Molren stepped down and strode through the crowd to see for himself.

'My Lord, she looked like our scout,' Hog stammered. 'We had no idea they possessed cloaking technology.'

'We don't,' said Miri, speaking quickly and directly to Molren. 'Your scout is unharmed. We seek peace.'

Molren raised his hand to silence her and looked around at his fellow Raekeem. 'How many more of you are posing as us?'

'Only I,' Miri answered. 'You stand to lose nothing by taking a moment to consider our proposal.'

One of the Raekeem who had taken Lana's backpack found the document and handed it to Molren. He unfurled the scroll and looked from one frame to the next, taking in each illustration with growing interest. He glanced at Hog and to the people around him.

'It is not my decision to make,' he said finally. He held the paper high and raised his voice. 'The Wood Folk promise us better land, where we can fish and hunt game. There, we will have a place to raise our families. Do I sign?'

Murmurs started. People were nodding, and words were shouted. 'Food! Family!'

Molren pressed his thumb into his top right fang, broke his skin and signed the peace accord in his own blood. He handed the document to Miri and raised her arm so all could see that the two of them were in agreement. The entire camp roared in applause.

Hog spat at the ground, and Lana heard him mutter, 'That scum has poisoned their minds. He'll be dead before he knows of this.'

Lana turned her head and glared at him. 'What did you say?'

Molren heard Hog's words as well. 'Hog… What did you do?'

Hog cowered when his Lord stood over him, glowering. He tried to obscure himself in the crowd, but the Raekeem around him could see Molren's anger and seized him.

'My Lord,' Hog stammered. 'Hal is a traitor. He and his–'

Molren struck Hog with the back of his hand. 'What did you do?' he demanded.

Hog wiped the blood from his split lip. 'Two of Hal's group are ours. I ordered them to kill Hal and the others in their sleep. Tonight.'

Chapter 31

Hal's group were on their way to the Fyrst Born forest. They made camp at nightfall and all but one, who remained on watch, were soon asleep in their tents.

The man on watch had a Tarsier gene splice. His eyes were large and he could turn his head almost one hundred and eighty degrees. He sat hunched, his large hands and feet planted on a mound overlooking the path they had travelled on uphill. Luminescent bugs flickered in sparse groups over the rocky, bracken-covered field. He felt assured that should Hog come seeking a fight, he would spot the fool well before he could attack.

A noise caused his head to swivel and he pulled his knife. 'Announce yourself, Slither,' he scolded a male Raekeem who'd been given reptile DNA. 'I could have killed you.'

'Old habits,' Slither replied apologetically. He gazed up at the stars and sighed. 'Of all the ill fates, I never would have guessed being stuck on a planet like this would be ours. I was Feen's best infiltrator. Spotless record; after so many worlds, not once was my cover blown.'

'Your forbears would have been proud,' the watchman complimented him.

'Indeed. And I am proud to have carried on their legacy of skilled stealth and deception. A legacy lost since Telsta dropped us into the Three Kingdoms' meat-grinder.'

'Stark-raving mad fool,' the Tarsier grumbled. 'I wonder what became of him. Kordin said–'

He paused when Slither leaned abruptly into the shadows.

'What was that?' Slither exclaimed in a whisper. He waited until the watchman swivelled his head in the direction he'd indicated, probing the dark with his large eyes and ears, to plunge a dagger through the back of his neck.

Slither listened to the even breathing coming from the tents while his first victim clutched soundlessly at his fatal wound. Blood dribbled between his fingers, and he slumped and rolled off the mound to the rocks below.

Light from the campfire wavered over Slither's scaly skin as he entered Hal's tent. He knew he only had a couple of seconds to do as Hog ordered, before the Raekeem woman sleeping just a metre away would catch his scent and wake. Her genetic splice was with wolf DNA. Slither leaned over Hal, moved the tip of his blade to centre it over his heart and pressed his other hand on the hilt. Just as he began to bear down on it, a loud burning like a jet engine sounded above.

Hal's eyes snapped open. He saw the knife, grabbed Slither's wrists, but he was too late. Five centimetres of the blade sank below his left collarbone. He cried out, and Fang, the black wolf, tackled Slither to the ground. She pinned him and latched her jaws over his throat. Before she could clench and rip, Hal shouted for her to stop.

'We need him alive.'

He heard the jet engine cut out and looked up to see a woman land, deftly catching her weight. He thought it was Lana until she stepped into the light of the campfire. Her hair was pink, and she looked Asian.

Fang released her hold on Slither's neck and drew herself back a metre, her eyes growing wide. 'Talon!' she exclaimed.

Hal looked from Talon to Fang, confused and in pain.

Talon drew her side-arm and fired at somebody standing behind Fang. She returned her gun to her hip holster before the Raekeem woman, Hog's second assassin, dropped face-first to the ground. The knife she had poised to throw at Hal fell beside Slither.

He took the opportunity to scramble out of the tent. Talon kicked him in the gut and grappled his head when he doubled over. With a sickening twist, she snapped his neck with her arms.

Fang rushed to the blood-covered mound where she had last seen their watchman. She followed red smears and droplets down the rocks to the lifeless, twisted body below. She sank to her knees beside her Tarsier friend, pressed her hand to her mouth and shuddered. One of the others arrived and helped her carry him back to camp.

Talon was intrigued by Fang's genetically engineered form. Though short haired, her black coat looked warm. She was humanoid, with yellow eyes, wolf teeth and a bushy tail.

Fang wiped her eyes and ordered the closest Raekeem to fetch bandages and a needle and thread so she could treat Hal's wound.

'Hog planted them in our group,' she growled.

Hal winced. Slither's dagger was still sticking out of him.

Fang tore his shirt from the bottom of the knife handle and glanced at Talon. 'Thank you. You saved our lives.'

'Lana said Home Realm sent backup. She's not here,' Hal told her. 'She was taken to the Raekeem camp.'

Fang pulled Hal's shirt over his head. 'Oh, shut up, you big baby,' she scolded when he hissed. She wrapped the shirt around the knife handle as a Raekeem woman arrived with medical supplies. 'Lie down.'

'They're good people,' Hal pleaded to Talon when she turned to leave. 'Don't hurt them.'

He watched her fire up the jetpack and fly off into the night.

'You know her?' he asked Fang.

'I've told you I was a Sentinel under Feen's command before Kordin murdered him.' She took hold of the knife handle. 'Ready?'

She waited for Hal to nod before pulling the blade from his chest. He yelled and thumped the ground. The woman kneeling next to Fang handed her a clay bottle containing alcohol. She used it to wash Hal's wound and then began stitching.

'I was assigned to monitor chest cam footage relayed during missions,' Fang continued. 'I saw Sentinel Danin's strike on the factory that produced Automated Machines.'

Hal took the bottle and drank. After a pained breath, he asked her, 'What did you see?'

Fang didn't answer while she swiftly and skilfully sewed Hal's wound. Once she was done, she took the bottle from him.

'Talon killed them,' she said after a swig. 'Danin's entire squad.'

Molren led Miri and Lana back along the Tundra path. Hog was with them, watched closely by two of Molren's trusted guards. They each held a flaming torch, while Lana lit the path ahead with her console.

Molren gathered that Lana had somehow portaled in from what his people called the Realm of the Three Kingdoms and that her whole spiel about being part of a multiparty alliance with the Wood Folk was completely made up. After Lana confirmed his suspicions and apologised, he told her about what happened when the particle ray took him and his fellow Wardens.

'Not many of us survived that damned ray, which I assume the Lustitians shot at us,' he said. 'More were killed by the fall. The rest of us landed in thick snow or in deep water at the foot of the cliff.'

He watched the path ahead wistfully, the cool air blowing his thick mane.

'I remember waking,' he continued. 'I was being dragged out of the water. I could barely lift my head… it was so cold I couldn't feel anything. So I lay there and I watched while Hal went back and forth, carrying us out onto the river bank, one by one, until there was no one left to save.'

'We watched you march through the forest,' said Miri. 'The elders decided we should not make contact. They were afraid for the children.' She looked at Hog's tusks protruding over his top lip. 'We thought you were monsters. But you were headed for the icy cold of the Tundra. So my sister and I travelled ahead of you. We left clothing in your path.'

'That was you?' Molren turned to consider Miri with gratitude.

Lana understood now why Miri's sister was so angry with the Raekeem. But she was confident that the two peoples would become allies.

Miri stopped abruptly. 'Do you hear that?'

A moment later, a flaming glow appeared over the treetops. It grew louder, closer, until Talon swooped down and landed in front of them. The Raekeem drew stone knives, and in the same instant, Talon drew her gun.

Lana stepped in and swung her left hand under Talon's wrist, just as she squeezed the trigger. The bullet scraped the top of Hog's scalp and he fell to the ground.

'Hold your fire!' Lana shouted, holding her left ear, barely able to hear her own voice. 'Who are you?'

Talon holstered her gun while jabbing a finger at Hog. She raised two fingers and pointed behind her, to the path out of the Tundra.

'She found Hog's assassins,' Molren guessed. 'Must have flown over here from their camp.'

Lana heard Molren's underwater garble and turned to him. 'What?'

Talon's brow was furrowed, watching the Raekeem guards help Hog to his feet. She was annoyed that her shot had missed, but she glanced from Molren to Lana and nodded.

Miri's eyes were wide open with amazement, staring at the handheld object that had made a loud noise and knocked Hog down, and at the steel case on Talon's back that had carried her through the air. She couldn't begin to imagine the amount of knowledge and skill it would take for someone to engineer such tools.

With her good ear, Lana heard one of Molren's guards speaking.

'That's Talon, the machine that wiped out Danin's strike team,' he said.

Molren shot an accusing glare at Lana while standing to her right. 'You brought your finest warrior to kill us.' He jabbed a finger at Miri. 'Why the charade with this Wood Folk girl?'

Lana looked from Molren's angry grimace to Miri. 'Fine ass warrior… Wood Folk girl?'

Miri gave Molren an apologetic glance before leaning to Lana's left ear and relaying Molren's accusation.

'Oh. I came here to bring Hal home,' Lana confessed. 'Miri helped me, so I'm helping her. It's what civilised people do.'

Molren's eyes darted between Talon and Lana. He couldn't argue with the implication that the Raekeem were not civilised. *In all honesty,* Molren thought, *my people will have to assimilate into a functioning community in order to survive.* He gave Talon another uneasy sideways glance. 'I'm not going any further until she leaves.'

Lana took Talon aside. 'I read Lincoln's report on the Branner Factory.' She glanced over her shoulder at Molren and his guards. 'They're right to fear you.'

Talon's expression softened, taking Lana's words as a heartfelt compliment. She had seen news footage of Lana's heroic feats, and she knew the public idolised her and Rachel. But after seeing Lana here, trying to stop a conflict in a world she didn't belong to, Talon realised that she wasn't just a poster child for Universal Community ideology. She was also a woman trying to do the right thing.

'Hal and his people will probably have made it to the forest by now,' Lana continued. 'You go ahead. We'll meet you there.'

Talon nodded, fired up the jetpack and set off to catch up with Hal.

Molren watched Talon disappear before walking on. Nobody spoke for an hour. He broke the silence with a question. 'What happened to those under Kordin's command? The rest of us who were not forced to become Wardens?'

'They were captured by the Lustitians.'

Molren swore. 'They'll be executed. Damned puppets. And what of Lord Telsta?'

'Kordin killed his serpent. Telsta escaped.' Lana glanced at Molren curiously. 'Why do you call the Lustitians puppets?'

'They're not human.' Molren said this as though it were common knowledge. 'They take any form they can shape into.' He narrowed his eyes at Lana judgmentally. 'I suppose you're allied with them now?'

'Can they be trusted?' Lana asked.

Molren shrugged. 'I suppose, as long as you do not break any of their laws.' He was beginning to slow. He dropped his bulk onto a log to rest. 'Don't cross them. That's my only advice.'

Lana took a chance. 'Where does Telsta go when he trades places with the serpent?'

Molren gave her an approving smile. 'I was wondering when you were going to ask.' He wiped perspiration from his brow. 'Only I and the late Feen knew of what I am about to tell you.' He glanced about conspiratorially. 'Telsta is on an Earth that is infested with serpents. He has a compound built inside a mountain—'

'Earth has no reptile species that grow that large,' Lana said doubtfully.

Molren shot her an irked glance. 'That Earth — as far as we could gather — had sent a space probe to a passing meteorite. It landed, took samples and returned. Upon being exposed to oxygen, the contents of the sample became airborne.' He stroked the hair under his chin thoughtfully. 'The alien matter, which had been dormant for who knows how long, became an infectious disease. We trusted few who were assigned to Telsta's pet project had to be vaccinated every four months. Telsta — damned ghoul that he is — gave some of us a placebo jab in order to observe the transformation process.'

'They turned into serpents?' Lana asked, shuddering at how excruciating the change must have been for them.

'Humanoid abominations,' Molren answered gravely. 'They endured that horror for only a few days before the symbiosis failed and they, as hosts, expired.'

'So the serpent disease did the same to every animal on that Earth?' Lana asked.

'Every creature became a host and hatched larvae. The ecosystem was likely destroyed inside of a year. The serpents eat any bio matter, and they can multiply in great numbers.' Molren looked from Miri's captivated expression to Lana's. 'They're unstoppable.'

Chapter 32

Hal said some kind words at the grave of the Tarsier man Slither had murdered. Then he set off alone – despite Fang's protests – on the trail to the Fyrst Born forest. After a couple of hours, he entered their domain and bird-like warning calls sounded above. Hal could only make out the stone tips of arrows when he looked up. He heard somebody approaching, so he stopped and waited.

A thin woman appeared, walking barefoot, favouring her left leg. She was humming a sad tune, watching Hal with grey, sunken eyes. She stopped and reached out her bony hand.

Hal took an entranced step toward her.

Wind blew catkins and pine needles between them, and she changed into a tall Fyrst Born warrior before Hal's eyes.

'Come no further, you fool,' she commanded gruffly. 'State your business.'

'Lana sent me,' said Hal, looking around for the Mutated woman.

'Fine. Where is my sister?'

'With the Raekeem.' Hal saw the woman's jaw clench. 'I know their leader. He won't let any harm come to them.' He gestured behind him. 'I'm travelling with a small group. We need food, shelter. Can you help us?'

Miri's sister looked up when one of the archers alerted her.

Hal heard the sound of a jetpack engine. 'Don't be alarmed by what you're about to see,' he cautioned. 'A friend of Lana's is approaching. We come from an advanced world, where people build things that can make you fly.'

Talon descended slowly between the trees and moved her hands away from her sides when she saw the archers. Miri's sister signalled them to stand down.

'Come inside. I will send somebody out to guide your people in.'

That evening, Lana and Miri arrived at the edge of the forest with Molren. 'Make camp here,' Molren ordered Hog and the two guards. 'Await my return.'

Fyrst Born guards greeted them and showed them to where Hal's group were housed. It was a treetop dwelling similar to Miri's home. Miri said it was a guest house, used to accommodate travellers and traders from allied lands.

After a meal, Hal and Lana finally had some time alone. From Hal's perspective, over four months had passed since they'd been separated. They sat by the light of what the Fyrst Born called fire beetles, which lived in miniature trees. The bonsai were in plant boxes mounted at head height along every wall of every room.

Hal told Lana about the first day, when many Raekeem had died and more still on the long journey through the cold. He had saved their lives, so the Raekeem followed him as their leader. Over time, Hal had formed friendships and even a special bond with one of them, Fang.

He related the night he and his group had arrived at what would be their Tundra camp. There was a blizzard coming, and Hal had a fever. They dug a deep trench and created a roof out of pine branches. They huddled together. Fang held Hal close to maintain his body temperature. She was the only reason he survived the night.

Hal returned to where he and the Raekeem had fallen into Ether Realm every fortnight for two months. He did so to see if there was any sign of Lana. During this time, he found it difficult to ignore Fang's affections. He knew he may never see Lana again, but he couldn't shake the feeling that he should remain hopeful and wait for her. And so he did.

Fang tried to understand when Hal expressed his reasons for being distant and why he was unable to commit to her. She didn't want to be with any of the Raekeem men. She loved Hal. He had saved her life, and she had saved his.

Lana saw the warmth in Hal's eyes when he spoke of the wolf woman. And her heart sank.

'I'm sorry, Lana,' he said when she turned away from him. 'I couldn't see a way of ever getting back to you. Eventually, I realised this is my home now.' He moved Lana to face him. 'I can't leave. These people need me.'

Lana wiped her eyes. 'You did a good thing.'

Hal took her hand. 'You will always be welcome to visit.'

There was a knock at the wall outside the curtained doorway, and Miri spoke. 'Lana, may I speak with you?'

'Just a minute,' said Lana. She looked into Hal's eyes. 'You're sure?'

He smiled knowingly and nodded.

Lana could see gratitude in his expression. She said goodbye to him. When she left the room, she walked steadily and with dignity, and she did not look back.

Miri followed, concerned by the sadness radiating from her. When Miri looked back to Hal's room, she saw Fang arrive at the curtain, and Hal's arm circled around the wolf woman's waist.

She understood what had happened. 'This is a bad time,' she said. They descended from the tree house and met with Talon. 'I'll find you later.'

Lana swallowed her emotion and faced Miri. 'I'm going now.'

Miri hesitated for a second. 'I want to come with you,' she blurted out. 'To my world?'

'If it is permitted.' Miri made her explanation brief. 'The elders have requested an accord be delivered to the leaders of your world. We would like to form an alliance.'

'Of course.' Lana breathed out a heavy sigh of frustration and sadness. She looked at Miri and smiled apologetically. 'I'm sorry, it's just that I came all this way to find him, and…'

'Let us leave,' Miri suggested. 'Your grief will be easier once you are home.'

Home Realm

Lana, Talon and Miri stepped through the portal, and they were greeted by Rachel and Sam. Pete closed the portal from the control room and joined them in the briefing room. Lana introduced Miri to them, explained briefly what had happened over the days that she had been in Ether Realm, and finally asked, 'How long was I gone?'

'A little over a day,' Rachel replied. 'You haven't missed much. Kordin found that Telsta's teleportation logs have been erased. There's no record of his movements. Dead end.'

'Maybe not,' said Lana optimistically. 'A Raekeem survivor called Molren told me he was ordered to erase those logs. But he was a senior technician on board Telsta's ship, so he has access codes, which he gave to me. He said Telsta didn't understand that you can't erase data completely without physically destroying the hard drives.'

Rachel followed what Lana was saying. 'We should be able to recover the teleportation logs using Molren's codes.' She typed a message on her console to inform Lincoln of the latest development.

'You said he was a senior technician,' Pete said. 'Why was he changed into a Warden and deployed with the others?'

This question made Lana realise that deceit may have motivated Molren's effort to change the path he and his people were on. 'Molren said he was subjected to the mutagen by force. He suspected Telsta did the same to everyone who knew about his serpent.'

Sam looked to Miri and admired the woollen vest she was wearing. And she noticed the small woman had not left Lana's side since her arrival. 'There are really four-legged people in your world?' she asked Miri.

'The Mountain Folk are our most valued allies.' Miri made a welcome gesture to everyone at the table. 'You must come to my world. I would be happy to introduce you to them.'

Pete was humbled by the invitation to experience such a vastly different Realm.

'We've been through a lot, guys,' said Lana. 'I think we oughta turn in. We can talk more in the morning.'

'Of course,' Rachel agreed. 'It's a pleasure to meet you, Miri.'

Lana showed Miri to a spare room down the corridor from the lounge. She watched her pick up the white bath towel from the end of her bunk bed and press the soft cotton to her cheek.

'Where is the warmth in here coming from?' Miri asked, looking around the room.

'We use energy harnessed and stored from our sun. That energy is converted to heat, and it's circulated through the roof and out of those vents,' Lana said, pointing to the ceiling.

The two of them continued on to the shower room, where Lana left Miri to wash while she spoke to Rachel outside.

'Miri said her people have been around for millennia,' Lana commented curiously. 'But they haven't developed their technology.'

'I guess they've settled on what works for them.' Rachel looked Lana over, seeing no visible injury. 'I'm glad you're home safe.'

'Whose idea was it to send Talon?' Lana asked.

'Lincoln's.'

Lana watched Talon sit down on the couch in the lounge and turn the TV on. 'She's one serious woman.'

Rachel could detect the tired sadness Lana was trying to hide. 'So… Hal.'

'He's staying in Ether Realm, with someone else,' Lana confirmed.

'But he's okay now.'

Lana understood what Rachel meant. Hal had lived a truly difficult life. Now he was part of a large family, in a place far removed from Haze Realm and its broken, polluted city.

Rachel hugged Lana close. 'I'm sorry things didn't happen the way you wanted them to.'

Sam came at Lana with a hug from behind, and she squeezed tightly. 'I was so worried about you!'

'I was safe, thanks to Miri and her people.'

'Well, I'll go and thank her for taking care of our girl.'

'Wait,' Lana cautioned, too late.

'Oh!' Sam exclaimed in surprise.

Lana pulled her out of the shower room while Miri stood under the hot water mid scrub, with an eyebrow raised at the commotion.

'What?' Rachel took a peek. 'Oh my.'

'Rachel…!' Lana tugged them both away. 'Could you please be cool?' she steamed.

Talon looked over her shoulder, glared, and turned up the volume on the TV.

'Of course,' Sam agreed distractedly. 'Are all Fyrst Born intersex?'

'Most of them.' Lana shrugged. 'It's no big deal.'

'Fascinating.' Sam started speaking so quickly that Lana had trouble following. 'Fyrst Born progesterone and estrogen must have priority over their testosterone. They must have evolved distension, which means Miri has a womb as well as – what we call – "male" genitalia.'

'She said her people don't recognise the definitions our medical scientists use,' Lana explained. 'I guess they consider sex organs to be genderless. They only recognise people's nature, and her people are feminine in nature. Our term "intersex" doesn't mean anything to them.'

'So she's not a she or a he?' Rachel asked. 'Do we call her "them" or "they"?'

Lana held up her hand to interject again. 'When the Fyrst Born speak, we hear their language translated into English because the signals they emit fool us into thinking we're hearing English, right? Well, I've spent a lot of time with many of the Fyrst Born, and I only ever heard them refer to each other as female. So as far as we humans are concerned, the Fyrst Born are all women. Okay?'

'Makes sense,' Rachel confirmed.

'Miri's body and all her people's make more sense than ours,' Sam stated, looking from Lana's perplexed expression to Rachel's even more lost, floating eyebrows. 'Human men and women develop their sex organs from the same embryonic tissue. Fyrst Born embryos develop in a more efficient way.'

'Riveting,' said Rachel, rubbing her eyes. 'I'm going to bed.'

Sam gave Lana another quick hug. 'I'm glad you're safe.' She went into the shower room and apologised to Miri for startling her.

Lana hugged Rachel goodnight, and Rachel gestured discreetly with her thumb over her shoulder. 'She likes you.'

'Who? Miri?'

'Smitten.'

Lana gazed over Rachel's shoulder when Miri left the shower room wrapped in a towel.

Miri was looking up at the air ducts in the ceiling. She turned her head, somehow knowing that Lana was watching. Her hair tumbled, partially obscuring her face. She and Lana held each other's gaze.

'Don't just stare at her, ya big goof,' Rachel whispered.

Lana hushed her. 'Yes, thank you, Rache. Night-night.' And she approached Miri. 'Would you like to watch TV with me?' she asked, gesturing to the lounge.

'Yes, I was curious about that... thing Talon has been staring at.'

'Come sit with me, and you'll see why the TV is one of humanity's greatest inventions.'

Chapter 33

Lincoln returned to the Portal Hub in the morning with Kordin and Xera. They were no longer accompanied by armed guards. Lincoln trusted that they wanted to find Telsta more than anyone else.

Talon had disappeared and later texted Lincoln that she would be willing to help out again but only if it was Lana who needed her.

'We have recovered the teleportation logs,' Kordin announced when everyone was assembled in the meeting room. 'Molren's codes gave me clearance to all of Telsta's serpent projects.' He nodded to Lana. 'Including the compound's location on the Earth overrun by them.'

Lincoln pressed his knuckles on the table and leaned on them. 'The compound will be heavily fortified.'

'I can get us in,' said Kordin.

'How?' asked Lana.

Kordin gave Lincoln a sideways glance, knowing the Commander wasn't going to like what he was about to say. 'I must lead. And I will need two of my crew.'

Lincoln raised a "don't push your luck" eyebrow at Kordin and opened his mouth to dismiss his plan, when Lana interjected.

'Hear him out,' she said, with a nod to Xera. 'The first thing Xera noticed was amiss about Rachel and me was our scent.'

'What about AMs?' Lincoln suggested. 'We don't emit human scent.'

Xera shook her head. 'Worse. You do not emit a protein signature. You are too obviously artificial.'

Lincoln chose not to take offence and turned to Rachel for her input.

'Infiltrate,' Rachel said, with an agreeable look to Kordin. 'What can we do to become more convincing Raekeem?'

'You will have to stand at the back, or we can surround you and mask your scent,' Kordin suggested.

Miri stood up from the meeting table and changed her form to become the Raekeem scout she had posed as before. 'Perhaps I could be of assistance.'

Kordin and Xera took a moment to study her, both surprised and impressed. Xera approached Miri and pulled back after just one sniff. 'Your scent is Raekeem. How?'

'I am emitting signals that make you all sense me as I need you to.'

'Why did Xera sniff Miri?' Rachel asked Lana.

'She just changed into her Raekeem form,' said Lana. She watched Rachel lean toward and squint at Miri, as though she were looking at a Rorschach test. 'It doesn't work on you?'

Miri turned to Rachel and changed herself to look exactly like Lana. Everybody gasped in astonishment.

Rachel didn't react. 'What doesn't work on me?'

'I have never encountered anyone capable of resisting my signal,' said Miri, and she sat back down as her regular self.

'I'll explain later,' Lana said to Rachel.

'Miri, Lana, and Rachel...' Lincoln began, with a tentative look to Rachel. 'That is, if you're up for it?'

'I'm in,' Rachel answered firmly.

'That's what I wanted to hear. Suit up. I'll have Valhez release two of his prisoners.' Lincoln nodded to Kordin and Xera. 'You lead.'

Miri was given a bodysuit that provided protection from small weapons fire. It was something Hutch Branner had developed as an alternative to the Kiyol spray-on suit that some wearers found claustrophobic. Lana and Rachel donned the same, as it helped to hide their human scent.

Once dressed, Miri walked by Lana's room and saw a stuffed toy on the bed. She smiled when she realised it must be the animal Lana had perceived her people to look like. She entered the room and found a peach-coloured dress hanging over a chair. She couldn't resist picking it up to admire it.

Lana arrived in the doorway. 'That was Abbey Crone's.'

Startled, Miri spun around, unintentionally twirling the dress like a dance partner.

'She was taken and sold into slavery.'

Miri draped Abbey's dress over the chair. 'How old?'

'She's seventeen.'

An image of the man and woman Lana had strung up and left hanging naked by their ankles emerged from her memory. She told Miri about the mission to find Howard Crone, and how she had worn Abbey's dress to get into the home of the wealthy husband and wife who were trafficking minors.

'She told me to keep it. She didn't want it anymore.'

Miri read and interpreted Lana's distant expression, the anger in her frown at what people with power often did. Exploit others.

'You were very brave to go into that house, knowing what they were,' Miri said.

'I've faced monsters worse than them.' Lana pushed up her sleeve. 'And I have abilities.' She pulled her axe from its sheath and sliced her arm.

Miri gasped, immediately grabbing Lana's arm as though she was going to apply pressure to the wound. But there was no blood.

'You can armour your skin.' She held Lana's hand, imagining the many battles she must have fought over the years. 'It takes more than armour to do what you do.'

Miri's praise made Lana feel proud. She leaned in, her nose touching Miri's, but paused in case she was overstepping her bounds. She felt Miri's lips close over hers.

Lana pinned Miri against the weapons wall, knocking a sword from its mount. She pushed her fingers through Miri's hair with one hand and unzipped her bodysuit with the other.

'Kordin's ship is here,' Rachel called from the corridor. 'Lana? Miri?'

'Give us ten minutes!' Lana answered, and kicked the door closed.

The two Raekeem released by Captain Valhez were ready to follow Kordin into one final battle. A battle from which they did not intend to return.

Miri and Lana arrived on board Kordin's ship. Rachel guided them to the armoury, and she elbowed Lana when Miri wasn't looking. 'You saucy minx,' she whispered.

Lana smiled. 'Thanks for stalling.' She picked up a Raekeem blaster from the weapons rack in front of her. There was no clip in the handle.

'How do these work?' she asked Xera.

She stepped between Miri and Lana to instruct them both. 'You have two shots before the gun goes into a two-second automatic cool down. Firing rapidly for more than two shots will incur a greater cool-down time.'

She pressed an adhesive mimic device onto Lana's left collar and activated it. Rachel activated hers, and her body was mapped with a hologram that gave her a Raekeem appearance.

Lana showed Miri how to aim her weapon in the Weaver stance. Miri nodded once she was confident. She changed her form to the scout's, and she took her position. Xera, Kordin and the two other Raekeem Sentinels stood on the outside of their group formation.

Xera had cut herself earlier to draw blood into a bandage. She pulled it over her face and tied it at the back of her neck. It covered all but her eyes, which she further obscured by pushing her fringe across her face.

'Our entry is likely to raise an alarm,' Kordin said to everyone standing behind him. 'Keep your weapons holstered. Let me do the talking.'

Black tendrils swirled around the group of seven. They were enveloped in seconds and transported into Telsta's mountain compound.

When the inky cloud parted, they were standing in a corridor before large steel doors. An alarm boomed, and red lights flashed on the stone walls.

'Identify yourself.' A voice came from the speaker mounted below a security camera on the doors.

Kordin saw two long nozzles with pilot flame connections protruding from the walls either side of him. He and his team could be engulfed in flames at any moment.

'Lead Sentinel Kordin,' he answered. 'We are all that remains of Lord Telsta's carrier crew.'

There was a long pause before the sound of an electronic breathing apparatus came over the speaker. 'Kordin.' Telsta's voice was deep, with a synthesised rasp. 'How did you find this place? No one–'

'Molren,' Kordin stated honestly. 'He survived, and he helped us return to you.'

'I see. Tell me what happened.'

'The Lustitians attacked. Many were lost.'

'And what of my Wardens?' Telsta growled.

'Defeated, my Lord,' Kordin answered blankly.

Telsta breathed through the speaker for a moment. 'I do not see Xera among you. My serpent must have ravaged the stupid girl.'

Kordin clenched his fists, but maintained a respectful tone. 'We are the last.'

More heavy, artificial breathing crackled static through the speaker.

The doors opened, and Kordin led his group into another corridor. There were steel doors at the end. Kordin saw no surveillance equipment in this adjoining section, so he took the opportunity to reveal the rest of his plan to the others.

They entered a cavern. Screeching echoed against the walls. Dust drifted from the rock ceiling. In the centre, surrounded by a girded walkway, were cages housing serpents. They were brightly lit, reinforced enclosures, separated in groups of larvae, hatchlings and enormous, adult-sized monsters. Each cage was monitored by Raekeem men and women wearing black lab coats. And *they* were monitored by six armed Sentinels patrolling on the walkways.

Two large humanoid creatures stood with their backs turned to Kordin's group. *If those are Wardens*, Lana thought, *their gene splice must be with serpent DNA.*

Her eyes narrowed when she saw, past them, one of the prison inmates. He was strapped to a table. A lab technician was using scissors to cut his orange uniform and tank top to expose his chest while another rolled a trolley of clamps and scalpels to the table. The inmate was conscious and struggling.

Kordin watched a tall figure descend the stairs from the compound control deck. He was in shadow, each footfall pounding steel steps. When he entered the light, Kordin realised that it was Telsta.

Lana's stomach turned at the sight of him. *Abomination, alright. Molren wasn't kidding.*

'Welcome, my brave Sentinels, to the future of our race,' Telsta said, gesturing grandly to the cage and surgery area. Despite the failure of his Warden assault, Telsta's self-assured arrogance had not diminished.

Tubes ran from either side of his steel face mask, over his shoulders, to an oxygen tank on his back. He wore a mechanical exoskeleton that carried out his every move with a second of delay after each signal from his brain.

Telsta typed a command using the console on his wrist. Spotlights blinked on at the back of the cavern, above the rear walkway, revealing windowed cells.

There were about six inmates in each cell. Lana counted ten cells. She noticed that Xera and Miri had already slipped away, as per Kordin's instruction.

Telsta gazed over the caged serpents, turned back, and raised his chin at Kordin. 'This infested planet is the weapon we will use to wipe out the Lustitians.'

'You intend to teleport these creatures onto their ship?' Kordin asked.

'Yes, and once they are destroyed, we few, the final vestiges of the Raekeem, will grow a new army.' Telsta stared at him, unblinking. 'We will take to the stars. And we will conquer once again.'

Chapter 34

Telsta heard his two serpent-spliced Wardens trudging toward the new arrivals, and he addressed them with a delighted tone. 'Gentlemen.' Then he raised his voice for a grand introduction. 'Behold: our first serpent Wardens, Mr Williams and Mr Conroy.'

Lana's jaw dropped when she saw the two abominations enter the light and flash their sickly yellow eyes. The splice had made them twice their original size. They wore a carapace in place of human flesh. The process must have been excruciating. She wondered how either of them had survived.

Seeing her expression, Telsta shrugged. 'The transformation process could have gone a lot smoother had our extraction team found the *actual* O'Conner – idiots – but these two will be no less effective in battle.' He saw that Kordin was not impressed. 'Perhaps a demonstration.' And he swept his eyes over Kordin's group for the strongest-looking Sentinel. 'There were seven of you.'

'One of my crew was wounded,' Kordin explained calmly. 'My medical officer–'

Telsta pointed at Lana. 'You there. Come forward.' He nodded to Dennis Conroy. 'To the death.'

'Allow me,' Kordin volunteered.

'It is not necessary for you to prove yourself to me, Kordin. I am not your uncle.'

'I am merely eager, my Lord, to see your fine work in action.'

Telsta smiled and slid back, holding both arms toward Conroy like a ringmaster.

Conroy widened his stance, brought his arms up from his sides and extended his claws three extra centimetres. He leaned forward and bared his jagged teeth. When he roared, viscous phlegm was projected from his throat at Kordin.

Kordin weaved left to avoid the shot of acidic gunk and advanced on Conroy. He drew his sword and slashed at his head.

Conroy raised his forearm and deflected the blade. He took hold of Kordin's sword and slammed a shoulder into his chest, knocking him to the ground.

Xera had reached the command console and used Molren's code to gain access. She programmed a delayed cloud portal for everyone's escape, then typed commands that would corrupt the system and lock all controls. Two slave operators were working either side of her, saving surveillance footage to a hard drive. Xera saw that the footage was time-stamped two days ago. Two male humans, one with a sagging face, the other missing a hand, were strapped down to steel tables. They were screaming and writhing in agony.

Xera stood when she heard fighting and spotted Telsta with his back turned, watching Kordin fight one of the serpent Wardens. She ran the length of the deck to the edge, dove off the two-metre-high staircase, and launched herself at Telsta.

A breach tone alerted Telsta and he turned to the control deck. He saw Xera flying at him, raised both arms, and produced forty-centimetre blades from the mechanical housing attached to his wrists.

Xera kicked her legs in front of her, edging her feet between the blades before Telsta could bring them in front of his chest. She planted her feet in the hollow of his elbows. Her momentum parted his arms, and she used her falling body weight to take hold of his face with both hands and stab her thumbs into his eyeballs. She rode him to the ground, and her thumbs disappeared into his eye sockets.

Xera leaned heavily and penetrated deep into Telsta's skull. He screamed through his face mask while she kept his arms pinned.

'For my mother!' Xera growled, repeatedly slamming his head into the floor while his body shook and blood oozed between her fingers.

Telsta stopped moving. Xera stood and glared down at him, her chest heaving.

Kordin rolled left when Conroy brought his own sword down upon him. Conroy paused upon hearing a warning from Jericho Williams. And he turned to see Lana and Rachel advancing.

Jericho shot acidic muck at them from his throat. Rachel dropped to one knee, ducked under the flying gunk, slid side-on to Lana and provided a stepping platform for her.

Lana had turned her body and weaved to avoid the slime shot. She maintained her momentum and hopped lightly onto Rachel's knee. Launching herself at Jericho with Rachel's aid, she ducked into a mid-air summersault.

As soon as Lana was airborne, Rachel fired her blaster at Jericho. He swung his arm to slash Lana out of the air with his serpent claws but took hits in the shoulder that halted his action. Lana kicked her heels into his chest, knocking him to the ground.

Conroy let out a shrill screech and advanced on Rachel. Kordin got to his feet, ducked under blaster fire from the guards, and charged at Conroy. He jumped, rotated his body and delivered a heel-kick to Conroy's lower back, staggering the Warden serpent away from Rachel.

Miri had slipped away and taken position on the walkway with the other guards. 'Our Lord has been wounded!' she cried out, to take their attention away from the cells. They ran toward Telsta while she pulled on the unlock levers. The cell doors slid open, and the prisoners burst out.

Miri assumed the firing stance Lana had taught her and shot down two guards while the remaining three were occupied by Kordin's men. She ran down the steps to the inmate tied to the medical table. There was a shallow incision running down his chest. He was tugging at his restraints, screaming through a mask. Miri took a scalpel from a tray and rushed over to him while he yelled angrily at her. Then he was stunned silent when she changed back to her regular form and freed him.

'Get the other inmates to meet us at the entrance!' Miri yelled. 'Go!'

Miri looked to the gargantuan serpent men fighting Rachel, Lana and Kordin, and she ran to assist.

Jericho and Lana were fighting close, striking and blocking. Jericho's knuckles were serrated, ripping through Lana's bodysuit upon each blow. Lana was doing her fair share of damage to him, knocking chunks of scales from his body, delivering heel kicks and firing point-blank blasts.

Conroy was struggling against both Rachel and Kordin. Kordin had won back his sword, and he was slicing layers of carapace armour off Conroy's arms with every strike.

Conroy resorted to breathing out a noxious mist that repelled Rachel. He delivered a savage strike across Kordin's head and leaned in to enact another. Kordin weaved to Conroy's blind side and chopped down with his sword, severing Conroy's right arm at the elbow.

Conroy staggered backward, roaring and shrieking in pain. His serpent DNA kicked in, producing a long, sharp blade of bone from the stump in seconds.

The cloud teleport Xera had programmed appeared at the entrance. The inmates ran toward it, giving Conroy and Williams a wide berth.

Lana took a blow across the face and Jericho spear-tackled her to the ground. He leaned over her, bringing his face close to hers, taking satisfaction in having the upper hand. He opened his mouth wide, but before he could bite down on Lana's neck, his jaw slackened and he froze, as she connected her mind to his neural pathways.

A hue of murky yellow clouded Lana's vision, and a horrible shrieking pierced her senses. She could feel Jericho's hunger for the woman lying pinned beneath him. A shift of neural connection that she hadn't thought possible changed her vision. She was inside a cage. Prison inmates were running by. Another sickening jolt shifted her perspective again, and she could see Kordin. He had just been knocked down. Her vision turned to her right, and she watched Rachel driving the heel of her boot forward. The blow connected, and Lana's vision went black.

Another shift occurred with a pull so extreme that Lana felt its inertia in her stomach. Now she could see snow and rock. Serpent creatures were climbing. Lana was inside the mind of one, following the many hundreds ahead of it. They were on a mountain outside the compound. They snaked along at speed, unfurling their scales like blades to grip each surface before pushing off to the next. Mounted cannons were firing down on them from above. There was an opening. Steel doors were smashed. The serpent horde surged across the ground, along the walls, up to the ceiling.

Lana's eyes snapped open and she was face to face with Jericho.

He shook his head and blinked repeatedly, but he kept Lana pinned.

Miri's foot slammed into the side of his head. She helped Lana to her feet and pointed to the entrance. 'We have to go. Xera has opened a portal, but it will close soon.'

'They're coming,' Lana breathed. She accessed her comms and shouted to everyone. 'The serpents are coming in! We can't let them follow us back!'

Jericho rolled onto his feet and exhaled a cloud of gas at Lana and Miri. Lana coughed and staggered out of the fumes. She saw Jericho and Miri emerge. He was holding Miri from behind. Her arms were pinned to her sides. His claws were closed over her throat, squeezing.

'Throttled duck,' Jericho rasped, his words rising out of toxic vapour. 'We're going to walk out of here together. Or I'm going to rip this little cherub's throat out.'

Lana was still. Her heart ached at the sight of Miri's peril. But Miri's brow was furrowed in concentration. Electrical signals were tingling in Lana's brain, and she could see an image of herself projected in Miri's mind. Miri was giving her something.

Lana stared down at her body and at her hands. Her skin turned marble red. Black lines formed swirling patterns over her body. She tongued sharp teeth in her mouth. The images from Miri's perspective told her that she had become some kind of demon.

'What the shit?' Jericho exclaimed, as Lana morphed before his eyes.

Lana's adrenaline peaked. Jericho was forming words, but his voice sounded deep and slow. The inmates were filing through the cloud portal. They were all running but somehow in slow motion.

Lana ran at Jericho. She took his wrist and pried his claws away from Miri's neck. She pulled Miri away from him as her sense of time continued to slow.

Jericho saw Lana blur in front of him. Her fiery orange eyes were locked on his.

Lana drew back her arm, turned her shoulders and drove her fist into Jericho's face. Her speed reduced, and everything around her began to accelerate back to normal. Jericho's eyes widened in horror while Lana's knuckles ploughed through his nose, smashed his teeth, and shot out the back of his skull.

Time returned to its regular constant flow, and Lana pressed her knee against Jericho's chest to pull her arm free from the hole in his head.

Miri gazed at Lana in her demon form and took her outstretched hand.

Lana changed back to herself. The two of them ran for the portal.

Kordin deflected Conroy's bone spear and Rachel attacked with a scissor kick, landing a strike to Conroy's face, causing him to stagger backward.

Kordin circled the portal and ran out into the corridor. He saw the horde of serpents ablaze after they'd triggered the flamethrowers. They'd smashed through the steel doors at the far end of the compound and were rushing in.

Xera collided with Conroy, reaching him with a mid-air shoulder slam. He fell sideways and snapped his bone spear against the ground. Rachel jumped on his chest and jammed the barrel of her blaster into his mouth.

He stared wide-eyed at her.

She pulled the trigger, and Dennis Conroy's brains splattered through the back of his skull.

Chapter 35

'Can we close the portal from the other side?' Lana asked Xera.

'No,' she said, feeling partly responsible for the new threat Earth was about to face. 'Only from its origin. And the computers are corrupted.'

'How long?' Rachel asked.

'Forty seconds.'

'They're here!' Kordin shouted. He opened fire on the torrent of serpents surging along the walls, ground and ceiling.

Lana, Miri and Rachel ran through the cloud portal and into Kordin's ship. Rachel pushed through inmates being detained by security AMs. She found Raekeem grenades mounted on the armoury wall but no high explosives.

'We need a bomb!' she shouted.

'What's going on?' Lincoln arrived, immediately sensing something terrible was on the other side of the portal. He listened while Miri explained.

Kordin's ship was positioned outside the Portal Hub. Rachel called Sam's comms and asked her to send all of the high explosives locked in the armoury directly through a portal to the ship.

'Firing line!' Lincoln ordered his team. 'Serpents inbound! Fire on all targets!'

Xera and Kordin were dual-wielding blasters, firing on every serpent that came at them. Kordin glanced at the timer on Xera's wrist. Twenty seconds remained until the cloud portal behind them would close. The serpents were climbing over the bodies of their fallen, crowding in greater and greater numbers.

Xera swore in frustration at the cool down her blasters required after firing rapidly. The numbers on her timer seemed impossibly slow to descend.

'You have to go,' said Kordin.

'Don't you dare!' Xera shouted. 'You owe them nothing! We can disappear in the human world! The Lustitians—'

'They will never stop hunting us.' Kordin aimed above their heads and killed two more serpents. 'I would rather die here than be jettisoned into space by those self-righteous bastards!'

Lana's voice came through their comms. 'Xera, Kordin, bombs are ready!'

Bundles of high explosives flew through the cloud. A second later, the detonation switch clattered to Kordin's feet. Xera reached down to pick it up and felt Kordin's hand close over hers.

'No, Kordin, please!'

He kissed her then shoved her through the portal.

Xera rolled out onto the floor of the ship. Two serpents flew over her head and Rachel shot one three times to bring it down. Xera struggled when AMs grappled her, and she screamed out to Kordin as she was pulled down the ramp.

Lincoln and his soldiers destroyed the other serpent while everybody else moved clear of the ship. They took cover behind a barricade that Lincoln's team were assembling.

A line of eight serpents snaked out of the ship. Three of them were immediately shot to pieces, but one made it to the barricade, tackled an AM to the ground and killed him before it was shot. Three escaped down the hill. The last was riddled with bullets.

There was a loud thump inside the ship and it exploded into hunks of flying metal. The shockwave threw rocks, soil and pieces of serpent into the air.

When the dust and smoke cleared, there was an eerie silence as the cloud teleport became visible, impervious to the blast inside Telsta's compound and outside the Portal Hub. The black tendrils continued to writhe and swirl for three seconds longer.

Lana hadn't thought it was possible for sound to travel through a portal. But everyone could hear the clambering of carapace bodies, the roars of adult serpents, and the piercing shrieks of their young. The noise rose louder and louder, until the cloud shrank and vanished in the blink of an eye.

Again there was silence.

Xera pushed her way through the soldiers and staggered into the smouldering rubble. She shrank to her knees in the centre of the blast crater and buried her fingers in the hot soil. Her shoulders trembled, and she cried.

The Lustitian vessel arrived over the Portal Hub the following morning. Captain Valhez teleported into the portal room with Kim, and Sam guided them to the briefing room to discuss what happened at the compound.

Rachel reported that Telsta and the Raekeem under his command were killed. Valhez clasped his hands and gave her a satisfied nod. 'Given the threat of serpent infestation, your efforts went well beyond our expectations.' He looked to Miri, to Lana and, somewhat reluctantly, to Xera. 'Well done, all of you. Before we leave to deliver our prisoners, I would like to–'

Xera stood abruptly. 'You are not taking them.'

Lincoln motioned for his two security officers to stand down when their hands dropped to their side-arms.

Lana broke the tense silence. 'We may have an alternate solution to the Raekeem problem.' She glanced at Xera and saw that her words had offended. 'That is to say, their way of being,' she corrected, and gave Miri her cue.

'They are a tortured people,' said Miri. 'But they can change… given a chance.'

Valhez opened his mouth to dismiss any solution these women had to offer, but Kim leaned to his ear and whispered something. He paused to consider what she said. 'What do you propose?' he asked Miri.

'Send them to my world.'

Valhez glanced at Lana and back to Miri. 'You want me to exonerate them?'

'Only the people in this room need know,' Rachel offered in support. 'You could stage a breakout on your ship. Use the particle beam to clear your holding deck.'

Valhez turned to Lincoln for his input.

'Some of the serpents made it past us yesterday,' Lincoln said. 'They were found and destroyed during the night. They had already laid a dozen eggs down by the bay. Had ten or twenty escaped, the entire coast would have been populated by serpents. They would've moved inland, infesting all of California, killing thousands of people.' He turned to Xera and met her gaze. 'We would be in a state of crisis right now had Kordin not sacrificed himself.'

Kim could see Xera's eyes glazing, but she remained composed in the presence of the Lustitian Captain.

'Very well,' Valhez agreed, finally. 'I will make the necessary arrangements.'

Miri knew she had to return home and speak to the Fyrst Born elders before the Raekeem were freed and sent to her world. But first, she wanted to talk to Lana about what happened during the fight against Jericho Williams. She and Lana climbed the hill path behind the Hub and sat in the morning sunlight.

Miri stared at the Golden Gate Bridge, marvelling at the vast stretch of orange and vermillion, at the ingenuity and the amount of people-power it must have taken to build such a wonder. Wave crests sparkled and the wind blew cool against them. Miri explained that she had given Lana a gift that the Fyrst Born could only bestow once in their lifetime and to only one person.

'We call it Mutjal Jakti.'

'Moot-yahl Yahk-tee,' Lana murmured, mimicking Miri's pronunciation.

'Loosely translated, it means "power of the Fyrst".' Miri looked into Lana's eyes, and her hair glistened bronze in the morning light. 'This gift is for someone with whom I now have an unbreakable bond. Someone I love and cannot live without.'

Lana's heart fluttered. She realised that Miri was not speaking poetically. 'You're saying if I die…'

'My heart will fail,' Miri said, solemnly taking Lana's hand. 'But you must understand… giving you this ability in that moment was not an act of necessity. I would gladly have sacrificed myself if it meant that you could escape and live on. I gave it then because I thought I might not have another chance.'

Lana's mouth was moving while she tried to find words. *Any* words. 'I'll come with you,' she blurted out.

Miri shook her head. 'I think the Lustitians want to speak to you.'

'Me? Why?'

'I overheard what Kim said to Captain Valhez. Her advice was to listen to what you had to say. He must need something from you.' She stood to leave, still holding Lana's hand. 'Come and visit me tomorrow.'

'I will.'

Miri returned to Ether Realm, and sure enough, Lana's presence was requested aboard the Lustitian ship as soon as she returned to the Portal Hub. Lana teleported aboard and was greeted by Kim.

'I must apologise for the haste, Lana,' she said, guiding her to a briefing room. 'We're due to leave in ten minutes, so we'll have to make this quick.'

'Kim, what exactly am I doing here?'

'We're required to assign law enforcement wherever we can,' Kim explained. 'You might say we're making you sheriff here. You will enforce your people's laws under our authority in conjunction with your Council.'

Lana's eyebrows shot up. 'You're kidding.'

Kim glanced at the time on her pad and spoke quickly. 'We hope that you accept this assignment because it would mean we don't have to return here. Not that we don't want to, it's just that we have so many other systems to patrol.'

She activated a file on the hologram projector mounted on the meeting table and brought up images and descriptive captions for each item she was about to run through. 'Accept and we'll grant you the rank of Captain, which will be made official with your military as well as ours. That rank gives you access to a monthly supply of weapons and resources, including a case of rare metals that you can trade for any currency you need to cover expenses.'

'You're not kidding.'

'You will choose your own crew members, assign rank, investigate criminal elements, establish a network of contacts throughout the galaxy, and go out on your own missions to enact justice wherever you see fit. Any questions?'

Lana rested her hands on her hips and nodded as though she understood everything Kim had just said. 'Nope, I think that just about–'

'Good. Do you accept?' Kim asked hopefully, then added for effect: 'Are you ready to be Captain of your own crew of deputies?'

Lana blew through her lips. 'Sure,' she said, even though she could still feel the breeze of Kim's words flying right over her head.

'Excellent. I'll forward the details to your console. You can contact me at any time, should you need to. It has been an honour and a pleasure to work with you.'

'Likewise,' was all Lana was given time to say, before Kim teleported her back to the Portal Hub.

Rachel was carrying a bowl of spaghetti from the kitchen to the entertainment area. She stopped in her tracks when Lana appeared in front of her. 'That was quick. What did they want?'

Lana clapped her hands together and rubbed her palms. 'They made me Captain…'

Rachel beamed. 'Congratulations.' And she forked all but a hanging length of pasta into her mouth.

'Of the human-populated parts of the galaxy,' Lana added.

Rachel paused mid-suck, eyes locked on Lana's.

'Yup.'

Lana explained the assignment Kim gave her, and Rachel ate her meal and listened.

'Valhez actually approved this?' Rachel asked.

The reality of the task Lana had accepted was beginning to set in. 'I… I have to sit down.'

Rachel pulled a chair for Lana and she dropped into it. 'They're giving you a lot of power, Lana. And with that comes–'

'A shit-ton of responsibility,' Lana breathed. She thought it through while her heart rate evened out. *I'm prohibited from helping people in different Realms, but here in Home Realm, I could help anyone anywhere in the galaxy.*

There had been reports, following the Warden invasion, of deformed beasts that had escaped the Lustitian particle beam. And extremism still existed in the desert countries of the world. Attacks on innocents continued year after year. Colonies on the outer rim of the Milky Way galaxy were said to be lawless.

The Security Division of the Universal Community could only do so much. And since Hutch Branner's factory had been destroyed, there would be fewer AMs deployed to locations in need of policing.

Lana stood, nodding slowly, and looked at her friend and mentor. 'I'll need your guidance.'

'I'll be here when you want me. What about Miri, though? You two have hit it off.'

'It'll be easy to spend time with her in Ether Realm without neglecting my duties because time moves more slowly here.'

'Fair, fair. So who are you going to deputise first, Captain?'

The desert sands outside Liberty wafted against the vacant fracking machine disassembly building. Lana entered through a side door with her hands away from her sides. She paused when she heard the click of a Beretta ready to fire.

'I'm here to offer you a job.'

Talon circled Lana and holstered her pistol. A curious look suggested she wanted to hear more.

Lana explained the assignment and mentioned the long-term commitment that would be required. It was the only aspect of the job Lana predicted might be a deal breaker for Talon.

Talon stood at a workbench, cleaning her tools. She thought on the offer for a moment, raised one finger and gave Lana a serious look.

'One... condition?' Lana guessed. 'Shoot.'

Talon walked over to a wall panel and flicked the centre switch. The ceiling lights blinked on and illuminated the Black Heron. How Talon managed to manoeuvre it into the building without taxiing it in on wheels like one would a regular aircraft was beyond Lana, but she guessed what the machine woman's one condition would be.

Lana approached the ship and ran her fingers lightly along the advanced Raekeem armour of the Black Heron's tucked wing.

'We take your ship.' Lana nodded approvingly. 'Deal.'

<u>To be continued in Enter Portal III: Worlds Asunder</u>